Where Ravens Circle

Gaynor Lynn Taylor

malcolm down
PUBLISHING

Where Ravens Circle

The time came
when these doomed men would fall in battle.
There arose a loud clamour.
Ravens circled . . . eager for carrion.

(The Battle of Maldon: Anglo-Saxon Chronicles)

1
Maeldun 991

Wood splintered as vibrations rocked the Saxon church of St Mary the Virgin to its core.

"Can it hold?" said Esme, hardly able to breathe.

Father Aidan stood beside her with lips pursed in grim finality. "Not under this barrage."

Behind them, a handful of frightened women crowded into the narrow chancel in the vain expectation of greater safety. A bemused girl stood alone, separated from her mother, swinging her tiny frame. A tatty rag-doll flapped beneath her elbow. The priest scooped up the child in the crook of his arm. She nestled her head in the folds of the brown wool encircling his neck.

Esme swallowed hard. Her heart hammered. Perspiration crawled across her clammy flesh, sapping her strength. A cloud of lime-washed plaster floated onto the colourful tapestry that she had painstakingly repaired. Carved, ornamental angels juddered. Candle-holders rattled. At last the pounding ceased; an uncanny silence descended; then, the deafening crack of a final blow confirmed an awful realisation: their men had lost the battle, slaughtered by the Wolves of the North.

The door jerked open, demolishing a makeshift barricade. Torchlight emblazoned clouds of fine particles with an eerie glow. Gradually, the suffocating dust thinned, unveiling a diabolical silhouette. Behind this unholy vision three more grotesque figures jostled for a place, eager to weigh the spoils of their labours. The battering ram – a water trough – lay discarded at their feet.

Esme tried to recite the Lord's Prayer, but the phrases became muddled in her head. Energy drained down her legs, settling in the soles of her feet like lumps of clay. She stood transfixed as a broad-shouldered beast ducked to avoid the lintel, kicking wreckage from his path. A winged monster gilded his helmet. Congealed blood spread across his silver chain-mail and smeared the blade of his axe. He scanned the scene, weapon poised. Muffled murmurings penetrated the silent fear.

Sensing no threat, the brute relaxed his weapon and removed his iron mask. Esme shuddered as the force of his unwelcome gaze settled upon her. For several seconds he appraised her; then spoke using the Saxon language, his voice resonant. "Where are the others?"

The confrontation startled her. She looked to Father Aidan for guidance, but the grizzled chin was bowed in a spiritual communion that appeared to render him insensible to the situation.

"Well? Will you give me an answer?"

Although terror was paramount, Esme was conscious of her indignation growing stronger. The heathen had defiled the sanctuary of Christ. She summoned a deep-rooted reserve of courage. "There's no one else here. They've all escaped."

The corners of his mouth twitched. "Bravely spoken! I regret to disabuse you of your comforting belief, but no one has escaped, nor will they."

His focus lingered on the untidy tresses of her hair. She baulked at the insufferable arrogance and tried to marshal her thoughts: keep talking; ask questions; use any tactic to divert his deadly intent. In a voice as determined as she could muster she said, "Our militia held the causeway and slew many of you dogs before the tide came in. We were winning."

The Viking's reply pierced deep. "And now, it seems you have lost."

Anxiety clawed at her stomach. "How could that happen?"

"Your leader, Byrhtnoth, invited us to fight face-to-face on the mainland knowing he was outnumbered."

Esme clenched her fists. "The Ealdorman would never throw away lives needlessly."

The Viking shrugged. "He succumbed to flattery." There was no hint of condemnation.

Taking a deep breath, the pitch of her voice rose. "He was an English lord. You mistake pride for dignity." Then, unable to stop herself, she said, "Something you pagans would know nothing about."

The Viking's jaw tensed. She regretted the outburst and took a step back. He moved towards her. "It's an unwise leader who allows his sensibilities to overcome good strategy."

Heat emanated from his broad hauberk. Shoulder to shoulder the iron links bore witness to the death throes of those who fought to protect Maeldun. She longed for a knife and the strength to be rid of this condescending victor. In truth, the only weapon she had was her tongue.

Cheers sounded from the porch as a fair-haired youth leapt over the ruined barricade. "Lord Eirik, the men await your orders. They won't take any from Olaf Tryggvason." He examined the motley group wrinkling his nose. "Is this all we got for our trouble? It was hardly worth the effort." He fixed his eyes on Esme. "Except for her," he said, with a wolfish grin. Brandishing a knife, he swaggered over to Father Aidan. "Shall I kill the old priest? We don't need him."

Anguished cries arose from the chancel. Esme's concern for Father Aidan and the child in his arms emboldened her. Flinging herself in front of them, she shouted at the newcomer. "Leave him alone."

The young man wrapped an arm around her waist and lifted her off the ground. "Out of my way, girl."

She brought back the heel of her shoe and kicked him hard on the shins. Her flailing knuckles caught him full on the nose, and her nails dug into his cheek. He yelped. Leif threw Esme to the floor, smearing blood across his face with the back of his hand. "She's a wild cat."

Father Aidan had finished his prayers and set the small girl on her feet. Without warning, he looped his arm under the shoulder of his youthful opponent. Twisting his body, he levered the younger man up and over. Leif lay stunned. His dagger clattered on the flagstones. Esme grabbed it, scrambling to her feet. "Lay down your weapon or your boy will feel his own blade."

The Viking's next gesture was a blur. He seized her wrist, squeezing so hard that a searing burn forced her to let go. "Enough," said Eirik. "Leif, get up. You've been soundly beaten."

Leif scowled. "I only meant to scare them."

"And they were only defending themselves." The Viking cast a curious glance at Father Aidan; then he turned to Esme. "So, woman, you would have me cast into the next world." There was no rancour in his tone.

"You murdered our men."

He released her and wiped sweat from his brow. "True, I have killed many men, but murdered none – not yet."

She hissed through her teeth. "And women and children, do you kill them, too?"

"Not while they behave," he said in mild amusement.

Esme's fury rose; her breath came fast and shallow. She stared into his eyes, expecting to see the hard light of one without compassion. Instead, what she saw unnerved her. Their blueness suggested life – life in its fullness.

Leif was in petulant mood. "Lord Eirik, do we sail tonight or on the morning tide?"

The Viking continued to look at her as he answered. "Neither. We wait for Sweyn Forkbeard."

"Shall I report to the men?"

Eirik swung round to face the young man. "No. I have a task for them which they'll find distasteful. Persuasion will be necessary." The Viking donned his helmet. "Stay on guard. Pull the door closed. Keep out Olaf's thugs. Don't let anyone touch these people. There are enough to serve us well."

Esme's guts churned. So his intent was to make them slaves.

Eirik flicked his fingers towards her. "Watch this one! She has enough barbs to kill a man. And no more attacks on the priest. I have a use for him." He marched off, flanked by his supporters.

Leif growled, "You're surrounded. Don't move – if you want to live." He shoved debris away from the door and tugged it shut.

2
London 1979

A thunderous roar and blast of warm air herald the approach of the tube train at Notting Hill Gate. Departing passengers surge forward, reluctantly making room for those arriving. Emma grabs a pole, one hand among many, as they lurch into the next black hole. She alights at Victoria.

News-stands everywhere are sporting the headline: Margaret Thatcher Wins Election. The air is filled with an unusual buzz of excitement. People who would otherwise race by are pausing to comment on this historical event: the country has a lady Prime Minister. "She's as strong as any man," one woman says.

Josie, Emma's flatmate, raised a fist on hearing the announcement earlier, declaring, "That's one up for Women's Lib." Emma never has been a supporter of the burn-your-bra brigade, but wonders whether behaving like a man is the answer to equal rights. She appreciates how blessed she is to have had an education and, more important, to have male colleagues who respect her.

Crossing Vauxhall Bridge, she briefly watches the boats bringing life to the river; then hurries towards a high-rise building on Albert Embankment. Stepping into the lift, she presses the button indicating *Bailey, Shawcross and Stuart*, and enters her office. The spectacular view from her window of the Thames, with the Houses of Parliament on the north bank, is always a delight. On her desk is a memo written on the firm's headed notepaper. It's from Ben Shawcross.

To: Dr E. Stuart BSc, MD, PhD

Jens Bjorn Erikson telephoned to say he will be half an hour late. He sends his apologies for the inconvenience.

She sighs, thinking how very Scandinavian this is. Generally it's a bonus if clients even turn up within the appointed hour. Ben, one of the partners, is a genealogist. He chases records back through time. However, improvements in carbon dating and chemical analysis mean that investigations probe increasingly so far into the past that archaeological input is needed. This is Emma's role.

A middle-aged woman in blue overalls knocks and sticks her head round the door. "I've made coffee – freshly percolated."

"Thanks, Brenda. I can smell it. I'd love some."

Emma opens a filing cabinet, pulls out the relevant folder under the letter 'E', and throws it onto her desk. Hanging her jacket over the back of her chair, she re-reads the letter received from Jens Bjorn Erikson.

Dear Dr Stuart,

As Scandinavia is one of your areas of expertise, I would be grateful for your help. I have a whetstone, dated from the early eleventh century, found on our family farm. A runic inscription etched onto its surface reads: Magnus, son of Edgar, son of Eirik. Our family saga, which may be fanciful, says Eirik was a leader of the legendary Jomsvikings, a band of warrior monks said to be present at the Battle of Maldon of 991 in your county of Essex. Since Edgar is an English name, I hope to discover more.

She scans the notes of her preliminary inquiries: the enduring three hundred lines of a poem entitled 'The Battle of Maldon' from the

Anglo-Saxon Chronicles; quotes from the less reliable Icelandic Jomskinga Saga; a conversation with the curator of the National Museum of Denmark. When Brenda announces the arrival of the visitor, Emma is absorbed in an article on bio-archaeology. Grabbing her jacket, she steps forward to greet Mr Erikson. He is not unlike her image of a modern-day Viking and quite handsome too. About forty is her guess. His eyes twinkle as he smiles. She hopes her unbidden reaction is indiscernible.

"Good morning, Dr Stuart. Many apologies for my lateness." His speech is rhythmical and accented as he grasps her outstretched hand. There is no hint of disdain for her gender.

Emma wishes she had checked her appearance instead of delving into the latest version of *Current Archaeology*. She clears her throat. "Please take a seat. Would you like coffee?"

"Thank you. Black. No sugar."

Brenda is hovering in the corridor and raises her eyebrows with a smirk. Emma frowns to discourage her from whispering an embarrassing comment about the newcomer. She orders the coffee then settles back into her green leather chair. "Have you had a good journey?"

"I had to meet a flight from Heathrow, which is why I'm late."

Emma's imagination is in overdrive. She envisages him greeting a sophisticated Danish wife with two good-looking children. "Is your hotel comfortable?"

"Actually, we're in an apartment – a flat, I believe you call it. I come to London quite often."

So, he's a businessman who brings his family with him occasionally.

Brenda delivers the drinks in the best blue mugs from Harrods, and discreetly closes the door. Mr Erikson picks up his coffee and stares out of the window. "What a magnificent sight. Is that why you sit with your back to it, to avoid distraction?"

She nods. "I found your letter most interesting, Mr Erikson."

"Please, my name is Jens, although most people call me Bjorn. May I call you Emma?" Then he adds, "Forgive me. I saw it on your nameplate."

She is slightly taken aback. The American-style usage of first names has not yet reached London. "Yes, of course . . . Bjorn," she says, with uncertain emphasis.

She shuffles her notes. "What is it you're hoping to achieve?"

"Let me show you this." He opens a leather satchel and hands her a package wrapped in linen. "This is the whetstone I mentioned."

Emma parts the cloth and examines the weighty lump in her palm. "The inscriptions are quite clear considering its age. Have you had it carbon dated?"

"Yes. I have authentication to prove it." He reaches inside the bag. "It definitely fits the time span. We are said to be descended from Magnus. But who was Edgar? Did he and Eirik ever live in England?"

She returns the whetstone and watches as Bjorn carefully covers it once again. "I've done a little research already. I'll go to Maldon and see what I can find out."

"Do you mind if I come with you?"

She hesitates. "It's not our usual practice, but, in this case, yes, you are most welcome."

"Good. Please allow me to drive us there when you are free."

3
Maeldun 991

Esme spoke urgently. "Father, is there any way out? I must get help."

Aidan scrunched up his face. "No, it's too dangerous."

One of the women took issue. "Who else *is* there, Father? Esme is younger and faster than the rest of us and has no children."

"You know what will happen to her if she's caught."

"The same as will happen to all of us if we're left here."

"Please, Father," said Esme.

The priest pinched his lower lip between thumb and forefinger. "There's a grate in the crypt. It's loose, roughly two-feet square. You could clamber out, but it's risky."

"I'm willing to take the chance."

A dark-haired woman, a few years older than herself, who was grasping a small child in each hand, spoke up. "I would go with you, Esme, you know that, but I have the children."

"Rowena, bless you, I wouldn't expect you to come."

"I have no children," said a voice. A woman, whose laughter lines traced down weather-beaten cheeks, stepped forward. "I'll come."

Esme took her hand, "Thank you, Astrid. But it is best I go alone and find Lord Edmund. He's a friend of the king." The thought of Edmund stabbed Esme's conscience. He had been her guardian – now, they were betrothed. "He doesn't know I'm in Maeldun and will be displeased, but I'll have to deal with that. He's the only one who can save us."

Rummaging in her basket, Esme fetched out a pair of scissors – two blades joined together with a single twist of metal. She tucked them in a pocket specially sewn into her cuff to keep the tool within reach while embroidering.

Aidan waggled his finger. "Promise me you'll only use those in self-defence."

"Of course, Father. But they could give me a moment's advantage."

Esme followed him into the crypt by light of a candle. Aidan indicated the grille. "Forgive me. That was a ruse to deceive the women. It is best they don't know in case they're questioned. I'll remove it so it looks as though you went out that way, but you must use the tunnel. It was built for priests in case of attack. Be careful. Some of the wooden staves might be rotten."

"Where does it lead?"

"To the woods beyond the field, but men will be combing the area."

"Kizzy, my mare, is grazing up there."

In the middle of the crypt, a small baptismal font was positioned on a dais. Bending his knees, Aidan grunted, heaving it aside to reveal a trap door. Curling his hand around an iron ring, he yanked it up, exposing a dark hole wide enough for a body to squeeze through. "It hasn't been used for years. The passage points in one direction only. You must keep going."

Esme gazed into the gloomy abyss. "You're putting yourself at great risk, Father, when they know you helped me."

"Don't worry about me, child. Besides, you heard the Viking – he has a job for me. I'll pray for your safety." Aidan knelt down, placing his hand beneath her arm as she descended the rungs. When she reached the bottom, he leaned over and handed her the candle. "God speed."

The candle guttered and she cupped her hand around the flame, stooping to avoid clouting her head on the roof beams. The air was thin and progress was slow. She forced herself to concentrate, counting the strides, reciting poetry, imagining the safety of the wood and, above all, freedom.

At last, a faint chink of light appeared in the distance. With it came a shaft of air. The sun was nestling on the horizon as she pulled herself onto a bank of dried moss and dead leaves. The pithy smell of matured ferns filled her nostrils while she waited for her pulse to steady. She crouched and set off, creeping along the line of trees bordering the fields, listening for signs of a patrol. Every cracking twig, rustling leaf and agonised squawk of a bird made her heart leap in alarm, filling her limbs with the impulse for flight.

Reaching the edge of the coppice, she emitted a low whistle. A gentle whinny floated on the breeze. She hurried to meet the easy welcome as the mare's hooves padded softly towards her on the harvested earth. A shelter made of willow branches housed her saddlery. She slid the bridle over Kizzy's head then clutched the little mare's mane and leapt onto her back.

Coarse voices sounded in her ear, speaking a tongue she didn't understand. The mare jibbed. "Let go," Esme screamed, lashing out with her legs. Muscled arms dragged her from the horse's back. Landing on her feet, she brought up her knee, but the man anticipated her move and it struck nothing more than a rock-hard thigh. Thrown onto her back, air was driven from her lungs. A sharp pain shot up her spine while a resolute hand held her throat, crushing, suffocating.

One attacker stood behind her head while the other tugged at her neckline, ripping the dress at the shoulder seams. Stale breath wafted over her face as stubby, blood-stained hands pawed her skin. Bile rose into her throat. Then she remembered the scissors. A desperate shake of the wrist released them from the tuck inside her cuff. She swung her arm wildly upwards and thrust the blades into his neck, splattering drops of warm blood over her cheeks. He sat up, fingers pressed against the wound, and howled with rage. A fist struck her jaw; her teeth bit deep into the inside of her mouth. The assailant dragged her nearer and held up the scissors. His cruel laughter froze her mind. Her eyelids fluttered as she lost consciousness.

4

Eirik returned to the church. The girl had gone. He stormed out, bellowing Leif's name. "Where in Thor's teeth have you been? You disobeyed my order. The girl is missing."

"Sorry, lord, I was called away for a few moments. But I checked first. There's nowhere for any of them to go. She'll be quite safe."

"Safe!" Eirik roared. "With Olaf's fiends on the rampage?"

"Don't worry. I'll get the truth out of them." Leif unsheathed his dagger and grabbed a small boy. "This scrawny Anglo-Saxon waif can easily be dispensed with."

His mother gasped. "She's in the crypt."

"See? It was easy."

Eirik spoke to Aidan. "Show us."

Aidan led the way to where the grate lay on the floor, wrenched from its mortar. Eirik looked at the almost perpendicular bank immediately outside the opening. He glared at the priest. "Do you take me for a fool? There must be a tunnel. Where is it?"

Aidan's eyes flickered, but still he said nothing.

Eirik glanced around the crypt fixing his attention on the dais. "It must be under there, and no doubt leads to the woods. Leif fetch two horses." He stabbed a finger at Aidan. "Let it be on your conscience if any harm has befallen her." Eirik's fury at Leif's disobedience was outweighed by his concern for the extraordinary young woman who had challenged him. Fire danced in her brown eyes yet she had a strong conviction that he envied.

Leif arrived, sitting astride a dappled-grey gelding. Beside him a great bay stallion stamped and reared. "Sorry, lord, he won't let me get on him. He's a beast. You're a better rider than I am."

"A beast, you say. So is Olaf. Search the thicket to the left. I'll take the other side." He sidled towards the horse then remained still, inclining his head. The stallion snorted but grew curious. Moments later Eirik was galloping headlong into the woodland with a rope wound over his shoulder. He emerged onto the edge of a field where a highly agitated little horse paced up and down. Two men were kneeling over a woman. He raced towards them, bellowing through the gathering dusk, "I wouldn't do that, if I were you."

They looked up, startled, but seeing he was one of them they waved dismissively. "Clear off. We found her first."

"Wrong," said Eirik. He swung the rope above his head. One attacker cried out in disbelief as a noose ensnared his neck, flipping his head backwards. His fingers clutched the abrasive fibres branding his throat. Uttering an asphyxiated croak, he passed out.

Eirik jumped to the ground, leaning adroitly to one side as the second assailant sprang forward aiming a great fist. He caught the man's wrist, twisting the weighty arm backwards, and slammed his head into a tree trunk. The body slumped. He trussed the two men together, back to back, and looked round for the girl. Neither she nor her horse were anywhere to be seen. He spotted the discarded scissors and picked them up. "Headstrong woman," he muttered.

Leif appeared out of the gloom. "Did you find her?"

"The wretched woman has escaped again." Eirik gathered his reins. "I'm going after her. Tow these two ogres to the village and dump them in the pond to cool off. Go to the church. Make sure the women and priest are safe. Wait for me outside."

He took off through the woods and saw Esme galloping past the church. Reining in, he watched as she steered her horse through a gap in a tall hedgerow where the land flattened out. She'd ridden into the battlefield. Disturbed ravens flew into the air, circling in unison, before resettling on their feast. Her horse reared. The girl lost her balance, falling into the soft mire of death. All around her lay corpses: disembowelled, beheaded, limbless. She bent over, retching. Eirik doubted her brain could absorb this vision of torment. He cantered towards her. "Let me help you."

Panting hard, Esme spat some vile substance from her mouth. "I need no help from you. Finish me now, let me die with my countrymen." Ashen channels of tears streaked through the grime on her cheeks.

"That is not necessary. Nor do I wish it."

As she tried once more to grab her horse, the effort overcame her. She fell heavily, hitting her temple on a severed head. Then lay still. Eirik dismounted, wading among the viscera, and knelt beside her. Satisfied that she was alive, he gathered her in his arms. Even through the gore, he could see how lovely she was.

The little mare waited obediently. She allowed him to carefully place Esme onto her back. "Treat her gently. Keep her warm," he said.

The church was built on a hill leading down to the estuary. Lighted candles flickered from the high, round windows. Drunken, raucous laughter rose through the thatched roof of a wooden barn-like construction situated on a shoulder of land below. Slowly, he helped the girl to the ground.

5

The rhythmic sway ceased. Terrible, frightening memories stirred. Esme opened her mouth to scream, but fingers were pressed over her lips. "Quiet, woman."

Images flitted across her mind: a dark tunnel; rough hands; torn clothes; a battlefield; death; scissors. Scissors! She gasped. What had he done with them? She stared down at her wretched clothes and shook violently. Mortified, she attempted to cover herself. The futility of the action crushed the last vestiges of self-respect. "What have you done to me?"

Eirik shook his head. "Nothing, I saved you. Olaf's men attacked you."

Esme caught her breath. "Did they . . .?"

"Dishonour you? No."

"Where are they?"

"Taken care of for the time being."

Esme could endure no more. She swayed and a supportive arm wrapped around her. For several minutes her sobs purged the terrors until they came to an uncertain, juddering halt. Eirik untied a kerchief from around his neck. "Here, blow your nose. You need to wash. You've been lying in men's innards. There's a rainwater butt and a bucket at the side of the church." He looked her up and down. "Take off your dress. It's soaked in blood and excrement. Don't worry, I won't look at you. Besides . . ." He turned away and unbridled the bay horse now grazing on consecrated grass – nose to nose with Kizzy.

The unspoken words hung pregnant in the air. Esme discerned their meaning. He had already seen more of her than she would willingly allow. Hot, stinging drops trickled down her cheeks once again. But she refused to give in. "At least I am clean inside," she said with venom, "unlike your dark, heathen heart."

The Viking reached for a mantle slung over his shoulder. "Heathen or no, my patience is wearing thin." He pointed to a bush grown thick with leaves and handed her the cloak. "Undress behind there while I cleanse the horses' hooves."

Esme shook as she let the dress drop to her feet. He was right. It was covered in foul substances. She heard Leif's voice. Eirik was issuing instructions. Despite the blanket, she shivered with nerves and shame. Never before had she undressed in the company of a man – not even Edmund. Even as a child he had allowed her total privacy.

"Are you ready?" said Eirik.

Esme had no will or strength to argue. He led her to the water butt and filled the bucket. "You'll need several of these. And see to your hair. It's covered in blood." He turned. "Good, Leif found one of your friends. I'll leave you." He placed the bucket on the ground and disappeared.

Esme looked up. "Astrid!"

Astrid hugged her. "My dearest girl, what happened?"

Esme choked with relief. "I landed in the battlefield. I must wash. I thought that Viking leader was about to . . ."

"Wash you himself? How humiliating." Astrid pulled a face. "That aggressive young man came in demanding a volunteer to help you. He also asked Aidan for some clothes."

"Aidan? What clothes can he possibly have suitable for me?"

"Don't let's worry about that now. I've got a cloth to dry you."

With Astrid's help, Esme rinsed the dirt from her skin, but knew she could never remove the stain of her abuse. Her friend tried to untangle the matted hair, to little effect.

They heard Leif's voice again. "I found what you wanted. It's as you thought, the priest sometimes tutors boys who think they've been called to serve their God. There's a leather cap too, and I found a comb."

"Good. Not a word of this to anyone. Let the horses loose in the field. Then fetch Olaf's men out of the pond."

"Have you finished?" said Eirik to Astrid. "If so, come and get these clothes. Make sure you dry her hair. I don't want it dripping all evening."

Astrid retrieved the garment – a habit. Esme slipped it over her head. The coarse linen irritated her skin. "I remember making this over a year ago for one of Father Aidan's pupils. The boy's father asked for the fabric to be as rough as possible to discourage his son from becoming a monk. It worked. He soon gave up."

"This is dreadful," said Astrid. She went to find Eirik. "Surely this is not necessary? I can find a dress for her."

Eirik shook his head. "She offended her assailants. They won't give up looking for her. But they'll not notice a skinny lad trying to follow the ways of a weakling god. She can live in the church with the priest. I have work for her to do."

Astrid cast a look of loathing at Eirik. He ignored it. "Go now. I want the names of everyone in the church. I shall need their help too, and yours. See the children get home safely." She was reluctant to leave, but Esme insisted she did as he asked.

Eirik held up the leather cap. Esme recalled how the boy insisted on being tonsured. His mother had commissioned it to keep his head warm.

"Turn round," said Eirik. He began tugging at her scalp. When he finished she looked in horror at what he held in his hands: strands of fair curls in one, her scissors in the other. At first she was shocked, then anger flared. She traced her fingers through her hair to assess how much he'd cut off. "How dare you," she said. "No respectable Saxon woman would have her hair shorn."

"You're no longer a respectable Saxon woman. You're a young trainee monk. I've only cut out a few tangles which still had bits of flesh stuck to them. Besides, you'd never be able to hide all your hair under that cap." He held out a comb. "Use this. Straighten what you can."

Esme glared at him with hatred in her heart. Tiny muscles worked in his jaw and suddenly he caught hold of her wrist. "Don't underestimate what these men will do to you if they guess who you are. Their revenge will be infinitely worse than anything they first intended. You must vanish from their sight."

He released her and Esme began to tremble, with anger or fear she couldn't decide. She took the proffered comb and set to work smoothing her hair close to her scalp. Then tying back the strands, she piled it under the cap. The Viking had spoken plainly about the peril of her position. This man, it seemed, was her protector. But even he couldn't guard her every waking moment.

Guilt disturbed her soul. She glanced at the darkening sky and a disapproving moon rebuked her. The Viking stripped off his leather tunic, splashing water over his torso with evident relish. A lambent glow from the windows sparkled on the great silver rings round his upper arm. He pulled his tunic back over his head and assessed her appearance. "Come with me."

6

Esme followed him into the church. Father Aidan was sweeping the floor with a broom. Dirt and debris filled an ample barrel. A cord hitched the habit above his knees, exposing solid white calves and bare feet. A box of basic tools lay open; on top was a hammer with some nails that he'd used to repair the broken lock.

Hearing the door creak, he stood and stretched his large frame. Allowing the besom to drop, he knuckled his back and peered at Esme with a puzzled squint. Then suddenly his broad, weathered face broke into a smile and he hurried to greet her with arms outstretched. "Thank God you're safe, my child." He gave her a chaste hug, taking the opportunity to whisper in her ear. "The Viking was angry when he saw you'd gone. He went after you."

"It's as well he did. I let you all down and made things worse."

"We admire you for trying, child."

Eirik interrupted them. "You'll be needed tomorrow, priest. Come, both of you."

They followed a path along the southern side of the church leading to the building below. Once a barn, it had been transformed into a hostelry for itinerant traders. Now, heavy-boned, inebriated men were slumped over long trestles in the main hall. A covered way led to a separate kitchen used for storing, preparing and cooking food. Great cheers filled the hall when Eirik appeared. Women from the village, some of whom were trapped in the church earlier, were serving at table. Among them was Rowena who surveyed the young monk with a curious, oblique stare. Esme inclined her head with the slightest movement. Suddenly recognising who occupied the habit, her friend quickly averted her eyes. As for the warriors, they completely ignored Esme. It occurred to her how cleverly disguised she was, and had Lord Eirik to thank for it.

At the top of a long refectory table slouched a man whose size was such that he could have wrestled a bear with ease. His long beard was plaited. His lank hair, tied in the nape of his neck, was as golden as the amulet hanging from his throat. Eirik now spoke in the tongue of her aggressors. She looked at Father Aidan and raised her eyebrows.

"Old Norse," he whispered.

"Do you understand it?"

Father Aidan's nod was barely perceptible, his translation restrained.

Eirik shouted across the room. "Olaf, it seems I lost our bet today. I never thought Byrhtnoth would fall for your charms. I owe you a day's wages."

Olaf guffawed. "In the name of Thor, can you believe it? I offered him a truce paid for with gold. He turned it down. Then I convinced him that picking off my men one by one at the causeway was unfair, that he should let us cross and fight man to man. He actually invited us over. I wasn't sure if he wanted to kill me . . . or kiss me."

The men howled with laughter, banging their mugs on the table, slopping the contents over the sides. Mead ran through cracks in the wood and dripped onto the flagstones, only to be absorbed by the reeds strewing the floor.

"It was Eirik saw off that ealdorman," a voice boomed. "He killed at least twenty men to get near him. Even when the hairy old goat was dying, he still kept pressing the fight – until his white head struck the earth."

The assembled company hooted in delight.

Father Aidan said, "They're making fun of our militia."

"That's hateful. How is it you understand them, Father?"

Aidan fidgeted with a wooden cross around his neck. "I interpret old documents."

Esme hesitated. "I thought they were in Latin and Greek."

The priest brought a finger to his lips as Eirik prepared to speak again.

"It's true that my axe took his life," he said, filling his mug. "I thought that the Saxon cowards would run for their lives seeing their leader gone. But I was wrong." He stepped up onto a bench. "Some battled on with the same blind fury that comes from the guts of Vikings. Their wicked swords were hungry for our blood and they faithfully followed the spirit of Byrhtnoth, even after he'd gone to meet his Christ." He lifted his cup in the air. "Thor and Odin would say they earned a place in the Hall of the Slain. I therefore raise a toast to those men. They deserve as much glory as any of us. Tomorrow, I intend to see them buried. Their priest will give them their last rites."

A hush filled the room. Then murmurs ran around the table. "Buried?" Olaf roared. "Has the enemy's axe turned your brains to pulp? Since when have we taken up spades to consign our foes to the ground? Leave them to the crows."

Eirik was undeterred. "If they choose to rot among the worms rather than freeing their spirits in fire, that's their decision. It's their way. But there is no honour or glory for us in what happened here today. It was a foolish act of suicide, not war."

As Aidan interpreted what was being said, Esme felt the back of her neck bristling with pride. Or was it shame? Byrhtnoth had lost, needlessly throwing away all those lives. Olaf's men were celebrating a conquest – one that Eirik was telling them they did not deserve. All eyes turned now to their leader, awaiting his reaction.

Slowly, a smile crossed Olaf's face as he got to his feet. "Come, we can be generous in victory." He raised his goblet, "To the Saxons of Maeldun."

The mood relaxed as the men breathed out in relief. They gave their approval, "To the Saxons of Maeldun."

Aidan smiled. Esme was perplexed. The Viking had killed so many Saxons, yet here he was praising them, planning to give them proper burials. How, she wondered, did a man cope after killing opponents for whom he had admiration? Did it sit well with his conscience?

"Eirik," Olaf hollered, reclaiming his seat and indicating a place beside him, "I hear you've given a couple of my men a good hiding for attacking your wench."

"A good soaking at least."

"What's happened to the little maiden?"

"She vanished," said Eirik, opening his hands, palms upward.

Olaf shuddered. "These Saxon women are said to have mysterious powers. Maybe the witch turned herself into a raven."

"In that case, I'm better off without her."

"I'll drink to that," said Olaf, raising his cup. "There are plenty of women to be had. I can arrange to send you one."

"Thank you, but I prefer to choose my own."

Olaf retrieved a piece of stewed pork from his plate. "You always were too finicky for your own good," he said, stuffing it in his mouth.

Eirik picked up the jug. "It's time we had a refill." He beckoned to Esme. "Come here, boy."

At first Esme was unaware that he was addressing her. She felt the soft pressure of Father Aidan's hand in the small of her back. This was her test. She approached, apprehensive. Olaf did not spare her a glance. Eirik handed her the pitcher; his eyes twinkled. Esme wanted to burst into hysterical laughter. For the moment at least, she was invisible.

7
London 1979

Having dictated several replies to urgent enquiries, Emma stuffs the papers needed for the weekend into her briefcase. Passing Ben's door she stops. "I'm off now."

"Ok. Have you got your usual tutorials at Cambridge on Monday morning?"

"Yes."

"How'd you get on with that Danish chap?"

"He's coming with me to Maldon on Tuesday."

"Well, be careful. He might want to run off with you."

Emma laughs. "No need to worry, he's married. I expect his wife will be accompanying us."

Ben grins. "You should be safe enough then." He leans forward and picks out an envelope from his in-tray. "Before you go, let me give you this. I received some correspondence this morning for your mother. Probate has been approved. How does she feel about inheriting a sixteenth-century house from an unknown relative?"

"Bemused. She's never even heard of Reginald Reed."

"Well, the house is hers. Keys are with the estate agent in Norwich."

"Thanks. We'll go and take a look."

"Good luck."

Doors are slamming and the barrier is closing as Emma runs to catch the Norwich train. Arriving at Thorpe Station, she takes a taxi home. The Victorian house is set back from the road. Border plants and shrubs skirt a lawn divided by a central path. She opens the dark-red front door. Its inset stained-glass window and overhead fanlight give the lobby a welcoming feel. A polished banister curves around the bottom step of the staircase.

Jack, her ten-year-old son, runs from the kitchen down the carpeted corridor and barrels into her. "Mummy, guess what? I've been picked to play second cornet in the school band. We're practising for a summer concert in the cathedral."

She hugs him. "Well done. Your dad would have been proud."

"I've already told him," says Jack.

A fleeting shadow passes over her. She knows the boy means he has spoken to his father's photograph standing on the mantel in the dining room.

Emma's mother Sonia appears – a tea-towel over her arm. "Wash your hands, you two. It's time to eat." From a window above an enamel sink, the flushed, orange sky streams directly onto the reddish-brown floor tiles. A family-sized pine table is already set with cutlery. Sonia carries a steaming pie-dish to a placemat in the centre, and she serves each of them before taking a seat. "Would you like to say grace, Jack?"

"Thank you, Lord, for this food, and thank you for Grandma, who cooked it, and thank you for bringing Mummy home safely again."

"Amen," they chime.

"So, what sort of week have you had, love?" says Sonia.

"Well, I had an interesting client this morning from Denmark."

"Really? Did you practise your Danish?"

"No."

Sonia sounds disappointed, "My mother spent many hours teaching you her language."

"Mum, I understand it, but can't speak it fluently like you."

"You don't try. What did he want anyway?"

"He believes one of his ancestors took part in the Battle of Maldon."

"Essex, 991," says Sonia.

Emma's eyes widen. "Yes, that's right."

"I've read about it. One of our most well-known aldermen, named Byrhtnoth, allowed the Vikings to cross to the mainland so it could be a fair fight."

Jack swallows his mouthful. "And who won?"

"The Vikings."

"Daddy wouldn't have allowed that."

"Your daddy was fighting for peace," says Emma.

Jack snorts, "Don't you fight to win?"

"But war brings peace when it's over."

"Only when one side has got their own way," says the boy. "The other is a loser."

Emma looks at her son. One day she will have to tell him how his father died. "Mr Erikson believes his ancestor was a member of the Jomsviking monks."

"Mercenaries who dedicated their lives to Thor and Odin," says Sonia.

"What's a mercenary, Grandma?"

"Someone who works for the person paying the most."

"Doesn't everyone do that?"

Emma laughs. "I suppose they do."

After dinner Jack goes to his bedroom where one half of the space is given over to his musical instruments. Emma and her mother stroll outside to a circular patio with a table and chairs. Trees arch their branches into a delightful tunnel which leads to a small lawn. Beyond is a garage housing her father's BMW – once his pride and joy. Double wooden doors provide access to a driveway. Emma hears the gentle strains of 'The Old Rugged Cross' from Jack's window above. Leaning back her head, she closes her eyes and allows the notes to wash over her. Blues and greens form the soft shapes of moving clouds.

"You're watching the colours," says Sonia. "It's strange how synaesthesia pops up after skipping several generations."

"Sometimes it's a nuisance." Emma fetches the envelope from her pocket. "Ben Shawcross gave me a letter for you. The property is now yours."

Sonia unfolds the paper. "Why didn't Reginald Reed make a will? He was nearly a hundred. How can he have lived there all that time and I never met him? Do you know where the house is?"

"Not exactly, it's somewhere south of the city."

"I'm expecting them to ring back any day to say they're very sorry but they've got the wrong person. I don't deserve it."

"You deserve something good after nursing Dad for so many years." Emma pats her mother's hand. "I'll pick up the keys tomorrow. We'll go and take a look."

8
Maeldun 991

The pale-grey strokes of dawn filtered through the window of the church meeting room, which doubled as a vestry or place of private worship. There, Esme had spent a few restless hours on a straw-covered pallet. Her head ached. She sat up, massaging her elbows. Eirik had instructed her and Rowena to prepare dough for the following day, and the two women had worked steadily, side by side in the kitchen, until their backs and arms ached.

Esme struggled to her feet, entangled in the over-long habit. Tying a knot in the cord around her waist, she lifted the garment to a comfortable length. On a sturdy wooden chest sat a bowl, beside it was a copper jug. She stared into it. The distorted image of a dishevelled young monk glared back, wild-eyed. She was in the middle of a nightmare but unable to force herself awake. Only a few nights ago she had slept peacefully on her feather-filled bed with soft linen sheets, safe, secure, each day predictable.

She tried to breathe deeply to steady her nerves, but air refused to enter her lungs in anything more than short bursts. Slumping onto the edge of the pallet, she began to pray. Whatever she had to face, her faith would help her through. Of that she was certain. A sense of calm gradually filled her soul and she stood, filling the bowl with cold water from the jug and splashing her face. She peered down at the churned water, determined to stay in control and abide by the rules of the new regime until help came. She had played that game most of her life. The ways of gaining freedom and true independence were similar – by winning trust. Was that really any different from her relationship with Edmund?

The desolation of that day, ten years ago, overwhelmed her. For a moment she was carrying her baby-brother in a sling, returning from foraging for mushrooms to be told that her parents had been subjected to an indiscriminate and fatal Viking raid. Since that deadly attack, which left them orphans, Lord Edmund, an adjacent landholder, had been guardian to Esme and young Brand. She was grateful to him and now had agreed to marry him, if only for the sake of her brother, although he had never shown her any affection. In fact, he didn't even seem to like either of them very much. She had run his household, organised the chores both inside and outside the home and looked after baby Brand. Edmund came to rely on her totally and left her alone to do as she saw fit. Disobedience or protest would not have achieved her position of authority. Esme straightened and drew back her shoulders. God had given her intelligence, good health and a stubborn nature. She resolved to use them in order to stay alive.

Father Aidan was ensconced in a space below the west tower. The door was ajar. He was on the floor in a foetal position clutching the cloak that wrapped around his body. His long and regular breaths were punctuated by an occasional snort. She spotted her sewing basket. Aidan must have recovered it the night before. A few threads and skeins of wool were dangling from beneath the lid where it had toppled over. Careful not to wake him, she retrieved it and took it back to her room.

Outside, the fresh morning breeze caressed her face. She looked up at the top of the black timbered tower which for many years had been a guide for sailors seeking moorings. She followed the same path as the night before, noting the rounded, split trunks of aged oaks that formed the church walls. They were fixed to a base of roughly-coursed stone, giving the whole a feel of solidity. Surely nothing could undermine its permanence?

The tavern sounded and smelt like a pigsty. The locally produced mead was celebrated for its strength, and the Norsemen had imbibed copious amounts. Bodies lay everywhere: on, over and under the tables. Olaf was slumped in his seat. His head lolled at an angle, mouth agape. His golden hair, which fell in disarray over the wooden arm of the chair, shifted in a light draught wafting through the shutters. Globules of pallid wax hung like carbuncles on the candles, or were poised at the table's edge, solidified by the cool night air. Like Lot's wife, turned to stone.

Esme hurried through to the kitchen. None of the women had yet arrived. She pulled out the trays of coarse dough from the warming oven. The natural raising agent had done its work, filling the bread with air. Not that there had been much wheat content. The bulk of the newly harvested grain remained at the mill while the men were engaged in fighting. She stoked up the fire then unlocked the rear door which swung open in silence on well-oiled hinges. A spider's web clung to one corner. The creature scurried to hide. Tiny dewdrops bounced on the gossamer, waiting for the daily warmth to liberate them from their nightly entrapment.

She stood in the doorway, closed her eyes and absorbed the rich scent of August, grateful to be alive. When she opened them, she was startled by a movement and retreated with haste into the shadows. The dark-haired figure standing next to the well was unmistakable. A bucket of water, freshly drawn, perched on the surround. A whetstone lay beside it. In his hand was a sword. It had none of the blood and gore of battle but was clean and polished, belying its devilish work.

Unaware of his observer, Eirik faced the dawn and inhaled deeply. He moved slowly and deliberately, bending at the knee, raising the sword above his head. His actions quickened as he skipped backwards allowing the weight and momentum to follow through each parry, thrust and slash: man and weapon as one. The exercise complete, he began another, more complex than the last. Esme was spellbound by the sequence of movements, each muscle of his body stretched to its limit. He used his legs as cudgels, aiming at differing levels of his enemy's body – knees, groin and neck – followed by sudden agile twists, rolls and leaps.

He stooped and picked up a second sword. The blades moved in different directions, fighting off unseen enemies. Esme visualised an increasing number of opponents. The speed and grace with which Eirik defended and attacked was such that her vision distorted. He kicked and slashed, and men fell.

He stopped with no sign of fatigue. Lifting the bucket from the well, he allowed the water to stream over his torso then began to remove his leggings. Esme glanced away, conscious that she was intruding on a private moment. When she dared to peek again, he was dressed, and wore a sleeveless leather jerkin which hung open. Droplets trickled down his arms and chest as he picked up his swords, sheathed them and made towards the building, heading straight for the kitchen.

9

Esme darted out of sight. Did he know she'd been watching? Would he be angry, as she had been when she believed he was intending to watch *her*? How different was this – just because he was a man? But Eirik gave no indication that he'd seen her and strode to the kitchen with an easy gait. He reached the open door and squinted into the gloom, leaning his swords against the architrave. Esme began kneading a lump of dough and wiped the back of her hand across her forehead.

His gaze was alert, attentive. "Morning, I'm glad you're up. Do you know how to milk cows?"

Esme pursed her lips. "There are very few chores on a farm with which I am unfamiliar."

"The cows will be pleased. There are several wandering this way with heavy udders. And hens still lay eggs even in battle."

"The children can collect those."

Eirik nodded his approval. "I see you're baking bread. We'll need a constant supply while we're here. I've found more wheat. It'll be delivered to you later."

"Oh, I'm so pleased. Anything else, lord?"

He stared at her for several seconds ignoring the irony. "As a matter of fact there is. Come. I've something to show you."

He led the way to a few small, cone-shaped, stone buildings. "Mind your head," he said, bending as he went inside. She hesitated, aware that his presence consumed the whole space.

"Are you afraid?"

"No. Why should I be?"

He stepped outside, a grin on his lips. "Then go in and take a look. It's only dead pig."

A metal pole, embedded in the stone, ran across the centre of the cell from which hung several sides of smoked ham attached to hooks. "They're freshly cooked. Take them down. Slice them. Olaf's men will be hungry when they're sober."

He gripped her elbow and guided her to a large vegetable garden, well-planted and tended. "See to it these are dug up. Now let's examine the orchards." He strolled towards the trees. "There are apples, plums, pears and mulberries. Some are ready for gathering. Make sure it's done."

Esme knew that under different circumstances, she would be enjoying this encounter. At home she loved nothing more than inspecting the results of her toil. Now, the conditions forbade such pleasures. Part of her wanted to trust this charismatic Viking, but rational thought counselled otherwise.

Beyond the orchards were the beehives that produced honey for the mead and other sweet foods. "Can you handle these?" he said.

"Yes, I can empathise with the bees. They're free to leave, but their return home is never in doubt – unless fate intervenes, as it has for me."

Eirik searched her face intently, but made no comment. They reached a large wooden barn and he pulled open the solid doors. A heady aroma filled the senses. Bunches of fresh herbs hung drying from beams. Others had been chopped ready for use in herbal teas. Crushed lavender plants were waiting to be macerated in oil, heated and filtered; some of the delightful results had been funnelled already into small pots and lined up on a bench.

"Good astringents for cleansing wounds," said Eirik. "Are you familiar with herbs?"

"My friend Astrid knows all there is to know."

"Then she shall help you. My men are camped on Northey Island, the other side of the causeway. Some have deep wounds. Generally, each man tends his own—"

"Then they can have no need of me."

Eirik frowned at the interruption. "It's not always easy for them. Their hands are large and they cannot control the fine bone needles. Others struggle to see close-up. Your skills as a seamstress will be useful." He opened his hand. Her scissors lay across his palm. "By the way, I still have these."

Esme took them, recalling how she had last used them. A cold shaft ran down her spine. They hadn't inflicted as much damage as she'd wished.

"I trust you won't be too squeamish for such a job?" said Eirik.

Esme eyed him steadily. "No."

"I thought not. Their clothes need mending too. They'll be grateful. There's plenty of work to keep your little fingers busy. They will expect it of a young monk."

Esme felt heat rise to her cheeks. "It would seem that my fingers, little or not, are in demand."

His mouth twitched. "Yes, they are. When I first laid eyes on you, I had no doubt you would be proficient in many ways."

Esme bristled. There was an awkward silence. Eirik cleared his throat. "I didn't intend to belittle your skills." He pointed to a cart lying in the field. "Once the food and medicines are ready, harness your mare and drive down to the island. Leif will be waiting to help you unload."

"And how should I behave with the men? Like an uncouth lout? Expected to drink to excess, indulge in vulgarity, help myself to what is not mine, and brutalise whomever I please?"

Eirik turned her to face him. The scorching fury of his eyes in no way melted the frost in his glare. "My men are unlike Olaf's. They're disciplined. Treat them with respect. They'll do likewise. Remember, you are for the moment a man of God, albeit not their god. They'll be mindful of that fact. You'll not be troubled if you do as you're told." He hesitated. "You may even find the experience enlightening."

Esme examined his strong grip. "Enlightening?" He judged the rebuke in her tone and stepped back. "You do me a disservice, lord, if you believe that a Viking can instruct me in the improvement of my manners, or indeed any aspect of good conduct."

Eirik's fists clenched and unclenched though he remained controlled. "Your courteous treatment of others is a consequence of your privileged upbringing. You can know nothing of the heart of a man obliged to delve into the darkest side of his humanity, having to follow hideous forces, killing and maiming against his inclinations."

Esme was taken aback by the intensity of emotion she had unlocked. She paused before answering. "You're right. But just because a woman wears beads, that's no indication her upbringing has been without torments. You presume to know too much about the circumstances of my life."

"By Thor's hammer, woman, you're enough to try a man." He rubbed a frustrated hand over his face. "Must you always have the last word on every matter?"

"Only where justified," said Esme, squaring her shoulders.

He stepped closer, catching a fold of her robe between his thumb and finger. "This material is harsh. Can I make a suggestion?"

Esme did not demur. "By all means."

"Remain disguised as a monk. The man you stabbed last night thinks you've escaped, but may still try to find you. He's looking for a beautiful young woman with long hair. Dressed like this, he'll never recognise you. However, I'm sure your friend could find you an undergarment that would lessen your discomfort." He sniffed. "And it may improve your mood."

"I have no wish to confront that disgusting thug again. I'm happy to stay dressed like this. The discomfort is of little consequence." She knew this was a lie. She would give anything to feel soft linen against her skin.

"There's one last thing I'd like to show you, if you're willing."

Esme noted his conciliatory manner. He led the way to a low building housing five stables. "There's a mare in here, not far off giving birth. Will you keep an eye on her?"

A sleek, black head appeared over the top of a stable door and whinnied as they approached. "She's beautiful," murmured Esme.

"Yes, she is." Eirik's voice softened. "Judging by the look of her, it'll be no more than a few days." He opened the door and walked inside. "She's had fresh straw and hay, and I've filled the trough. If you could do that each morning, I'll see to her in the evenings."

Esme felt a surge of joy. She loved horses. "Yes, I can do that," she said, trying to moderate her evident delight even as she fondled the horse's mane.

"I'll walk back with you to the kitchen."

"And what plans do you have to pass the day while we labour?"

"Not that it's any of your concern, but we'll be rounding up the Saxon cowards who fled the field before battle began yesterday."

Esme's pulse raced. "And what will you do when you find them?"

His glance hinted at mischief. "What would you have me do?"

"I'd show them mercy. I . . . I'd let them work on the land."

"You think they would find that preferable to death?" Eirik pouted his lips. "A Viking would disagree with you."

Esme tossed her head. "These men are not Vikings. They would be grateful for another chance at life."

"To do what? Break their chains and rise up against us?"

"Many of them are farmers, dragged into the militia. They are husbands and fathers, not fighting men."

"I applaud your defence. However, Olaf's men enjoy a good execution." He claimed his swords from the doorway. "It's their entertainment."

She stared at him, speechless. So he was nothing more than a butcher after all, despite his elegant words of the previous evening.

Eirik bowed. "We shall meet later, my young monk. By the way, if you don't want the hall smelling like swine, I advise you to fill up the troughs with fresh water. Olaf and his men might then be tempted to wash. Prepare a good potage for their evening meal. But if they ask you to do anything unreasonable, remind them that you work for Eirik." Turning to leave, he spoke over his shoulder, "And I would advise against trying to escape. There may be no one to help you next time."

10

Shortly after, her friend Rowena arrived. She hurried to greet Esme and gave her a hug. "How are you today? Thank goodness you're safe."

Esme put a weary arm around her companion. "Dear Rowena, you're always worrying about me."

"Someone has to," grumbled Rowena. "Why won't that Viking let you come and stay with me?"

"It's best if I stay with Father Aidan."

"Why? It's bad for your welfare staying in that cold, draughty church. It's no place for a woman."

Esme took a quick glance in the covered way leading to the tavern. "Rowena, please keep your voice down," she whispered. "I'm no longer a woman. I'm a monk in training."

Rowena lifted her shoulders and let them drop with a sigh. "I suppose so." She jerked her thumb at the hostelry and smirked. "Have you seen that bunch of murderers this morning? I can't hear a peep out of any of them, except snores. Our bread saw them off."

"What makes you think it was the bread?"

At that moment Astrid walked through the door and kissed Esme's cheek. She answered the question. "We added mouldy rye and poppy seeds with hemp and darnel scavenged from the hedgerows. That's enough to make anyone crazy. I've noticed the effect of such concoctions on folk in previous years. It makes them light-headed – a sort of midsummer madness."

"The Viking tells me ground wheat is being delivered today," said Esme.

Astrid grimaced. "What a shame!" She peered into her friend's face. "I don't like how you look. The light has gone from your eyes."

"Little wonder," said Rowena, "after that crack on the head."

"I might have something to help that – a compound from the leaves and bark of the willow tree."

"Thank you, Astrid," said Esme. "You should see the list of duties the Viking has given me to organise, including cooking for Olaf and his men."

Rowena clicked her tongue. "That's totally unreasonable. Don't you worry, we'll help you and so will some of the other women."

Astrid agreed. "So, what jobs are lined up for us today?"

"There's one which will make use of your special talents, Astrid. A barn over yonder is full of medicinal herbs."

"I know. They're mine."

"The Viking wants me to take some astringents to his men on the island. They stitch up their own wounds but some can't do it, their fingers are too fat."

Astrid choked with mirth and patted her chest. "Oh dear, that image is too much for my old heart to endure. Does he also want poultices to draw out infection, and herbal teas to calm their troubled brows?"

"That's exactly what he wants." Esme smiled. "Now look what you've made me do." She dabbed her mouth. "I've split open the cut on my lip and it's bleeding again."

"I've got just the thing for that too," said Astrid.

By mid-afternoon the cows' milk was in churns; sides of ham were sliced; potatoes and carrots washed. Rowena's children collected eggs, wrapping them carefully in straw, and picked any ripe fruit from the orchard. Astrid selected astringents and healing herbs. The women who joined them kneaded yet more dough and helped to prepare vegetables for the men's evening meal. They brought whatever linen was left over from mending or making clothes, and tore up strips for bandages. Esme gathered essential thread and whatever needles were available for stitching wounds, and, when food, drink and medicines were ready, she loaded the cart and harnessed Kizzy.

"Do you want one of us to come with you?" said Rowena.

"No – you've enough to do. It's best you stay together. Leif will be there to help me."

"Even though you punched his nose?" Rowena smiled.

"I hope that horrid man is not there," said Astrid.

"Don't worry, he'll never notice me. Men only look at attractive women, not at scrawny little monks."

Astrid grinned. "You take care now, boy."

Esme set off south towards the coast. All around there were signs of the detritus of battle. Ravens still scavenged the flesh of the dead. The sight revolted her. Kizzy trotted beside the hedgerows she had sped past the night before. The mass grave where the burials were to take place was hidden from view.

They reached the edge of the fields where a track rose to the west. It entered a wood before joining a road leading to the next village, and then homeward. Esme had ridden that way many times on route to Maeldun. But would the path be wide enough for the wagon? She reined in. If she drove into the trees and released Kizzy from the harness, they could get away. Her thoughts wavered between the exhilaration of freedom and concern for Astrid and Rowena. She looked down at the village. The church still stood proud: the arbiter of morality. The tiny, fragile community was adjusting to whatever conditions would now become its normality.

Esme closed her eyes, concentrating. She made a decision and pulled the rein hard to the right. A few yards into the wood Kizzy stopped. The foliage was too dense; the wheels constantly snagged on roots. It was time to release the cart. She jumped down and yanked the leather straps of the harness. Then a rustling caused her to panic.

"Leave that alone."

Esme looked up in alarm. He was observing her with a steady gaze from the seat of his great bay horse. "Lord Eirik!" she said, "I was just—"

"I can see what you were just doing."

Esme straightened and held her head high. "I'm a prisoner of war. What would you expect me to do?"

Eirik scowled. His eyes darkened. "Well, you will not be doing so today. Back up."

She refused to move. He leaned forward and, in one smooth gesture, picked her up. She landed awkwardly on the wooden bench, her buttocks bruised and pride crushed. Kizzy stepped backwards as she pulled on the reins, but a rear wheel became embedded and the wagon refused to budge. Eirik dismounted. She slid to one side as he lifted the wagon out of the rut.

"Keep it steady," he said.

She reversed slowly until reaching the edge of the field, at which point Eirik tied his horse to the wagon and climbed aboard. "I thought your enthusiasm for flight would be curbed after last night's unpleasant escapade."

"To which do you refer? There were several as I recall. I can think of none that I shall remember with pleasure."

Eirik laughed. "Not even the dousing by the butt? Surely that was a welcome event?"

Esme recalled the bitter-sweet experience. In shame she wished to obliterate it from her mind. "You tried your best not to make it so."

"My, you have a tongue on you that would shrivel fox fur at a thousand paces. What a shame it is that you're not a man. You alone could take on ten of our enemies."

"Your enemies are not mine."

"Take care. Some of your enemies may protect you yet."

"I do not care for your type of protection."

"Indeed? Well, it can be easily withdrawn. We're not far from the shore. Shall we put it to the test?" He shook the reins and encouraged Kizzy to step out. After a while he said, "Do you live in Maeldun?"

"No. I came to repair a tapestry for Father Aidan. Rowena and Astrid have been my friends for a long time."

"Where is your home?"

Esme could see no benefit in pretending she was anything other than what she was. "Saxstow Hall."

"A large estate?"

"Yes."

"Is it far?"

She shrugged. "An hour's ride."

"And you came alone?"

"Stephan, a farmhand, usually accompanies me to the edge of whichever village I'm visiting, but he's busy at this time of year. I told him I was not going far."

"A long way for a young woman to travel unescorted. Why do you take such risks?"

Esme turned to look at him. "There has been no risk, until now."

He chose not to retort. "You live with your parents?"

"My parents were killed – by marauding Vikings."

"Now I understand."

"No, you don't," said Esme, anger spiking her tone. "You can understand nothing."

Again Eirik refused to rise to her goad. "So who do you live with?"

Esme tossed her head. She wanted him to know that she was well connected, and he would be advised to note the fact. "Lord Edmund – my guardian. He owns the estate neighbouring that of my parents. After their death, my brother and I became his wards."

Eirik clicked his tongue. "And now he controls the lands left by your father."

She paused, shocked by the bald statement. What was he insinuating? Her answer was defensive and she was unsure if it was entirely correct, "Only until such time as Brand is old enough to take control." She was determined to change the course of the conversation. "And what of you? Are your parents still alive?"

Eirik hesitated for several seconds before replying. "They died of fever when I was twelve."

"What did you do?"

"I lived with an uncle and later joined the monastery at Jomsborg."

"A monastery?" Her lips parted in surprise. Never before had she imagined that fighting men could also be monks. "Did your gods teach you how to kill and maim?"

Eirik's reply was controlled. "I was well trained. The men became my family."

"Did you not wish for a family of your own?"

His body tensed. She bit her lip and instantly regretted the inquiry. It was a personal question of a different kind; one she should not have asked.

"I once saw it as a possible future. But it was not to be." The tone indicated it was unwise to push him further on the matter.

49

They continued in silence. Esme began to feel oddly grateful for the palpable strength seeming to ebb from him and flow into her.

11

Esme's first glimpse of a Viking longship was the prow, with the carved head of a snarling serpent whose body snaked into a smooth, polished bow. Even from a distance, she marvelled at the craftsmanship of the sleek boat.

More ships came into view, beached in the shallow waters of the island adjoining the causeway, their sails neatly reefed. She envisaged them slicing through the waves with ease, perfectly balanced as they rose on the swell and dipped into watery troughs. Esme had always thought of the estuary as a dispiriting place, barren, with ugly, grey mud-flats and scant vegetation. But filled with these exciting craft it took on a different perspective, that of an adventurous highway, giving access to new lands. This must be how the Saxon ancestors had viewed it; and long before them, the Roman galleys that pioneered these waters. It was strangely thrilling.

Her heart beat faster at the impending encounter with Eirik's men moving amongst the tents they'd erected. Some were engaged in combat training, using wooden poles as weapons. Laughter and derision emanated from onlookers. Elsewhere came the flurry of clashing swords. The warriors used every part of their bodies as Eirik had done. The muscle power needed for such a weapon was not lost on her.

Threads of grey smoke rose from the fires and meandered skywards, sending acrid whiffs of resin onto the breeze. Flames licked the sides of black cauldrons that hung over red embers. Some of the men were washing, trimming and combing their beards. Others had waded through the marsh grasses into the estuary, submerging their bodies. Washed battle clothes lay drying. Decks were being scrubbed and waste removed. Edmund had always called them filthy savages. He was wrong.

She inclined her head, listening in disbelief. The men were chanting, singing in deep voices, harmonising memorised verses. "What are they singing about? Victory, I suppose."

Eirik shook his head. "They're ancient folk tunes. We're proud of our heritage."

"Which ships are yours?"

"Just the ten you see in front of you."

"So where are Olaf's?"

"Moored round the bay. He has eighty or so."

As they neared the causeway, the full extent of the fleet was revealed. Ship after mighty ship was beached within yards of each other. The whole coastline was filled with small encampments.

"I didn't know we were so outnumbered."

"Byrhtnoth's militia had no chance against such odds."

Esme felt bile rising once again. "So where will you plunder next?"

Eirik shrugged. "Thorkel, the King of Denmark's first commander, is expected to visit at any time. It will depend on how much King Aethelred is prepared to offer. We work for the highest bidder."

"You mean you kill for money alone?"

Eirik pursed his lips. "We do not fight indiscriminately."

"Why are your men wanted when there are so many already?"

"As yet we have lost neither battle, nor ship, nor man. Odin has been good."

Esme had judged his age to be not yet thirty. "You must have been young when you began your illustrious career."

"Eighteen."

"It's hard to believe these warriors would accept a mere youth as their chief."

Eirik's reply was brusque. "I cannot control what you believe, nor can I stop the bitterness of your tone. Nevertheless, it is the truth."

Esme seemed unable to avoid these verbal confrontations. The tide was out. In silence, they drove across the causeway to the island. The men shouted greetings to their leader. Leif came striding in their direction. "Did you bring fresh bread?"

"Yes, together with other delicacies for your palate. Our young monk will attend to wounds."

"Good," said Leif, evaluating Esme's garb. Quite what he thought she was unable to tell. "Fenrir has a nasty gash on his leg, deep into the flesh. He stitched it up himself, but says his fingers are too big for fine bone needles."

"Let him be seen first." Eirik turned to Esme. "Fenrir is a hairy wolf of a man but he has a heart of gold."

"Gold stolen from English coffers?" said Esme, lifting the basket of potions from the cart.

Eirik grabbed her arm. She stifled a cry. "You're hurting me."

"In case you're in any doubt, I can hurt you a great deal more. I'm a patient man until my sympathy is lost." He pushed her away. "Now go. You have much work to do."

Esme followed Leif, chiding herself for not keeping to the rules. Obey. Don't antagonise. Keep your own counsel. Only by doing that could she possibly hope to win. That had always been her policy with Edmund. But this time she found it impossible. Her presence aroused very few inquisitive glances, just the occasional nod of acknowledgement. Nobody challenged her. Fenrir was indeed the largest, hairiest man she had ever encountered. Very little of his face was visible, covered as it was with a dark-brown beard laced with grey. His long hair curled round his neck.

He looked up as she approached but made no attempt to stand. "Have you come to help me?" he said in a booming voice. "I'd be mighty grateful." Like Eirik, he spoke to her in Saxon.

Esme nodded and set to work washing his wounded leg. Without a murmur, he allowed the administrations of hot water, potions, a poultice and fresh stitches. With every completed task he thanked her profusely and complimented her skill. "You're doing a great job, lad," he said continually, sometimes breaking into his own tongue. She was surprised by how much of the language she understood. Somewhere in the back of her mind was a recollection of sitting on Grandmother's knee, learning what the sounds meant.

Esme began to feel braver when it was clear that this hirsute, avuncular man was no threat to her. Dressed as she was in the habit, Fenrir did not question that she was any other than a young man of God. No doubt he'd seen many a youth whose face favoured the fairer sex. Although Esme was conscious of the odd strands of hair loosening from the encumbrance of the cap, they were not unlike the colour of several of the men.

"Eirik tells me you're training to be a monk."

"Yes," she said, almost beginning to believe it herself.

"We're all Jomsvikings from Jomsborg, a group of King Harald Bluetooth's most formidable warriors. It's a monastic establishment. No women allowed. I expect you'll get to know all about that, lad." Fenrir winked. "Don't worry, there are ways around it. We fight for Thor and Odin. I've heard your Saxons fight in the name of their God."

Esme reflected on his statement. Byrhtnoth fought because he believed he had God on his side. She remembered the book of Bible tracts inherited from her father. Many battles had been fought with the help of God. How different were these Vikings? She propped up Fenrir's leg on a log to make him more comfortable, offering him a cup of herbal drink to relieve his pain.

Fenrir sat back, sipping the infusion in his mug. "Thank you, laddie. We've been together a long time – Eirik and me. He's been our leader for many years. Worthy of it he is, too."

Esme was curious to know what he did to deserve it. But before she plucked up the courage to ask, Fenrir closed his eyes.

12
Norwich 1979

On Saturday morning Emma retrieves the key and the three of them drive out to find the property. Suddenly Jack shouts from the back seat. "There, I think I saw a sign. Turn around, Mum." The entrance is so overgrown it is easily missed. As Emma turns into the drive, branches scratch both sides of the car as the suspensions try to iron-out the ruts. After several hundred yards the bushes thin out. A house can be seen through the foliage.

The building is timber-framed. The brickwork is angled giving an attractive patterned effect. Oak frames surround leaded-light windows. Jack is the first to run off round the back and is soon yelling with delight as he investigates dilapidated stables, a coach house, outbuildings and hen-houses.

In the centre of the house is an enclosed porch. Sonia's hand is shaking. "It's stiff. It needs a bit of oil. Here, Emma, you do it."

Emma unlocks the covered entrance then uses a separate key to enter the house. They step into a hall about five-feet square. Facing them is oak-panelled fascia. A well-worn Barbour wax jacket and a herringbone flat cap hang from a row of coat-hooks. She shivers. "Gosh, it looks as if Reginald is still here."

Sonia frowns. "It's surprising no one has taken those away. Rounded arches lead off both sides. To the left is a spacious room with a beamed ceiling. A wide, open fireplace sits on the opposite wall. Its stone chimney breast is embedded with timbers. Grey ash spills over onto the rectangular hearth – the remnants of a long-dead log fire. Emma crosses the floor and, with uneven tugs, draws back threadbare, brocade curtains revealing French windows overlooking the back garden. There's no key in the lock and she notices dried mud on the floor. Sonia is more interested in the frames. "Yuck! They're black with wood rot."

"But look at how the room is instantly brought to life with light coming in from the front and back," says Emma.

Sonia pulls a face. "Yes. I can see all those lovely little dust mites dancing in the shafts of sunshine."

Emma sighs. Most of the furniture is covered with sheets except for an armchair and one small, round, three-legged table. On its surface is an ashtray, filled with the residue of smoked cigars, and a cut-glass tumbler glittering with golden hints of dried whisky. Beneath the seat is a pair of slippers, neatly placed together on a frayed piece of carpet.

"It looks like this was his last evening," says Sonia.

"This room can be made beautiful, Mum."

"But it's so old and tired."

A latched door to the right of the fireplace opens into a long kitchen. A well-used Aga fills the chimney breast on this side of the wall. The dated floor-units support very few modern conveniences other than an old twin-tub washing machine tucked under a wooden draining-board. An empty gap suggests a missing refrigerator. However, like the lounge, windows at either end allow light to flow through.

Sonia grimaces. "This will need completely renovating."

Emma can almost see the pounds tallying in her mother's internal cash register.

Back in the lounge, opposite the kitchen entrance, is another door concealing a curved staircase. The stairs are steep. Sonia complains her knees ache. A landing overlooks the front, providing access to two large bedrooms on either side – both totally devoid of furnishings. Peeling, whitewashed walls desperately need re-plastering. Sonia looks and makes no comment.

They retrace their steps to the entrance hall and into the other corridor. On the left, a door opens into a library with a fireplace similar to the lounge except the hearth is smaller. Shelves from floor to ceiling support books on nearly every imaginable topic. Small partitions divide each ledge into subject areas, neatly labelled. Emma is captivated.

Sonia removes one of the books. "These haven't been dusted for years. They're practically falling to pieces."

"But what a collection," says Emma in amazement.

At the end of the passage, the area which mirrors the kitchen and diner on the other side has been converted into a bedroom and a bathroom. Sonia puffs out her cheeks. "Looks like Reginald didn't want to face climbing those stairs anymore. I can't say I blame him." She walks to the window. "Look at that land, Emma. Does it *all* belong to this property?"

Emma joins her mother. "Yes, I would say so. There's no evidence of border fences or even separating hedges."

"Oh, my goodness! Emma, it scares me to death." Suddenly, her mother grabs Emma's arm. "Look, the latch hasn't quite caught. Do you think someone has attempted to break in?"

Emma gives the glass a gentle push. The window immediately swings open. "It's possible. There are scuff marks on the windowsill."

"Why would anyone want to come into an empty house?"

"Perhaps to see if there's anything worth stealing."

"Well, there's nothing here I'd give you tuppence for." Sonia grits her teeth. "I'm too old for this. I *must* sell it."

13
Maeldun 991

While Fenrir slept, Esme mended a rip in his jerkin. After about half an hour, he suddenly woke and smiled. "I bet you're wondering how Eirik became our leader," he said, as though the conversation had never been interrupted.

Esme kept her voice even, "Only if you wish to tell me, sir."

Fenrir laughed, "No need to call me sir, lad. We're all equal here." He wriggled his buttocks into a more comfortable position and began his story. "Eirik was the youngest to join the Jomsvikings. One Yuletide – Eirik was eighteen – we'd all had a bit too much to drink. King Harald of Denmark, whose side we fought for, was goaded into doing battle with his sworn enemy, Jarl Haakon of Norway."

"You did battle when you were drunk?"

"Aye, we did. Normally we could have taken Haakon's men without a problem, but our wits and speed were thwarted by drink. We were overwhelmed – totally defeated. Only seventy of us survived and the Jarl decided to behead us all."

Esme gasped.

"It's the truth, lad. We were being executed one by one. Ten of us had lost our heads already. The next in line was Eirik. So young he seemed, but he didn't fear death so much as love life."

She handed Fenrir a fresh infusion, pulled up her knees under the habit and sat with her arms round her legs. "What happened?"

Fenrir took another slurp and pulled a face. "Odin's ass, what's gone into this?"

Esme wondered what Astrid would say about the expletive applied to her special medicine. "I don't know. It's a secret."

"Best thing for it." Fenrir held his nose and swallowed the rest in one gulp.

"You were about to tell me what happened."

"Ah, yes, so I was. At the time, Eirik had long silky hair. One of the jarl's henchmen took a liking to it. Said he wanted it once Eirik's head was off his body. Eirik, cheeky young tyke as he was, saw his advantage. Said it would be a pity for his locks to be stained with blood. He challenged the henchman to hold onto his hair while the axe man did his worst. Someone from the crowd shouted, 'Do it, Gunnar. There is precious little of yours left, you can use it afterwards.' The dullard couldn't resist the offer." Fenrir guffawed.

Esme's eyes were wide. "And did he? – Take hold of it, that is?"

"Gunnar twisted the long strands round his hand and held on tight. But just as the axe swung, Eirik jerked his head taking Gunnar's lower arm with him. The executioner chopped that off instead, nearly up to the elbow." Fenrir laughed so much his eyes watered. "You should have seen the blood. It was entertaining, though, to see Gunnar's hand and forearm dangling from Eirik's hair."

A tremor ran through Esme's body. She reminded herself that despite the camaraderie, Fenrir was still a brutal heathen.

The old Viking wiped tears from his cheeks. "I'm sorry, lad, I was forgetting you'd be unused to such sights as I."

"Did Eirik escape?"

"No! Not exactly. The jarl himself had witnessed the event. He said it was the will of Thor that the boy be saved. Eirik thanked him for the gift of life and said he would like to give him something in return. He had a nerve, I'll say that."

Esme was so absorbed by the story that she almost forgot she was playing a role. "What did he have to give?"

"He offered Jarl Haakon the rest of the group as fighting men."

"And did he accept?"

"Not at first. I don't think he had too good an opinion of us after the battle. He called us a pathetic bunch of drunken marauders. But Eirik was clever. He told the jarl that by tomorrow we'd all be sober, with fighting prowess second to none. He said our allegiance was to the highest bidder, and life is the supreme bid of all. Quite a crowd gathered and Haakon asked the people whether he should accept the terms. There was a roar of approval."

"And Eirik was freed?"

"Not just Eirik, the rest of us too. We were all saved because of him. But that wasn't quite the end. The jarl made Eirik swear on the figure of Thor that he and his followers would dedicate their whole lives to Viking service, until they die or be slain."

Esme frowned, wondering the implication of that. "Did that mean none of you could marry?"

"At the time, yes. But many of us have wives now. They provide great support. And if we win and make money, everyone benefits."

Except the ones you've plundered, thought Esme, but this time she knew enough to keep her mouth shut. She felt more confident. "Do you have a family, Fenrir?"

The man slowly shook his head. "My wife died in childbirth and took the young'un with her."

"I'm sorry."

"'Twas long ago. Eirik is my son now." Fenrir pushed his lower lip forward. "I keep telling him to find a wife, so he can have a son. But there's too much resentment in his heart."

Esme frowned, not daring to ask further, but Fenrir continued. "She left him for another just before the ceremony, someone who had greater wealth and power. It was Eirik's childhood friend, so he felt doubly betrayed."

A tinge of something she couldn't identify coursed through Esme's veins. Then it dawned on her. Edmund had wealth and power and she needed the stability.

Fenrir was enjoying his captive audience. "Eirik's had plenty of offers mind. But he's not like the rest of us." He grinned conspiratorially, "Not that I expect you would know much about that. Not yet, anyway."

Fenrir punched Esme's shoulder. She balked at the sharp pain. "Sorry," he said. "I was forgetting you're nought but a lad." He sighed. "I'm sorry, too, about your leader and your men but, you must agree, your God is ineffectual compared to Thor. And Eirik is a good leader. He's fair-minded – a man by which others judge themselves. Most of us are found wanting."

Esme felt irritated by this slight on her God and their Saxon leader. Nevertheless, she spoke with conviction. "Byrhtnoth was a good man."

Fenrir shrugged. "Maybe – I suppose someone has to lose. Eirik – he has some unworldly quality. It's like his strength comes from Thor and Odin themselves. They protect him. He took a vow and has never broken it."

A shadow fell over Fenrir. Esme looked up to see Eirik holding a pile of tunics over one arm.

"I've brought needles and thread. Now, monk, see what you can do with stitching the rips made by the swords of Byrhtnoth."

Esme lowered her eyes, blinking hard.

"That's a harsh reminder, lord," said Fenrir.

Eirik glared, threw the clothes on the ground and strode away.

Fenrir put an enormous hand on Esme's shoulder. "Don't take any notice of him. Something's riled him and he's taking it out on you."

Esme understood full well what his source of that annoyance was – it was her. But she said nothing. As she sewed, Fenrir slept. Her nimble and skilful fingers worked quickly, the needle ducking in and out of each rent. By the time she had finished, the sun was low in the sky. Eirik was nowhere to be seen so she placed the clothes in a pile and went to find the wagon. It was where she left it, ready harnessed. No one stopped her leaving.

14

Rowena and Astrid were keen to know how Esme had faired. She recounted the tale that Fenrir had told her about Eirik. "So it seems Lord Eirik and his crew are all monks."

Rowena's mouth dropped open. "How could monks behave as they have?"

"They're followers of Thor and Odin."

"I suppose that explains it," said Rowena with sarcasm. "Our Lord told us not to take up swords."

"True. But I can't help thinking that many of our battles have been fought in the name of the Lord."

Rowena was silent. "That's different."

"How different, Rowena?" said Astrid.

Rowena turned over a piece of dough and slammed it onto a wooden board then hit it with her fist. "Entirely different."

Astrid smiled. "I'm glad you were well received, Esme. Sounds like this Viking called Fenrir is quite a character."

Rowena glared at Astrid. "Quite a character? How could you think such a thing?"

"You must admit it's an exciting story. That Viking leader is a true believer in his own way."

"In the wrong way, Astrid, perhaps we should try and set him straight."

Esme said no more, not wishing to cause a rift between her friends. She made her way over to the stable to see the pregnant mare Eirik had asked her to take care of. There was very little to do. Hay and straw were still fresh. He must have come over the night before. Esme stroked the mare's ears then moved to a neighbouring stable, fetched Kizzy and walked back to the kitchen where her friends had piled up fresh vegetables and milk. In the afternoon, she once again loaded the cart. Rowena insisted she take no more risks. "Lord Edmund will come looking for us soon, so no more attempts to escape, my girl."

"And make sure you come back before dark," said Astrid.

Esme kissed them both as she climbed aboard and set off. When she passed the battlefield she saw men moving about behind the hedgerows. Were they plundering the bodies of the dead or had Eirik kept his promise to bury them?

Leif came alone to meet her and help unload. There was no sign of Eirik. The cauldrons were already heating and she was surprised he hadn't come to berate her for being late. She hauled over the sacks of chopped vegetables and tipped in the contents, adding barley and fresh herbs. Leif ordered two of the men to add the water Esme had drawn from the village well, and instructed them to stoke the fires.

As she was stirring the potage pounding hooves crossed the causeway and Eirik pulled up in front of her. "It won't be long now before we have a foal," he said. "When you've done, come and find me over by the water's edge. I have something to show you."

When the broth was simmering, Leif pointed to Eirik sitting on a stool with his back to them, absorbed in a task. She walked slowly towards him.

"You came then, monk," said Eirik, somehow knowing it was her. The Viking shifted his leg and swung round. Her eyes were drawn to a knife in his hand. He was whittling a piece of bark – some four feet in length.

"I see you're interested in my carving." He held it up. "Inspect it! I would have your opinion, good or bad."

Esme's interest quickened. The shape was in the form of a cross. He had utilised the structure of the bark to imply the outline of a figure, hanging, crucified. Yet there were small details such as a crown of thorns, and nails in the hands and feet. Despite herself, she was unable to disguise the admiration in her voice. "Where did you learn to carve like this?"

"My father taught me. We may be heathens in this land but we are not without some god-given creativity. It's for your fallen men – a tribute to the dead."

Esme stared, aware of hot tears standing proud in her eyes. He had instilled a sense of reverence into a misshapen lump of wood.

"Do you like it?" he said.

"Yes . . . very much."

"Tell me why. To me it represents grief and defeat."

She swallowed hard. "It speaks to me more of joy than sorrow."

"But look! Your god is dying. He can no longer protect you because his power has been taken away by death. Surely that's a source of failure."

"No, it's a reason to rejoice, because after three days he rises again and overcomes death – just as we will."

"Do you mean that in three days those corpses will rise again? I have fought many battles against you Christians but never have I witnessed such a phenomenon."

"No, it doesn't mean that." Esme shook her head finding it more difficult to explain than she'd anticipated. "It means that their souls will go to be with Our Lord."

"Just as our warriors join Odin in Valhalla? And drink at his table until they fight beside him in the final battle?"

Esme's brow furrowed, mulling over the comparison.

"You see, we are not so different, are we?"

Making her point more forcibly, she said, "Well, our God preaches peace and love, not war and hate."

Eirik's gaze lingered on her face. "Then those brave Saxons were not doing your Christ's work after all, because they fought with hate in their bellies. I saw it in their eyes. They could not have done so much damage otherwise." He let out a dramatic sigh. "Perhaps I should destroy this cross since all of them must have displeased their God." He pretended to toss it in the air with heedless disregard.

Esme stepped forward. "No! That would be sacrilege." She grasped his arm. His muscles tightened in response and she snatched her hand away.

Eirik frowned. "In that case, we'll give it to your priest and allow him to make the decision."

The cauldrons were emitting delicious aromas. Eirik's voice adopted the harsh, commanding tone with which she'd become familiar. "See to the food. Serve my men. Leif will help." Then he added, more gently, "After that, come and eat with us."

15

Esme had decided not to join Eirik, but she was hungry and needed something to eat before the return journey. Broth was followed by slices of ham, bread, boiled eggs, cheese and apples. Most of the men drank the cows' milk or the fresh water. Others preferred the ale they brought with them on board, but nobody became drunk. When they finished, there was a rota for washing and clearing away. The men whose turn it was argued that the monk should do the chores, but Eirik intervened. "He's done enough for you today, preparing this excellent repast." Further argument ceased.

They sat in small groups, each defined by an activity: talking, telling stories and jokes, arm wrestling, playing board games, or making music. Esme sat between Leif and Eirik. The fire offered a warm orange glow, softening the hardened faces of men who, little more than two days ago, were engaged in fierce hand-to-hand combat. Esme yawned, overcome with weariness. She had eaten well and the atmosphere was soporific, although she was acutely aware of fraternising with the enemy. She would rest a little longer then muster the energy to drive back.

"Come, Eirik, play us a tune on the pan-pipes," encouraged Fenrir.

Eirik pursed his lips and blew into the instrument; a haunting melody filled the evening air. For Esme, each note evoked the colour green or blue, and soothed her anxieties.

"And what colour was that tune, lord Eirik?" said Leif in a mocking tone.

"Green," said Eirik, with no suggestion of awkwardness.

"Occasionally blue," Esme blurted out. She blushed as they turned to look at her.

Leif rolled his eyes. "Not you as well, monk, green with hints of blue?" He laughed.

"The lad's right. There were touches of blue. So you see colours too?" said Eirik, with ill-disguised astonishment.

Esme nodded.

"In the name of Odin," said Leif, "you're both as mad as each other. I don't see the colours and glad of it I am too. There's enough variety for me in the world already."

Eirik jerked his head towards Leif but addressed Esme. "I thought everyone did, until I met this unimaginative bunch."

Esme glanced at Fenrir who took another swig of ale and examined them both with a wary eye, keeping his own counsel. "Right," he said finally, "what's next? Let's have some well-known ballads. Eirik will accompany us."

She found it difficult to follow the meaning of all the words, but understood the essence of the songs. They sang nostalgic sagas of war, ships at sea and bravery in battle, but she was amazed when they also crooned about love, faithfulness and friendship.

As Eirik finished playing, Fenrir turned to Esme. "This time each of us makes up words to a tune," he said. "Perhaps you'd like to join in?"

Esme shook her head. "I must get back."

"No, no, plenty of time yet, youth. You must sing for us. We all do it – your voice has not yet broken. It'll be birdsong to our ears."

"Not like yours then, Fenrir," said Leif. "Your notes are like the horns that foreshadow fog."

Fenrir aimed a clout at Leif's ear. The younger man ducked his head and laughed.

Esme protested her reluctance but Fenrir reassured her. "It's easy, even I can do it. Just let the words come."

She listened twice to Eirik's simple tune then, to her relief, she found the words flowed easily.

"Those were the days when my love and I
Sat beneath a starry sky
And stole a kiss and made a wish
My love and I."

A man in their small group clapped. "Very good, lad, and what would you wish for after you've stolen that kiss?"

"Leave the poor lad alone, Osric," said Fenrir. "He's not had time to think about that yet. We all know what you'd be thinking of." Fenrir cupped his hands expansively over his chest, creating more laughter.

As the evening wore on, they played or devised lyrics until the sun dipped below the horizon, brushing the sky grey. Stars began to emerge one by one and shone with startling brightness. Esme suddenly panicked. "I must go at once."

Eirik stood, yawned and stretched. "No. It's too dangerous. Besides, the tide's coming in. Go back at first light. Leif, snuggle up with Fenrir tonight – the young monk can sleep in your tent."

Leif protested. "Why me? Fenrir snores rattle his bones enough to burst his new stitches. Let the boy sleep next to him in case it proves to be so."

The man called Osric roared with mirth. "Come now, Leif, you may never get another offer as good as this one."

"The lad can have my tent, then," said Eirik. He beckoned to Esme. "Come, I'll show you where it is."

He led Esme to the outer limits of the main encampment beside a small copse beyond which ran a narrow tributary. When they reached his tent, he held open the flap. She hesitated, biting her lip.

"Don't worry, I'll not trouble you," he said, clearly noticing her concern. "Neither will anybody else. Nobody ever comes to this part of the island. They like to stay close to their ships. On a night like this I prefer to be outside."

"May I ask you something?" she said.

"Of course."

"How long have you been seeing the colours – those that appear with the notes?"

"All my life. But I've come to understand that it's not an ability given to everyone. I wish I didn't have it. Sometimes I see the auras of people too. Often a man's colour defies the truth of his words."

"That must be hard to bear."

Eirik gazed at her for a moment before entering the tent and fetching a rug for himself. "Sleep well. You've another busy day tomorrow."

Exhausted, Esme slumped down and sat cross-legged. How could she have been so foolish as to leave her return until it was too late? Astrid and Rowena would be worried about her. What on earth would she say to them in the morning?

She heard rustling outside and peeked through a gap in the opening to see Eirik lighting a fire. Fresh sap hissed and spat; erratic flames cast livid shadows. Feeling strangely protected by his presence, she lay back and tucked a woollen blanket tightly around her. Once her heart settled its pace, the physical and mental ordeal of the past two days overcame her.

16

Eirik lit a fire, spread out his rug and lay down with his arms tucked under his head. He gazed at the blackness above, now filled with tightly packed stars. Their eternity mocked his lowliness: a mere man ineptly taking control of his future. It was a peace he craved; he longed to be released from his vow to Thor. He loved this woman's conversation, quick wit and even the barbed comments with which she tried to strike his core. He longed to take her in his arms. Trying to drive the vision from his thoughts, he rolled onto his side and pulled the blanket around him. His situation was untenable, one from which he must extricate himself as soon as possible before he did something to regret.

He woke at first light and kicked over the embers of the fire. Dawn rays struck the surface of a still visible moon as thin grey clouds scurried across its orb. He knew his men would all be asleep, and there was no sound from the tent. Nothing stirred. His body was drenched in sweat; hair stuck to the nape of his neck. He longed to submerse his body, to be cleansed.

He strolled through the trees and headed towards the tributary that ran from the estuary. Remnants of the tide lapped softly against its banks and morning fog clung to its surface. He took a deep breath and pulled off his clothes, allowing the invigorating air of a new day to cool his skin. Coarse, dew-soaked grasses massaged the soles of his feet as he stepped onto the gravelly mud of the embankment. Cupping the chilly water in his palms, he splashed it over his face, across his chest and shoulders. Then he crouched and surrendered himself to the river, first swimming underwater; then turning onto his back and bringing his arms rhythmically above his head. Closing his lids, he soaked in the bourgeoning beams of sun. Satisfied, he pressed into the shallows. Sleek eddies swirled around his legs as he strode towards shore.

An unexpected splash penetrated the silence. He squinted through the suspended haze, immediately alert. At first he could see nothing, but directed his gaze towards the sound of ripples made by regular movement. Then he saw her. Esme! She was emerging from the water. Eirik stood quite still, hoping the mist would conceal him and save her embarrassment. He watched, mesmerised, as she scrambled up the bank towards him. He knew he should turn away, make a noise and pretend he hadn't seen her, but his feet refused to move. Instead he was unwilling to rend the mystery of the moment – until it was too late. They stood facing one another, motionless.

There in the swirling fog Eirik felt as though they were both new creations: man and woman, so different, yet inexorably drawn to one another. Without thinking, he smiled and stretched out his arm towards her. She responded calmly until their fingertips almost touched; the unspoken communication complete. A warm glow ignited within him. The world faded and for the space of a few precious moments they were no longer enemies.

Suddenly, an ugly, intrusive noise reverberated somewhere in the estuary – the loud, unearthly drone of a horn. The bubble burst and the world surged through with all its soul-destroying reality. Eirik stepped aside and looked up; the moment shattered. He drew in his lips, struggling to regain composure. His eyes narrowed. Esme was shaking. "Dress at once," he said. "Return to town. Forkbeard has arrived." He grabbed his clothes from an overhanging branch and marched off into the trees.

*

Esme had been careful to rise early. To be seen would expose her disguise. Eirik had reassured her that no one ever came over this way, and by the time she emerged from the tent he had gone. Overnight, the coarse wool irritated and reddened her skin. The prickly heat chafed unbearably; the temptation of the river was too great. She had dragged the rough fabric over her head, relieved to be rid of its bulk. As she waded in, cold water crept up her thighs and over her waist, numbing and soothing her inflamed flesh.

On seeing him in the mist, she had felt no embarrassment – something she could not later explain. He had held out his hand in welcome as though they were the only two people in the world. A feeling of joy and belonging had overwhelmed her. What could she have been thinking? The horn had hardened his demeanour. He rebuked her. Now she felt nothing but shame.

Dressing quickly, she hurried back, full of self-reproach. The camp bustled with activity by the time she arrived. Fenrir came out of his tent pulling up his trousers and fastening his belt.

"What's happening?" Esme asked him, seeing yet another fearful fleet of Viking longboats. A ship had moored next to Eirik's. Two men jumped into the water, heading for shore. One was the tallest man she had ever seen. "Who are they," she whispered.

"Sweyn, the King of Denmark, son of Harald," said Fenrir. "He drove out his father and put himself on the throne. The other is Thorkel the Tall – once a leader of the Jomsvikings, now one of Sweyn's lieutenants."

Both men heartily embraced Eirik, slapping him on the back. Esme watched the scene, aware that they were enlisting Eirik's help to plunder and loot more of the countryside. She felt mortified by her behaviour; she was nothing more than a collaborator. How could she have sat with enemies last evening, allowing the music and song to overcome her reason? So many people had been slaughtered, and now the three of them would be making more plans against her fellow men.

She glanced at Fenrir. He, too, was her enemy. But what were the words she had been taught? 'Love your enemy, do good to those who hate you.' Her inclination was the antithesis. She determined to pray about it.

To her surprise, Eirik, Sweyn Forkbeard and Thorkel mounted horses and rode across the causeway. "Where are they going?"

The old Viking shrugged. "Back to the village, I shouldn't wonder, to talk to Olaf."

Esme harnessed Kizzy and followed not long after.

17
London, 1979

On Tuesday morning Emma is back in the office having spent Monday in Cambridge tutoring students. She also spent part of the day in Cambridge University Library and now has a good understanding of tenth-century Viking plunderers, and even finds mention of the legendary Jomsvikings.

Bjorn Erikson telephones. "Do you mind if I bring someone with me to Maldon?"

Emma has been expecting his wife to join them. "No, not at all. There's a car park below this building. How long will you be?"

"About an hour."

The vision of a woman with immaculate clothes and flawless make-up comes to mind. She sighs. There is no way she can compete with that and is glad she's worn a summer frock instead of her usual navy suit. She feels more relaxed in the swirly skirt, cinched at the waist with a matching jacket, even if it is from Selfridges and not Harrods. And she has released her hair so it curls over her shoulders. After all, Maldon is the next best thing to the seaside.

Bjorn arrives. He is wearing jeans and an open-necked shirt with a casual leather jacket.

She glances at her watch. "You're exactly on time," she says with a smile.

He grins. *White, even teeth! He really is a handsome man.*

To her astonishment, a chauffeur opens the rear door of a Rolls Royce and introduces himself as Karl. Emma settles into a beautifully moulded, cream leather seat, and imbibes the aroma. A young girl is sitting in the middle. "Hello. I'm Greta."

"I'm Emma. It's nice to meet you," she says, shaking the girl's hand.

Bjorn Erikson opens the opposite door and takes a seat. "I see you two have been introduced. This is my daughter."

Greta speaks in Danish. "We have, Papa. She's very pretty."

Bjorn frowns. "Where are your manners? Speak English."

Emma is reluctant to assure him that she understands perfectly; they would then expect her to speak Danish. Perhaps, if the occasion arises, she will tell them about her Danish grandmother, who sadly died a few months ago.

Greta keeps up a continuous chatter. Emma begins to feel more and more comfortable in the company of Bjorn and his daughter. She wonders why Greta's mother has not joined them, but doesn't dare ask.

Greta's curls bounce as she speaks and her eyes glint with mischief, like her father's. She talks about the horses her father rears and trains to race.

"They're not all my horses," says Bjorn. "I have stallions which cover mares for a price. Then I rear the young colts or fillies and assess their potential as winners."

The child nods wisely. "A stallion can have many wives and many babies," she says, totally unabashed.

Bjorn turns to Emma, "How did you come to be interested in archaeology?"

Emma shrugs. "My father lectured in History and was a good friend of our County Archaeologist in Norfolk. He took me along to the digs."

"But you qualified as a medical doctor?"

Emma grimaces, "My mother's influence. She was a midwife. What about you? How did you come to rear horses?"

"In my blood, I'm afraid, inherited from my grandfather."

"So you're not really a farmer. You said your whetstone was found on your farm."

"The land was farmed for centuries, but times changed. You mentioned Norfolk. Is that where you used to live?"

"I still do. I go home to Norwich at weekends to spend time with my son. He's nearly eleven."

"Bit older than me, then," says Greta. "I'm only just ten." Unexpectedly, the girl changes the subject for which Emma is grateful; she hates talking about herself. "Will there be skeletons on the battlefield in Maldon? How many people died?"

It occurs to Emma how well Greta would get on with Jack.

Soon they arrive in Maldon and find a parking space. Emma notes the Rolls Royce has a right-hand drive and assumes it must be kept in England. It is a glorious day. "We'll be an hour or so," says Bjorn to Karl, who is staying with the car.

The three of them begin the walk down London Road and onto High Street. Greta comments on how old and lovely some of the buildings are. Emma has to agree, it is a delightful town. She asks a passer-by if there is a borough museum. "Yes," is the reply, "but unfortunately it's closed today. A water main burst last night. If you want to know about the battle, we have the Maldon Archaeological Group. They hold meetings on Wednesday evenings in the local community centre. You'll find information in the cafe on The Hythe below St Mary's church. Try there."

They stroll towards the river and St Mary the Virgin church, which, they discover, stood at the time of the battle, but which was rebuilt by the Normans. They gaze at the beautiful coloured-glass windows and wander up the nave into the chancel. A sudden icy shiver runs down Emma's spine.

Bjorn picks up a leaflet. "This says evidence of a timber Saxon church was found on this site dating from the seventh century. The building provided not only religious services but also acted as a warning signal for shipping, and a lookout for invaders."

"Do you think the Vikings invaded this church, Papa?"

"It's possible, Greta."

"I can imagine them barging in through that old door," she says, "the one with the curly hinges and iron studs. Do you think they broke it down? I bet all the people inside were very afraid."

Emma experiences the shiver again. "It is a little cold in here."

"That's because you've come in from the sunshine," pronounces the all-knowing Greta. "Can we go and eat? I'm hungry."

"Yes, love. Let's find the place that woman was talking about."

They walk out into the warmth. A short stroll and they are in the restaurant below the church. Greta chooses a table on a patio overlooking the estuary. She is fascinated by the moored boats with their high masts and furled red sails. Inside the entrance is a notice board for tourists. There, as the woman has said, is a poster advertising a meeting the following evening, starting at 7 p.m. The Archaeological Group have invited a speaker, Bernard Johnson, to give a talk entitled 'Aftermath of the Battle of Maldon'.

"It might be helpful," says Emma.

"Can you come back tomorrow evening?" says Bjorn.

"Yes. I wouldn't want to miss it."

"I can pick you up from your office and then take you home, if you'll allow me."

At that moment, there is nothing Emma would like more.

"Do you suppose the Viking raiders sat here?" Greta asks. "They would need to eat, wouldn't they? They'd take the townspeople's food, and drink all their mead. I bet they got drunk and made the women wait on them."

Bjorn and Emma laugh, but Emma knows the girl is right.

Greta continues. "Can we go to the battlefield? I'd like to look for old bones."

"Of course," says her father.

Greta finds no bones, but they see the proximity of Northey Island to the mainland, and the exposed causeway when the tide goes out. Emma tells how Byrhtnoth was persuaded by the Viking leaders that the fight was unfair, unless the warriors were allowed to cross to the mainland and fight man-to-man.

"It couldn't possibly be fair if there were more Vikings than Saxons," says Greta, matter-of-factly.

"Well, we'll find out more tomorrow night," says Bjorn.

"Can I come?" says Greta.

"Absolutely not. It will be well past your bedtime."

Greta pouts, speaking Danish. "You just want her to yourself."

Emma catches her breath, but Bjorn ignores the comment and his daughter's choice of language. "You're staying at home. And that's final."

Greta speaks again in Danish. "Anyway, it doesn't matter. Karl is teaching me how to play poker."

18
Maeldun 991

As soon as Esme arrived, she went in search of Father Aidan. Recognising her footsteps, he called out, "Good day, child. I was worried when you didn't return last night."

"I was well looked after," said Esme, thinking how God had protected her from ultimate ignominy only two hours earlier. The moment of disgrace still penetrated deep into her conscience. What made her stand there with the Viking, without guilt, in an unreal existence for a few seconds only?

The priest massaged his legs. "Glad to hear it. The old knees are finding all-night prayers more and more difficult. I was working on a manuscript."

Esme looked at the burned-down candles on Aidan's writing table. "You'll strain your eyes, Father."

"It's too late to worry about that. I have little time to finish all I must do. This one is for Eirik. He wants a translation of one of Paul's letters."

Esme's jaw dropped. "How can that be?"

"He's searching for a more satisfactory answer to life and death than Thor and Odin provide."

"He didn't give me that impression yesterday. He had me convinced there was little difference between our gods."

"I think that's the way he confronts us, to make us defend our point of view. But I'm sure he's seeking the truth. We had a long talk that first night, after the battle, when everyone was asleep."

"You, Father, and the heathen, you talked?"

"Oh yes. He was curious about Christ."

Esme stared at him. "Really? Why?"

"King Harald tried to impose Christianity on Denmark and Norway, but many rejected it. That's one of the reasons they supported Sweyn."

"I can understand that. I'd hate having belief in Thor's hammer forced upon me in place of the cross of Christ. Did you know Eirik has been crafting a crucifix?"

"I did. It will mean a great deal to be able to display it to the wives and children of the deceased. Some of their husbands will help to fill in the mass grave."

"Their husbands?" Esme took a breath. "I thought they were dead."

"The warriors are dead. But there were those who ran away. Not out of cowardice, but through lack of experience. Those who wield a scythe to cut grass cannot easily transfer its purpose to killing a man."

Esme frowned. "Eirik said he would execute them if found."

"Clearly he hasn't. They were roped together and made to work."

"So it's true about the Vikings burying our warriors."

"Yes, child, the men have been busy for two days digging graves."

"I saw them in the field. I wasn't sure I believed it and wondered if they were looting the bodies."

Aidan hobbled over to his jug of water. "Eirik has asked me to say appropriate words over our dead as they prepare to meet with God. It's far more than would normally be expected of a victor. By the way, I thought I heard a horn this morning. Is it Thorkel the Tall?"

Esme wondered why Aidan would assume that. Did he know already? "So I've been told," she said, "together with the King of Denmark and another contingent of ships. I don't understand what the king's doing here. My little brother is staying with his sister, Gunhilde."

Aidan spluttered. "Gunhilde, the King of Denmark's sister! I didn't realise you knew her."

"Yes, I know her. She lives an hour's ride from Edmund. My grandmother was from Denmark. Many people from the northern lands settled here and had families. You'd think the battles would be over by now. Instead, they seem worse than ever."

Aidan ran a hand over his stubbly chin. "The Norsemen are from many different groups, Esme, who are often enemies of each other. Some come to kill, but others come to protect us – at a price."

She gave him a swift glance. "That's awful. How do we know it's not just one big plot to extract silver from us which they then split between them?"

Aidan shook his head. "I suppose we don't."

"Do you think that's what Sweyn Forkbeard is doing? Come with a promise to protect us from Olaf's invaders? I bet they're all in it together – Eirik, the king and Thorkel. They're conniving."

"I doubt Eirik is involved in such a conspiracy," said Aidan, brushing white dust from his robe, "but it's possible." Aidan splashed his face and towelled it dry as he turned back to her. He put a hand on Esme's shoulder, lowering his voice. "I'm sorry, child. This must bring back the most awful memories."

"The conversations you and I had, Father, after my parents were killed, helped me to accept my new life with Edmund."

"Speaking of Edmund, will he know you're here by now?"

"I would have thought so. He left a couple of weeks ago to see King Aethelred."

"I confess I was not happy when Edmund assumed responsibility for your father's lands. I had reservations about his motives."

"It made sense for him to do so since his lands adjoined ours."

Aidan hung his towel on a hook. "Even so, it is *your* fields that are rich and fertile. Your sheep provide valuable wool, and your woodlands favour oak and ash for building Aethelred's war ships." He pouted his lips as he blew out a breath. "Are you happy to marry Edmund?"

Esme sighed. "He says it's time our relationship is, what he calls, regularised. We must observe the proprieties and prevent gossip. Marriage would secure the future. I see it as my duty."

Aidan shrugged, "Only as a duty?"

"Come, Father, don't you remember telling me the biblical story of Ruth – the penniless young widow? By marrying Boaz, an older, wealthy man, she secured the future of herself and her mother-in-law. If God approved of *her* behaviour, then surely he can have no quarrel with mine."

"You are set on the union, then?"

"I am sure it will be satisfactory, for both parties."

The priest suddenly raised his head, startled, as more light filled the room. Esme swung round to see Eirik standing on the threshold. She wondered how long he'd been listening, but soon knew the answer.

"Go about your business," he said to her. "Most of the men will be here tonight. There's no need to go to the island today." Then he added with a tinge of bitterness, "It will give you practice for when you're in charge of Lord Edmund's household."

So he *had* overheard. Well, it mattered not. She was no more to him than a temporary servant, and he was no more to her than an arrogant heathen.

Astrid and Rowena were in the kitchen. "We missed you last night," said Rowena.

Esme felt her cheeks warming. "I didn't get back until late – there was much to do."

Astrid looked doubtful but said no more. "I've brought you a soft undergarment. I made it myself. I'm sorry it's taken so long."

Esme was delighted. "Thank you, Astrid. I'm so grateful."

"I was making you a soft shift anyway, but then that Viking came to my house and asked me to provide one for you. He said the material you're wearing is too abrasive for skin like yours."

Esme stared at her friend. "He came to your house? When?"

"Yesterday, late afternoon, after you left."

Esme remembered that Eirik had turned up on Northey Island after she arrived. This news confirmed that he'd been in the town, but the reason astonished her.

"He's a strange one," said Astrid. "Commits murder on the one hand and insists on soft undergarments on the other. It seems he's taking care of you."

Esme grimaced. "I don't pretend he has any care for me – or for anyone. It's to make sure I can continue working for him." She noticed a small smirk on Astrid's face and was anxious to change the subject.

"Rowena, do you have any prepared dyes to colour skeins?"

"Yes. Which colours do you want?"

"As many as you have."

"It just so happens that I collected woad and lichen not long ago for blue and purple, and weld for yellow."

"Any reddish brown?"

Yes – from madder, and a range of greenish colours. I made some mordant too from clubmoss. When we've finished here, come with me and take a look."

"Thank you. I will."

"Why do you want them?" said Rowena.

"I thought I might design a tribute to our men."

19

That night, despite her tiredness, Esme lay on her pallet unable to sleep. Eirik had allowed her to think he intended to kill the captured men but, in fact, had saved them. Had she misjudged him – unable to see when he was taunting her because of her own prejudice? On the other hand, he was involved with Forkbeard.

It was still dark outside when Esme awoke to a hollering that was filled with so much pain it wrenched her heart. She sat bolt upright and picked up the candle. The cry was familiar: a horse in labour. The church was pitch-black. The feeble flame cast eerie shadows on the floor not daring to penetrate the crevices of the walls. She unbolted the door and ran to the stable block.

Inside the stable a lighted torch nestling in an iron sconce revealed the source of the problem. The mare was lying on her side on fresh straw, distressing moans coming from deep in her throat. Eirik was kneeling behind her.

Esme's shadow fell across the stable floor and Eirik lifted his head. "The foal is in the wrong position."

"Can you help her?" Esme whispered.

"Yes – if you help me."

She nodded enthusiastically. "What shall I do?"

"It's a breech birth." Eirik beckoned her. "The waters have ruptured. Look, one hoof is visible." Esme peered at the tiny protuberance covered in a white, rubbery coating. "I need fresh water and grease to find out what's causing the blockage."

She did not hesitate, knowing exactly where to find Astrid's ointment. Then she ran to the well. Slops from the bucket soaked the front of her clothes as she hurried back. Eirik submerged his right arm, washed it clean to the elbow and smeared it with the oil. Gently entering the birth canal, he followed the length of the foal's protruding leg. "I can feel the problem," he grunted. "The head is turned backwards and one foreleg is tucked underneath." He withdrew his arm. "Help me to get her to stand."

Esme lifted the animal's head uttering soothing reassurances, while Eirik kneeled down and placed a shoulder beneath the mare's neck. The strain of trying to push out the foal had drained the mare of energy, yet she seemed to understand what was expected. With one final surge, she was on her feet.

"Well done!" said Eirik. "The foal has slid back inside her. Now I can try again."

Esme waited, holding her breath, excited by the thrilling expectation of new life. "Can you do it?"

"The bent foreleg has straightened. If I can just tip the foal's head forward. Come on you little beauty." Then he shouted triumphantly. "The head has shifted. It should come out easily now." He stood up, a gleam in his eyes. "Keep stroking her nose. It'll relax her."

The mare moaned and slumped onto the straw as the powerful contractions started again. Two small hooves appeared as far as the knees, followed by a muzzle and then the head. Esme raised clenched fists and shook them in joy. The mare rested for a few minutes until, with a final thrust, the foal emerged fully and lay close beside its mother, still joined by the umbilical cord.

"We'll let them stay like that for a while," said Eirik, wiping fluids from his arm. "The foal needs vital life-blood from his mother."

Esme turned to face him. "It's wonderful. You saved them both."

Eirik picked her up and swung her round. She laughed. He slowly let her slip down his chest, through his arms until her toes touched the ground. Without thinking she kissed his cheek.

"A kiss is worthy of a response," he said, and his mouth covered hers, tender but brief. With a reluctant sigh, he released her.

Esme's pulse sprinted like a young horse. She could still feel his lips on hers, warm and soft, but guilt charged through her. She was betrothed to be married. Edmund and Eirik were enemies. She pretended to ignore the kiss and focused instead on the mare, which was licking and nuzzling her foal. After a while the newborn creature staggered uncertainly to its feet.

"It's a colt," said Eirik. "Just look at how sturdy he is! No wonder the poor old girl had trouble. He'll make a great warhorse." He glanced at Esme. "Thank you for your help."

"It's a wonder everyone else isn't awake," said Esme.

"The men will have drunk enough ale to keep them asleep all night. Come to think of it, we should celebrate too." Eirik picked up a small pitcher.

"Local mead?" said Esme.

"Yes. I was about to have a swig of this when I heard the mare and came running. I think a small celebration is in order."

He handed the jug to Esme. She shook her head.

"Have you tried it before?"

"Never." She looked at it, wrinkling her nose.

"Then I insist you do. Who knows, you may like it!"

Esme put the brim to her lips and sipped. "It tastes better than I thought."

"Good. Have some more."

They stood in the stable taking gulps in turn. The mead was strong and the alcohol went straight to Esme's head. She began tottering like the foal, which was now suckling his mother's milk.

Eirik retrieved the flagon and laughed. "Here, sit on this bale before you fall over. Father Aidan would never approve if you return in a drunken state."

"I'm not drunk," said Esme, "I'm . . . relaxed."

Eirik helped her to sit. The warmth of his hand on hers seemed to penetrate right into her heart. Then he sat on the ground beside her, legs bent, elbows resting on his knees.

"How do you know so much about animals?" asked Esme.

"My father reared horses. When he died my older brother took over. So I became a warrior monk instead. You can see where it's got me." He smiled ruefully.

"Perhaps it's got you just where you want to be."

Eirik shook his head. "I'm not where I wish to be, but I made a solemn vow to Thor and it cannot be easily broken."

"We're told to love and forgive our enemies."

"Tell me, what does your holy book mean when it says we must love our enemies?"

"We must try to separate the deed from the man who did it. Hate the act but love the enemy. If someone strikes you on one cheek, you should turn to him the other also. If someone takes your tunic, do not stop him, and if anyone takes what belongs to you, don't ask for it back."

Eirik frowned. "So if the Vikings strike you, you are not meant to strike back? And if they take your silver, you should give them more? That makes no sense."

Esme was quiet for several moments. "Perhaps if we did that you would leave us alone."

"It would encourage more to come. But make no mistake about the ruthlessness of your people – or the Romans before them. The Saxons came from Germany to conquer England. The Vikings are no worse. Who will invade these shores next? Each has come in violence and been subjected to violence."

"True. But our holy book tells us that we reap what we sow. Violence begets violence. No one gains, and many lose their lives. If only we could be satisfied with what we have, our souls would be at peace."

"Is it in man's nature to be at peace?" asked Eirik.

"It would appear not, but that doesn't mean we shouldn't pursue it."

Eirik looked at her. "Are you at peace, Esme?"

She wrung her hands. "Not since Vikings came – you and those before you."

"I'm sorry about that. I've spent many years trying to achieve the condition, but it eludes me. I'm not at peace. I trust yours will return when we've gone, and I hope you will find it in your heart to forgive your enemy."

Esme smiled. "I shall pray about it."

"Will you pray for me too?"

She stared at him and then, against her better judgement, she leaned over and kissed his cheek again.

"I would advise against doing that," he said. "I cannot be responsible for my actions if you do. I know you're slightly drunk, so I'll forgive your teasing. But you're not so inexperienced with animals that you're unaware of what I'm talking about."

Esme pushed herself up and stood. "I'd better go." The world wobbled disconcertingly.

"You're as bad as this young one," he joked, getting to his feet. "But in the morning, both of you will be steady, and I want no regrets."

Esme felt an arm on her back as Eirik walked with her to the church until they reached the safety of the door.

"Good night," she whispered.

"Good night. Sleep well."

Eirik went back to the stable to check on the foal and to finish off the jug of mead. The memory of being close to Esme awakened a longing to love her and become one flesh; body and mind. But she also needed to love him, and that could never happen. Soon the English lord would whisk her away to his marriage bed. His response was one of anger: anger at his weakness in allowing the girl to affect him so quickly, and anger that he was powerless to change the outcome.

20

Sunbeams drenched the room from a high window. They bounced off the copper water jug into Esme's eyes. Light shimmered between her lashes.

Lifting her head, she immediately felt sick. The pounding in her temples enforced each fresh wave of nausea, and she slumped back on the lumpy mattress. She had drunk too much. The events of the night flooded her brain. Some thoughts elicited pleasure, others horror. She had never met a man who aroused in her so many conflicting emotions that within the same evening she could feel hate, resentment, respect and admiration.

Snippets of the conversation on forgiveness drifted hazily into her mind, but the mead had controlled her tongue, of that there was no doubt, and she could scarcely recall whether what she said made any sense. He had kissed her and she had kissed him! The drink must have encouraged such disgraceful behaviour. Or had the desire to behave in such a way encouraged the drinking of the mead? If she was honest, she was unsure. Esme remembered that she was responsible for the morning visit to the stable. Opening her eyes more fully, she bemoaned the lateness of the hour. If she didn't rouse herself soon, someone would come looking for her.

She walked to the stables, conscious of each careful step, and found that Eirik had been there already. Everything was in order with fresh hay and straw, troughs filled. The foal was suckling, and the mare was content. Suddenly the mead attacked her stomach and she heaved in a corner. Ashamed, she cleared up the mess and dropped it into a pile of dung. This was her first experience of alcohol and she vowed it would be her last. She felt as though she'd been poisoned and wondered how the men could consume so much.

Esme made her way to the kitchen. It was empty. She heard the cows' constant lowing, the burden of their udders causing them pain. She stooped to pick up a small stool, and, grabbing a bucket, she set off across the field.

Rowena was there. She had already started the milking and looked up as Esme approached. "Are you alright?" she asked. "Astrid has gone looking for you. You're very pale."

Esme examined the expectant animals. Having decided which one deserved her attention first, she settled on the stool and began squeezing the udders. "I've been to the stable. One of the mares gave birth last night."

"That's wonderful," said Rowena, beaming. "It'll probably be the last of the season. I'll go and take a peek when I've finished here."

A pang of guilt struck. Esme knew that was not the real reason for her lateness, but was unwilling to confess to her friend the effect of the alcohol. How could an encounter which had seemed so right, so exciting, so almost . . . noble, suddenly seem so wrong and sordid? Esme grasped for the first time how little she had experienced the emotions of life in all its shapes and variety. Perhaps the death of both parents and the subsequent responsibility which she felt towards her brother had numbed all other feelings.

There had been very few occasions which she recalled as truly joyful, and almost none which engendered the gut-wrenching guilt that now overcame her. But now, seeing Rowena's delighted face, an event which should give her great pleasure merely intensified her self-reproach.

Rowena stared at her. "You look dreadful. Are you sure you're not ill? Don't do too much today. We can take care of everything. Here comes Astrid now."

Astrid arrived panting. She smiled. "So there you are. We were worried sick about you. Your bed was empty and I couldn't find you. I see there's a young foal in the stable. Is that where you've been?"

Esme nodded. "It's a colt. He's going to be a beauty. The mare was having difficulty pushing him out. He was round the wrong way. Eirik manoeuvred him into position."

Rowena stopped what she was doing. "You were there, with Eirik, in the middle of the night?"

That simple question! "Early this morning, actually," said Esme, blushing.

"Was that wise?" said Astrid, tightening her head scarf. "I'm nearly old enough to be his mother but can't help thinking he's something of a handsome devil. He's not like some of the other pigs we serve." Her disgruntled cow gave a throaty grumble. She pushed her knuckles into an udder to start the milk flowing.

Rowena tutted, "He may be outwardly handsome but has a heathen heart."

Esme felt obliged to speak in his defence. "Father Aidan told me Eirik has spared our men who ran from the battle field. He's interested in our scriptures and is beginning to read them. He's seeking peace, I think."

"Well, good for him," said Astrid. "Then he's not going the right way to find it in my view."

"What do you mean?" said Rowena, filling one pail with milk and picking up another.

Astrid waved her stool at a cow, shooing it away. "Neither of you will like what I've just overheard. Olaf and his friends plan to attack more of our coastline."

Esme looked aghast; her insides lurched, overcome by a fresh wave of nausea. All that talk last night about forgiving your enemies had been just that – talk! All any of them wanted was money. "Why can't men be more peace-loving," she said with vehemence.

"I've seen too many killings to pass comment any more," said Astrid. "I think we Saxons may have done our share. While ever men are in charge of this world, there'll be sorrow. When women rule the world things will be different."

Rowena gave a hollow laugh. "That will never happen."

Esme let out an expletive as a cow's hoof caught her wrist. She stood up but immediately felt faint.

Astrid grabbed hold of her. "Take it easy. You look like you need rest."

"It's only a headache."

"I insist you leave the milking to me. Take a gentle walk over to the barn. Fetch some fresh lavender oil. I'll massage those aches away. On the way, stop by the bees and gather some honey. It'll do you good."

Esme protested. "But there's so much to do."

"Not as much as you think. Now get going and take some deep breaths."

"Are you sure?"

"Yes."

Esme wiped her hands feeling too ill to continue. "I'll not be long."

"Take as long as you like," said Astrid.

Esme hated deceiving her friends in this way. How foolish she'd been, taken in by Eirik's caring treatment of the foal and its mother. As if someone like him could feel anything beyond the fact that the colt would make a good war horse.

The exercise refreshed her and the sickness began to fade. When she reached the barn, she was surprised to see the doors were open.

She peered into the gloom. Several barrels had been upended and clouds of billowing dust made her cough.

She could hear rustling and called out. "Who's there? Show yourself."

21
London 1979

Ben Shawcross puts his head round the office door. "Morning, Emma. How was your visit to Maldon?"

"Interesting. We're attending a talk this evening on the battle."

"You're going back? Is our client going with you?"

"Yes," says Emma, dismayed to find her cheeks are warming.

"Did your mother inspect her new place?"

"We went on Saturday. She wasn't impressed and may sell."

Ben nods sympathetically. "Well, not everyone would thank you for a sixteenth-century house. We've traced ownership back as far as relatives of a Bishop of Norwich, who built cottages for managers of the church estates. He was a staunch supporter of Roman orthodoxy and fell out with Henry VIII during the Reformation. The Benedictine priory, which was built on the same site, was dissolved in 1538."

"What happened to the properties?"

"Oddly, the next owners were Dutch Calvinists escaping persecution by the Catholics! Several generations lived there until the eighteenth century when the Danes moved in. The link to Reginald Reed is through your maternal grandmother."

"My mother is rather horrified by the responsibility."

"Well, it's freehold. Selling would give her financial security."

Emma rings Bjorn Erikson and arranges for him to pick her up at the office at 3.30 p.m. She wishes she could go home to change her clothes and make herself look a little less like a headmistress, but there is too much paperwork to cover.

She barely lifts her head from the desk until 3.15 p.m. at which time she refreshes her makeup, and rearranges the wisps of hair loosened from her chignon. Her Danish client arrives on time, as expected. Today he is driving. He helps her into the Rolls Royce as his chauffeur had done, only this time in the front seat. He seems less easy than he did the previous day, and, oddly, Emma is feeling the same. She asks about Greta.

"She's quite happy. A friend of hers has come round to play and will probably stay the night."

She smiles, "So Karl won't be teaching her how to play poker?"

Bjorn laughs, "Unless he teaches them both." Suddenly, he frowns.

There is silence for several moments. He must have remembered. Emma's stomach churns. Greta had been speaking Danish at the time. The comment will be deeply embarrassing for him if he knows Emma could interpret what the child said.

"You understood?" he says.

She sighs. "My grandmother was Danish."

Bjorn tenses his jaw. "Why did you not say so?"

"I'm sorry but it didn't seem important."

"I very much regret my daughter's remarks concerning you. I hope you will ignore them as the silly rant of a ten-year-old."

"Of course, I thought nothing of it."

For some time they continue in self-conscious silence until Emma attempts to explain. "I don't speak the language well, and I don't always understand either. But as soon as I tell anyone I had a Danish grandmother, they expect me to be fluent, which I'm not. So I really must apologise."

Bjorn takes a deep breath and smiles. He speaks in Danish, "I shall have to test you. I suspect you are better than you say."

"No, I'm not," says Emma. "I may understand but I can't reply."

Bjorn briefly turns to look at her. "I think I've made my point." The tense moment passes. They both relax and conversation begins to flow more easily again. He tells her how much he loves England, and she speaks of the property her mother has inherited.

"What will she do with it?" Bjorn asks.

"Probably sell. It's too much for her."

"If she decides to sell, would she mind if I take a look?"

"Not at all. Are you thinking of buying a house?"

"I need a property with land – not too far from Newmarket – so I can perhaps develop my horse-training business here."

Her heart skips a beat. "The property has been owned by Danish or British families for generations."

"Perhaps I should carry on the tradition," he says lightly.

22
Maeldun 991

Eirik emerged from the murkiness. "Good morning. There's a treasure trove here. Someone's been collecting for years."

"What are you stealing now?"

"Pitch. It must have been left here when the church was built. Let's say it's on loan."

"What will you use to repay – blood-money after your next attack? How could you speak to me of forgiveness and peace when you're threatening more violence?"

His face hardened. "I still owe allegiance to Norway."

"You disgust me." Esme turned away.

He jumped down from a bale and spun her round by the shoulders to face him. Esme was alarmed by the suddenness of the gesture. She could feel Eirik's breath on her and smell the musky aroma rising from his body. For a brief moment she thought he would try to kiss her again. She knew what her response would be. But he made no such move.

"Your protestations are becoming tiresome. Have you ever thought why it is you understand so much of our language? Or how your parents acquired vast tracts of privately owned land? Don't imagine your ancestors lived the lives of saints. Before you damn others to hell, perhaps you should study the mote in your own eye. Is that not what your Christ teaches?"

Esme was stunned. For several moments she made no reply. She knew her grandparents spoke Danish, but it had never occurred to her that they might have come here as aggressors. Then she thought of her mother and father and responded angrily. "You push me too far. My parents were killed by people like you."

Eirik held her gaze. "I'm sorry. I see the suggestion distresses you." He let her go. "Perhaps you should ask your guardian. I'm sure Lord Edmund will know."

Esme noticed the acid in the comment and she struggled to hold back her tears. "Even if I am of Viking origin and my ancestors gained land in the same way as Olaf and Sweyn Forkbeard, that doesn't excuse any of them."

Eirik rubbed a hand across his chin. "There's something you should know. There are traitors in the country who wish to be rid of your king."

Esme stared. "That's untrue. All Englishmen support the king."

"I'm afraid it is true."

"And who are these traitors?"

"Those with influence. Wealthy landowners. Even Danes who settled here several decades ago."

"Why would they betray him?"

"England needs a strong central power to control the country. They believe Aethelred is not the man to do it. Even his own Archbishop has suggested he pays us to stop raiding the coastline. He's indecisive and lacks the stature of some of your former kings, like his own father, King Edgar, who brought unity."

"And what will happen to King Aethelred?"

"Some want him dead."

"They would kill their own king?" Esme shuddered.

"They see it as a stand for a united England, and have no objection to the provenance of a new king. He may be Danish, Norwegian or Norman providing he's powerful, with resources to support his position."

"And what do they gain from such treachery?"

"Power. Land. Money."

She was still for a moment while her mind struggled to absorb what he was saying. "How do you know this?" she whispered.

"Because these people have offered us silver, not to *stop* the raids but to *increase* them – against Lunden and other strongholds– until Aethelred gives up his throne."

Esme's nausea returned. "That's utterly terrible."

He stared at her. "Sweyn wishes to be King of England."

"Why? He's already King of Denmark?"

"The traitors also wish it to be so. He ousted his own father from the throne of Denmark and wouldn't hesitate to do the same to Aethelred. Besides, Sweyn's sister already lives here with her husband and family."

"I know. Her name is Gunhilde. My brother is staying at their house."

Eirik's lips parted. He took a breath. "You have close connections with that family?"

"They're friends of Edmund. Pallig, Gunhilde's husband, is also a close adviser of Aethelred."

"Then you could be in danger."

Her eyes flashed. "Don't be absurd. They are not my enemies. As long as I cannot persuade you to stop killing my countrymen, it is *you* who is my enemy. Why are you telling me this?"

He hesitated. "We suspect that one of their leaders is your betrothed, Lord Edmund."

She glared at him. "That's an outrageous thing to say. He's one of Aethelred's most trusted advisers. I'd know if he'd been practising deception all this time." Her cheeks flamed bright red. "Edmund would never support a foreign king."

"Nevertheless, if true, you and your brother could be at risk."

"Why? We've done nothing." Esme swayed, unable to focus. Eirik caught her arm but she shook herself free. "Don't you dare to touch me."

"You're connected to this man. Not only is he your guardian, you are soon to be his wife. The king may suspect your involvement."

"You're saying these things to upset me. There's no truth in them. You're hateful." She held up both fists.

Eirik grabbed them, holding them close. There was desperation in his eyes. "I'm telling you for your own safety. If Edmund is involved, and he turns up, he could suspect you've heard of this treachery. It may be advisable to keep your presence here a secret."

Esme struggled to be free. "I have no need of protection from my guardian. The sooner he comes to save me the better." She could no longer hold back the tears of frustration, and looked directly into his eyes. "I loathe everything you stand for." Her tone was one of revulsion.

Eirik released her hands and massaged his temple; a look of intense sadness crossed his face. He bowed briefly. A muscle worked in his jaw. "Sadly, our paths seem destined to clash. Perhaps one day we will understand one another better."

Esme's reply was spoken with passion, "Never!"

Eirik walked into the sunlight and out of sight.

Unexpectedly, a deep sensation of loneliness overwhelmed her. She slumped onto a bale of hay, feeling the blood drain from her face. It was inconceivable that Edmund was a traitor. His motive to unify England had merit, but at the cost of Aethelred's life? And power for himself? That was unforgiveable. He was one of the king's closest friends. It couldn't be true. Otherwise, how could he have successfully deceived her all this time?

She wondered now whether Eirik would reveal her presence if Edmund did come. If her guardian was a traitor, would that really put her life at risk? Everyone knew the punishment for treason was death. But if Forkbeard's sister knew of a plot to put her brother on the throne, Brand could be in grave danger also. A frenzy of anxiety and confusion spread through her body. She was sick once again.

23

Feeling less nauseous, Esme made her way back to the kitchen. She was surprised to see the two women standing in the middle of the room with their arms around each other, their faces wet with tears.

"What's the matter?" she asked.

Rowena gulped. "Oh Esme, Astrid and I have done the most awful thing."

"Surely it can't be that bad. Whatever is it?"

"We've killed a man – one of the Vikings."

Esme clasped a hand over her mouth. "How?"

"In self-defence," said Astrid. "I think it may be the same man who tried to attack you."

Rowena explained what had happened between sobs. "I left Astrid doing the milking. I came back – to prepare the food. I was alone. The man came in. He was offensive. Disgusting. Then he grabbed me." Rowena could hardly get out the words.

"Sit down," said Esme. "Take your time."

Rowena drew a ragged breath. "He forced me to the floor. Lifted my skirts over my head. Said he didn't want to see my ugly face while he was . . ."

Esme held her hand. "What happened?"

Astrid took over the story. "I came back just at that moment and saw what he was doing. I grabbed one of the heavy iron pans hanging from the ceiling and hit him over the head."

"Heavens above," said Esme. "Is that what killed him?"

Astrid nodded. "He slumped on top of Rowena. I had to push him off. It was dreadful. He lay there on the floor in a great heap."

Esme looked round the kitchen. "What have you done with the body?"

Astrid pointed to a pile of sacks in the corner.

"He's under there?" Esme looked incredulous.

"God help me, yes, he is. He was so heavy we couldn't carry him. We thought about putting him in one of the outhouses, but it was impossible to drag him all that way. We can't leave him. Someone will find him and then we'll be executed. He'll start to smell soon."

Esme sniffed. "Can't be worse than how he smells already." She looked at Rowena's distraught face. "I'm sorry. I didn't mean to be frivolous, but, in truth, I suspect we'll all be safer now he's dead."

"I'm sorry, too, sorry that I've put us all in danger," said Astrid. "Someone is bound to notice he's gone."

Esme shook her head. "I don't know. There are so many men around, now the Danes have arrived. It's possible he'll not be missed for a while. And even then, I doubt they'll suspect he's been murdered, especially if we hide the body well."

"But there's nowhere to hide it," said Astrid.

Rowena blew her nose. "Perhaps they'll think he's gone off with one of the women. Everyone knows he can't keep his hands off us. What should we do?"

Esme bit her lip. "There's a large empty barrel outside. Do we have a hammer and some nails?"

"Yes, one or two," said Astrid.

"That's enough," said Esme. "We need to keep the lid on until we can get him to the church."

"Where are you going to put him?" asked Rowena.

"You'll see. Don't worry. I have the perfect hiding place, where nobody will find him."

Esme peeped outside. "Let's get him in there now."

They turned the barrel on its side and rolled it into the kitchen. Esme looked at the man's face. It was Snorre, the one who attacked her. She was glad he was dead. Never before had she believed herself capable of rejoicing over the death of another human being. "Give me a hand to get him in here. I'll nail the top down and fetch Kizzy and the cart later. We'll never get him up the hill otherwise. No one will question me. They've seen me transporting mead often enough."

They closed the door. Astrid's face brightened a little. "We need to tie his limbs tight to his body. By this evening, he'll be stiff. We might not be able to get him out."

Working together as fast as possible, the women did as she suggested, then wrapped the man in the sacks and manoeuvred him into the barrel. Out of breath with the exertion, Astrid and Rowena resumed their duties, while Esme inserted the lid and banged in the first nail. She had turned to the table to pick up another when a sudden shaft of light fell across the floor. One of Olaf's men stood on the threshold. Her heart missed a beat. She placed the hammer beside a joint of raw beef, and slipped the nails in her pocket.

He regarded her with suspicion. "I heard banging. Why did you close the door?" He pointed to the hammer on the table. "You, boy, what are you doing with that?"

Esme forced herself to act naturally. "I'm softening the meat for your supper. Beating it before cooking makes it easier to chew."

To her relief the man chuckled. "Well, I must remember to tell my wife – if I ever get home. You must have learned a thing or two about cooking from these women." For the moment Esme had forgotten her disguise. She smiled. "They're good teachers. They'll give you a lesson some time, if you wish."

The man looked pleased. "I might take you up on that. Keep the door open in future. And don't any of you try to escape or you'll feel my fist. I'll get into trouble if they find any of you missing."

Esme shook her head. "We won't," she said. "We're quite content with our work, aren't we?"

Her friends smiled amiably.

He smiled too. "Yes, I can see that."

"If you don't mind I'd better get on, else I'll be in trouble too," said Esme.

He turned to go, but then changed his mind and walked over to the barrel, tapping its top. Esme drew in a quick breath as the lid tilted slightly. Hairs from the top of the corpse's head wisped into the gap, but the man seemed not to notice. "Could you give me a cup of your excellent mead?"

Astrid spoke up. "Sir, it needs more time to settle. But I have a barrel out back if you could just wait a moment." She began wiping her hands on her apron.

The Viking hesitated. "No. Thank you. I must report back. Another time perhaps. There's nothing quite like it for blotting out life."

Esme stared at him briefly. It was strange to hear that this man felt obliged to get drunk in order to cope with the life he was leading. Eirik had warned her she knew nothing about the darkness of men's hearts.

"Perhaps you could show me how to make it sometime."

"With pleasure," said Astrid.

He finally left. The women heaved a sigh of relief.

Later that evening, Esme drove the cart up the hill to the church. No one remonstrated with her. Astrid and Rowena walked separately so as not to attract attention. Father Aidan was out. They rolled the barrel into the room under the west tower and, with much straining and grunting, carried it down the steps to the crypt.

"Gosh, it's musty down here," said Astrid, sneezing. "Are we just going to leave him? Won't he be found?"

"Help me move this altar," said Esme, "I want to show you something."

Together they inched it to one side, then Esme used all her might to yank up the cover to the tunnel. She shivered as she looked into the abyss, remembering her frightening struggle to escape in the dark. Rowena raised her eyebrows as she gazed down into the hole. She glanced at Esme in sudden revelation. "That's how you got away, isn't it?"

"Yes. The tunnel leads to the woods. It's not unlike a grave down there. He won't decompose so quickly."

She climbed down the shaft while Astrid and Rowena wrenched the lid off the barrel and tipped it up. The body slipped out. There was a dull thud as it hit the bottom. Esme used the sack to drag the man into the tunnel. Then she climbed back up into the crypt and hugged her friends.

"Even if someone does open it up, there's nothing to see," said Rowena. "As you said, it's the perfect hiding place, but it's so scary down there. You did well to follow it all the way."

"It's something I'd rather forget."

They edged the altar back into place and hurried out into the dusk.

24

The Vikings constantly demanded mead and ale at the table. They were always hungry. Esme worked at their beck and call, together with Rowena and Astrid. But the two women always went home at night leaving Esme alone with her turmoil of thoughts. At such times she turned to Father Aidan.

His welcoming smile turned into a frown. "What's the matter, Esme? You look utterly dejected."

"I'm worried, Father. I've heard the Vikings are planning more invasions. Furthermore, there are those close to the king who want to dethrone him."

"How do you know that?"

Esme hesitated, knowing that she was prevaricating with a partial truth. "Astrid overheard some of the men saying that traitors are paying our enemies."

"And that worries you."

She selected a piece of linen to embroider. "Yes."

Aidan observed her closely. "Did Eirik tell you this?"

Esme sighed and confessed. "Well . . . I saw him removing pitch from the barn and asked him what he was doing."

"I see. It would have been better if he'd said nothing since it is now a cause of concern to you. I've been praying about it."

She put down her needle and looked at him. "You knew already, Father?"

"Yes, Esme, I did. Thorkel told me."

"Thorkel the Tall? You know him?"

"Yes."

"How?"

Aidan pushed his manuscript to one side. "Because, my child, I was once one of them."

Esme gasped. "I don't believe it."

"Well, it's true. I met a man of God in the south-west of England after one of our raids some years ago. I was converted and studied at a large monastery, which was well provided for until a prominent ealdorman at the time began destroying them. The landlords of large religious estates were seen as a threat to the influence of the local thegns. So I left, and eventually Our Lord sent me here."

Esme shook her head. "But surely you were never like them." She jerked her thumb towards the refectory.

"I rather think I was. My name was Hugin, the raven, a bird of carrion. I adopted the name of a missionary monk I much admired. He was the founder of a monastery and early church in Northumbria. It was attacked without mercy by Norwegian marauders. The event is history now. Nevertheless, the atrocities and deliberate destruction by the Vikings were unforgiveable."

They sat in silence for several minutes with Esme trying to assimilate this revelation. "Did you know Eirik, too? One of his followers, a man called Fenrir, told me the strangest story of how Eirik became their leader. He saved them all by refusing to accept freedom for his own life unless his comrades were also freed."

"Yes, I remember."

Esme's jaw dropped. "You remember?"

"I was there."

She could hardly keep still, wriggling in her seat. "Are you telling me that you witnessed the event?"

"Yes, my dear, I was in the crowd, watching the executions. I doubt very much whether the earl's henchman has forgiven Eirik."

"Gunnar?"

"Yes, that was his name. Eirik was about to be beheaded. Gunnar grabbed his hair and lost the lower part of his arm instead. He's a trader now. I saw him not long ago in Maeldun. He's a villain if ever I met one."

"So, did you recognise Eirik?"

"Not immediately, he was only a youth when I first saw him and this was the last place I expected to see him."

"Did he recognise you?"

"No. He didn't know me. I was a mere onlooker at the time. He had more pressing matters to attend to."

"Do you approve of what he's doing now?"

"He has no choice. He made a vow to Thor. But I believe him to be an honourable man. Trust in the Lord, Esme. That's all we can do."

Esme considered this admission for a moment or two. If Father Aidan turned from the Viking gods, why could Eirik not do so too? She thought about the incident with the man who lost his arm and how the vows to Thor came to be made. "Have you told Eirik you spotted Gunnar?"

"No. But I'll do so if I speak to him again. He should be warned."

"You think Gunnar still bears a grudge?"

"Definitely. I imagine he's making it his life's work to take revenge."

She took a deep breath to give her courage. "There's something else worrying me, Father."

"What's that, child?"

"These people who pretend to support the king yet are betraying him – supposing one of them is Edmund."

Aidan pouted. "That's ridiculous, Esme. He's a trusted adviser."

"He's bound to turn up soon. When he does, he'll insist I return home with him."

Aidan hesitated. "Just like that?" he said, clicking his fingers.

"Yes, why not?" Esme replied, puzzled. "I shall expect protection for us all."

Aidan perched on the edge of his stool; he leaned forward with his hands resting in the fold of his habit. "I don't wish to alarm you, Esme, but have you considered the possibility that some men may not be so easily disposed to take back a woman whom they believe might have been violated?"

Esme was shocked. "Surely he wouldn't think such a thing. Besides, it's not true."

Aidan waved his arm in the air. "We know that, and you know that, but *he* doesn't. Look how close you came to – well there's no need to dwell on it, but he will only have your word for it. You've spent time with the enemy. Think for a moment, Esme. How will that look to him?"

"He'll soon know the truth when we're—"

"Married?"

"Yes."

"He may need satisfying on that point before the marriage."

Esme pressed her fingers into her forehead. "I hadn't thought of that." In fact, she hadn't thought of Edmund touching her at all. He'd never kissed her in the way she presumed a man would kiss a woman whom he loved – in the way that Eirik had kissed her in the early hours of the morning. She shivered at the memory. "I think he prefers the company of men more than women. I doubt he'll be too bothered."

114

Aidan looked at her with one raised eyebrow. "It's a strange thing about human nature, we may not want something ourselves, but we don't want anybody else to have it either."

25

The next day there was no sign of Eirik or his men. They stayed on Northey Island, preparing for a battle in the Thames. Leif came to collect their provisions. The gossip in the village said the mercenaries were to carry out a reconnaissance, to assess the state of the opposition. Olaf's fleet was on standby, ready to annihilate Aethelred's ships.

Never would she forget the look of sadness on Eirik's face when she remarked that she loathed everything he stood for. Perhaps he despised himself and that was the cause of his disquiet, the lack of peace in his soul. It seemed a long time since he forced his way into the church, but in fact it was little more than ten days. It was incredible to think that Father Aidan had once been a Viking from Norway, just like Olaf and his men. God's word had transformed him. She now understood the priest's lack of fear under attack, and the ease with which he dispatched young Leif on that fateful day. She wondered if he knew something of her parents' background and made up her mind to ask him.

That afternoon, Snorre was reported missing. Olaf had roared with rage when he heard the news. Unexpectedly, though, he never seemed to consider the possibility that his follower had been murdered. Instead, he assumed the man had turned soft, and ordered him to be executed on the spot should he be found sheltering behind the skirts of a Saxon woman to avoid serving the fleet. Esme knew she must tell Father Aidan what she and her friends had done as soon as possible.

As usual in the evening Aidan was in the chapel with his quill and ink. A candle sat on either end of the table. They sputtered in the breeze drawn into the room when Esme entered. He placed his pen carefully in front of him and flexed his fingers until they cracked.

Then he lifted his head and circled his shoulders.

"Hello, child," he said.

"Do you mind if I sit with you again, Father?"

"It would be a pleasure," he said, smiling. "Thank you for coming to keep an old man company. I have so much translating to finish."

He resumed his work and she watched the concentration on his face as the tip of his tongue pressed into his lower lip. His skin was the colour of the parchment laid out in front of him. Deep lines splayed from the corner of his eyes like a fan, tracking across his cheeks. His hair bristled around his balding pate in a confusion of matted, grey wire. Yet his shoulders were still square-set. When she looked at his dark eyes, there was a sparkle of joy that was rare to see in anyone.

Esme began her stitching, wondering how to broach the terrible admission about Snorre. She began with another question. "Father, I've been meaning to ask you something. Do you know anything of the background of my parents? I think they were from Denmark. Did my ancestors first come at the time of King Alfred when lands were being apportioned?"

"I cannot answer that, Esme. I'm not *so* old, you know." He grinned. "But I agree it's a possibility. Why do you ask?"

"It was something Eirik said."

"He's a perceptive man."

"And an aggressive one! How can you like him, Father, after he's plundered our land and killed our men?"

"He has no deception in him. He speaks the truth. That's a rare quality in a man."

Esme shrugged. "Nevertheless, now he's leaving I must somehow get back to Brand."

"Do you dare to risk another trip down the tunnel?"

"I fear it is no longer an option. It's blocked."

"Has it collapsed at last? I feared that might happen."

"No, the stays are all intact," said Esme. She placed her sewing on her knee.

Aidan leaned back against the stone wall. "Is there something you want to tell me, child?"

"Father, I have a most dreadful confession to make. A few days ago, Rowena, Astrid and I killed a man and hid his body. I know it's a sin. We all need forgiveness."

Father Aidan quietly contemplated her admission. Eventually he took a deep breath and said, "Was it one of Olaf's men?"

She tightened her lips. "His name is Snorre. He's the same man who intended raping me."

"Well, no doubt he deserved it. What was he doing?"

"He was assaulting Rowena."

"I see." Aidan stroked his chin. "And what did you do?"

"Astrid hit him on the head with an iron pan. She didn't intend to kill him."

A glimmer of mild amusement glinted in the old priest's eyes. "I see. What have you done with him?"

Esme tapped the flagstones with the ball of her foot.

"I understand – the crypt. Well, I've not heard mention that he's been found."

"What will they do when they find out?" Esme sucked her lip and looked round to check that no one had entered the room surreptitiously.

"It could take a while now Sweyn has arrived. Olaf's focus is elsewhere for the time being."

Esme bowed her head. "I couldn't think of anywhere else to put him."

"It seems to me that it was self-defence rather than murder. You were protecting fellow sisters in Christ. I doubt the Lord will condemn any of you for that. Nevertheless, we will pray for His forgiveness. Don't worry about the body. I'll dispose of it for you. There's a large, freshly dug grave not far from here. When the time is right, I'll make sure he goes into it."

"With our own countrymen?"

"They'll be on their way to a better place by now and won't object."

"He was a big man. Do you think you'll be able to cope on your own, Father?"

"I still have some Viking strength left."

Esme smiled. "How can I ever thank you? You've given me so much help and advice."

"And long may I continue to do so." Aidan chortled. "Well, well, it is rare that I witness God's retribution against our enemies, but this does seem to be an exception."

They had been working in companionable silence for most of the evening when Esme heard the sound of footsteps in the nave. She looked up in alarm. "Father, someone's outside."

Suddenly, the door flung open and crashed against the wall. Eirik staggered in, his hair dishevelled; his face blackened by soot.

Her heart thumped. Had he lost the battle? Aidan stood to face him. Eirik glanced at her. "Leave us," he said.

"But . . ." Esme protested.

"Leave us," Eirik repeated, his mouth determined.

She turned to Aidan for guidance. "I don't want to leave you, Father," she whispered.

"It's alright, child. Go now. It's time you were resting. Come and find me in the morning."

Esme picked up her sewing and moved towards the door. Eirik stood to one side to let her pass. His eyes were firmly set upon Aidan. As the door closed decisively behind her, she heard him say, "I've come to a decision."

The sound of voices next door continued nearly all night. Sleep eluded her. Why had Eirik returned so soon? At one point, Father Aidan left. She waited then opened her door a little. Through the crack she saw him returning with a jug. Both men went into the church. Their mutterings were too muted to decipher. A dreadful thought struck her. Was it possible Father Aidan had become a traitor too? Was he in league with the Vikings? Her bewilderment was complete and she felt more alone than ever. She dismissed the thought immediately. It was too horrible to contemplate. Flopping onto the mattress, she cried until she fell asleep.

26
Maldon 1979

Bjorn parks near the community centre in Maldon. Bernard Johnson stands at the podium wiping a glistening brow. "Good evening. Thank you for taking an interest in Maldon's history. I'm sure you all know about the vicious battle in AD 991. Byrhtnoth, the Saxon leader, was an alderman held in high regard." He continues to tell them of the hero's blunders, and then questions his audience, "Tell me, would you have done that in his shoes?"

There are general murmurings, a few nods and much shaking of heads. He has grabbed their interest.

"However, the Vikings, having routed the Saxons, were so impressed by their courage they declined to destroy the town, as was usually their wont."

There are a few cheers from those feeling less inhibited. The speaker permits his audience to settle again. "It's generally agreed Olaf Tryggvason of Norway led the invasion, but was helped by the Jomsvikings – a band of mercenaries, and possibly by Sweyn Forkbeard. That year King Aethelred paid Forkbeard a substantial amount of Danegeld, amounting to 10,000 pounds of silver – a bribe to stop the incursions."

A boy in the audience is heard to say to his father, "What does incursion mean?"

Bernard smiles benignly. "Good question, son. It means raid." He continues. "A woman who was present at the time of the battle wrote down her own story based on embroidery she'd created. There is also a record of events that happened later which consists of diary entries passed down the generations. These were preserved by one of her descendants – a woman called Phoebe. The items appear to be lost. But there is no doubt they once existed."

Emma feels Bjorn tense. "How can we be sure?" he says.

"They were mentioned in a fifteenth-century inventory of the priory at Norwich Cathedral. It's not surprising they've gone missing when you consider churchmen had to cope with fires and riots," he says, adding rather pretentiously, "not to mention the dissolution of the monasteries under Henrician reforms."

"Is it likely a piece of embroidery could survive all those years?" someone asks.

Bernard Johnson rubs his chin and assumes a thoughtful, well-rehearsed pout. "The Bayeux Tapestry dates from the tenth century – embroidered onto linen using woollen yarn. It survived the sacking of Bayeux by the Huguenots, and the French revolution, during which it was apparently rescued from a cart by a lawyer who hid it in his house. Even the German S.S. tried to nab it." He laughs heartily and the audience joins in.

"We also have a monastic text from a document in Ely which mentions a wall-hanging that commemorates the deeds of Byrhtnoth, thought to have been made by his wife."

Bjorn put up his hand. "You mentioned the Jomsvikings were here at the time of the battle. Do we know who their leader was at the time?"

"Basically, we can only be guided by the sagas, which are not always historically accurate, bearing in mind there is still no direct evidence the Jomsviking monks existed at all. Be that as it may, it's believed that their leader at that time, Jarl Sigvaldi, was disgraced by defeat at the Battle of Hjorungavagr in AD 986 against Norway, and he allegedly took flight. After which a young man, whose amazing bravery and cunning saved the group from total annihilation, was made their leader."

"Do we know his name?"

"Well, the name of Eirik has been bandied about, but no one knows for sure."

"Did any of them stay in England afterwards?"

"Many Danes were living in England, having married and settled here, including Forkbeard's own sister, Gunhilde."

By this time, there were several people waving hands aloft. "See me afterwards and I'll give you the name of someone who might be able to help you."

As they walk away, Emma reads the name on the card Bernard gave her. "It says Matilda, The Mayflower Nursing Home near Ipswich. I'll phone tomorrow and ask for a convenient time to visit."

"I think it best you see her alone. You can speak woman to woman. Unfortunately, I need to fly back to Roskilde tomorrow and don't know how long I'll be. Please feel free to use Karl. He loves driving."

"It's very kind of you to offer, but I wouldn't dream of taking such a liberty," says Emma. "We have a small company car. I'll check availability and book it once I have a date. It's no problem, really."

"Will you let me know how you get on?"

"Of course I will."

He glances at his watch. "We should be back by 10 p.m. At least Greta will be in bed."

Emma laughs, "Or playing poker with Karl."

"Karl's wife will put a stop to that. She's Greta's teacher. They both live in."

"Well, Jack will definitely be in bed."

"He sounds like a good lad."

"He's just very structured. If 8.30 p.m. is bedtime, then he finishes whatever he's doing and takes himself off."

They reach the car. "You must let me have the secret of your parental skills," says Bjorn, opening the door for her.

"I think it's probably due more to my mother than me."

"Does your mother live with you?" asks Bjorn, settling in beside her.

"Yes, since my father died. Otherwise I wouldn't have been able to take the job in London four days a week."

"What does your husband do?"

Emma hesitates a little longer than she would have wished.

"I'm sorry," says Bjorn. "It's none of my business."

She sighs. "He died. No one mentions it anymore."

"Perhaps they're not insensitive louts like me."

"It's just that I rarely meet anyone new and my friends already know."

Bjorn makes no further comment as the engine throbs into life.

"Derek was working undercover in Ireland three years ago. He was betrayed and killed."

"I'm so very sorry. The memory will still be painful. I understand. Clara, my wife, died of cancer. Greta was six. It was unexpected. In August we were told it was in her liver. She died before Christmas."

"It must have been terrible for you both. It's so hard for children when they lose their mother."

His voice sounds strained. "I keep a photograph of her in the kitchen so Greta will never forget what her mother looks like."

"I do the same," says Emma. "In fact, Jack sometimes talks to the picture and tells his father what he's been doing. Last weekend he told his dad he'd been picked to play the cornet in the school band. He's thrilled."

"I expect you feel proud too."

Emma laughs a little, and the pain of stirred-up memories begins to evaporate. "Naturally, I'm his mum."

"Tell me more about the property your mother has inherited," says Bjorn, wisely changing the subject.

"The farmhouse needs renovation and the amount of land is overwhelming. Mum's definitely decided to sell, so if you're interested come and take a look when you get back."

"Would she mind?"

"I'm sure she'd be delighted to meet a Danish gentleman. I'll ask her."

They sit in companionable silence, driving through the twilight into impending darkness as they hit the outskirts of London. He pulls up outside the flat in Notting Hill. "I'll telephone you to find out your news." He momentarily squeezes her hand. "I'm so glad we met."

Emma hardly dares to reply.

27
Maeldun 991

Early next morning, Esme was surprised to find Eirik waiting for her outside the church.

"I need to speak to you in private," he said.

"Tell me why should I wish to talk to *you*?"

"Because what I have to say will be of importance to you and your brother."

"The only private place I have is my room."

She led the way to the vestry, stepping down into the compact cell. He followed, his presence overwhelming the humble space. A bench stood against one side, but he declined her offer to sit down. Instead, he paced the floor. He ran his hand over his face, a gesture Esme had seen him do many times when he seemed to be battling with himself. "Today is the one you've been waiting for," he said at last. "A representative of the traitors will be arriving soon."

Her look was cold. "Perhaps it's the day *you* have been waiting for – the one when you'll receive your reward for deeds done, and the promise of money for future treachery."

Eirik bristled but refused to rise to the taunt. "It will be for King Sweyn and Olaf to decide which course of action they choose."

"And tell me, my lord, do you have no opinion on the matter?"

"My views can be of no concern to you."

Esme clenched her fist. "How can they be of no concern to me when they directly affect those with whom I share my life?" She sat down abruptly, head in hands. For several moments there was an uncomfortable silence. Eventually she looked up to find Eirik watching her. Her pulse fluttered with unsettling feelings. She frowned in dismay. "I no longer know who I am," she said. "The anchors have been drawn up from under me, and I'm sinking in a new world that I don't understand."

"Perhaps we all reach a watershed in life when we have to consider our future."

"I know what my future must be, of that there is little doubt. It has been destined since I was ten years of age. I see that now."

"Esme, our lives are not predestined. Each of us can make our own future."

"Perhaps that would be possible if there were no one else to consider in our lives. But that's true for very few of us, except you perhaps. You have freedom most people never achieve."

"You think I'm free?" said Eirik, frustration creeping into his voice. "Let me tell you, I am not. I made vows to which I may still be committed."

"Vows to your gods, but supposing your gods prove to be false."

Eirik's retort was instant. "And supposing the one to whom you are betrothed proves to be untrue?" He began pacing once again. "Do you want me to tell the delegate you're here?"

She hesitated. "Is it . . . is it Lord Edmund?"

Once again Eirik rubbed his hand over his face before replying. "Yes."

Esme got to her feet. "It cannot be true."

"The reason we didn't proceed with our foray into the Thames last night was because he and another man warned us not to do so. Aethelred had gathered together many ships and was prepared for our attack."

"You think his warning was to protect you? I think it's more likely he was protecting the king."

"He and his conspirators planned our attack and paid for it."

She felt the blood drain from her cheeks as the full force of Edmund's treachery overcame her. But still she couldn't quite accept it. Perhaps it was his way of befriending the Vikings and gaining access to their camp. "Will you demand a ransom for me?"

Eirik placed his arms akimbo. "I would prefer to say nothing about you being here at present. Remember, even Olaf and Sweyn don't know who you are."

She scowled. "You'll have to tell someone eventually – unless you wish to keep me enslaved to you forever."

"With your permission, I'd like you to hear what he has to say before you make a decision."

"What would you have me do? Serve him wine?" said Esme, with sarcasm.

"Why not? No one will identify you. Father Aidan will act as interpreter, if necessary."

"I can't. I have Brand to think of."

"It's Brand I'm also thinking of," he said.

She was unable to reply for several moments, her mind bursting with possibilities. Was Eirik right? Was she putting her brother in danger if Edmund proved to be a traitor? But supposing Edmund was acting with the king's knowledge. What if there was a counter plot to dupe the invaders? "You are asking me to spy on the man I'm about to marry, to make a judgement about his behaviour."

"Yes, I am. I have a suggestion," said Eirik. "That after you've heard what he has to say, you speak to me before I tell him about you, in case you've changed your mind."

"I cannot change my mind. I have to go with him. Except," she remembered her conversation with Aidan, "he may not want me back." She stared at him with unseeing eyes for several seconds, considering whether Edmund would truly want her back, and, if so, for what reason: because he loved her, or because she was useful? She suspected it was the second. Eirik made a move towards her, but stopped when she quickly turned aside.

"I'll send for you when they arrive," he said, shutting the door firmly behind him.

It was Father Aidan who fetched her from the kitchen later that afternoon. Rowena and Astrid were summoned too.

"Is Edmund in the party?" said Esme, unable to form the words easily.

Aidan nodded.

"Is he really a traitor? Eirik says he has paid them to invade us."

Aidan pulled his mouth to one side. "Let's not pre-judge until we know for sure. He could be here to offer the Vikings money on behalf of the king to stop their incursions."

Esme's chest felt tight as they entered the refectory carrying trays of delicacies and wine. A tableau of men sat around the end of the table. Olaf was sitting in his usual place with Sweyn Forkbeard and Eirik on either side. Two other men also sat at the table, but they had their backs to Esme. She couldn't see who they were until she moved across the room. It was then she saw him.

129

28

Esme's heart sank at the sight of Edmund. Instinctively she pulled up her cowl. Was this the same man to whom she was betrothed? He seemed smaller than she remembered, with hunched shoulders. The grey hair at his temples served only to make him look older rather than distinguished. Heavy jowls and full lips masked the outline of his jaw. He made no attempt to look up as she entered with Aidan and her two friends. After all, they were servants. Why should they be of any interest to him?

She waited to see what he would say. He took the lead and spoke with ebullience. "May I congratulate you on your success? The king is greatly disquieted. As you know, he is offering a large sum for you to cease your harrying. The amount will weaken his coffers and his ability to strengthen his fleet. We, on the other hand, will continue to support your attacks."

"We'll drink to that," said Sweyn. "Let us consummate our future plans with food and drink."

Edmund raised his glass. "I propose a toast to a long and fruitful liaison, and to our next king – Sweyn Forkbeard of Denmark."

There was a general murmur of approval as the men saluted Sweyn.

Esme stood completely still; stunned by the knowledge that Edmund was not only fully conversant with the planned attack, but was in support of a foreign king. Eirik had been telling the truth. It was more than she could bear. She clutched her hand across her mouth to stifle a cry, and hurried from the room, nausea overwhelming her.

She sat in the kitchen alone, willing rational thought to take over her mind. Once her heart steadied, she considered her options – realistic options, not ones of fancy – those that encompassed not just her own future but that of Brand. She knew she could not stay here dressed as a trainee monk. Her life was not her own. She wasn't free to make decisions. Whatever path Edmund was following was probably one he'd pursued for most of their lives together. There was no reason why he should ever find out that she'd overheard his conversation with Sweyn and Olaf.

After a while, Father Aidan followed her into the kitchen. "Goodness, child, you look distraught."

"I don't understand. Why is Edmund acting so?"

Aidan puffed out his cheeks. "He's clearly a member of a powerful group who wish to see the king gone."

"What will happen if he's caught?"

"It will depend on the strength of the opposition to the king. It may be Aethelred who'll be in trouble. But best not dwell on that at the moment. You need to decide what you want to do. You may end up being married either to a traitor or one of the most powerful men in the country. What matters is whether you want to marry him now you know."

Esme took a ragged breath. Did she still want to marry Edmund after everything that had happened to her? Was she even the same person now? Conflicting emotions battled in her mind, but, despite Aidan's entreaties, she knew there was no possibility of walking away to an uncertain future, leaving Brand behind without her support. "I have no choice but to return with him. Did he ask about me? Did he mention me at all?"

"No, but we cannot condemn him for that. If he's not yet returned home, he'll assume you're still with friends."

"Will Eirik tell him?"

"Eirik will consult you first."

"How could Edmund be such a traitor, Father? He risks being discovered."

"I fear so. On the other hand, Esme, it is probable these men have been plotting for a long time. I'm sure the king would have discovered it by now if he were ever going to do so." Aidan took hold of her shoulders. "However, I still think it would be safer for you to stay here. Once Edmund learns you know of his treachery, he might fear you'll expose him and then—"

She interrupted him, unable to contemplate his insinuation. "I'm sure he would never hurt me. I'll never tell anyone."

Aidan sighed. "I can only urge you not to go. Edmund has brought silver for more raids. Nothing will stop Olaf and Sweyn except a higher alternative bidder."

"More plundering and killing," Esme spat the words.

There was a knock at the door. Esme glanced at Aidan.

"That will be Eirik now," said the priest.

"Please don't let him in," whispered Esme. "If we're quiet perhaps he'll go away."

"He knows we're here. Besides, you must speak to him. I'll leave you two alone." He opened the door.

Eirik glanced at Aidan and clearly sensed disquiet. "I can return later," he said.

"No, no, please come in. It's important you speak to Esme. I'm just going."

Eirik paced the kitchen twice; his mind clearly in a turmoil. Esme waited until she could bear it no longer. "You were right. I heard what he said."

Eirik raised his head and spoke with urgency. "I regret my involvement in that enterprise, but I promised Sweyn my help long before I came here."

"And never let it be said that a Viking breaks his word."

"You may mock all you wish, woman. It's the way of warfare that allies help one another against their enemy. However, it has been known for warriors to change sides."

"Does Edmund know I'm here?"

"Not at the moment. I'm asking you for the last time if you wish me to tell him."

"Yes, I want you to tell him. Whatever his reasons for choosing his present course of action, it has nothing to do with me or my brother. He's our guardian. It was my father's hope that Brand should take over father's land. I shall marry in order to secure both our futures."

"Do you love him?" said Eirik.

She looked up sharply. "That is none of your concern."

"A man may marry a woman for many reasons. There are alternative courses of action for you."

Her eyes glinted with indignation. "Oh yes, and what might they be? Stay here hiding as a monk; or become a kitchen maid; allow you to take me back to Denmark and be sold as a slave, or worse . . . become *your* slave." Her words were filled with bitterness.

Eirik's eyes hardened. "Then marry your lord and may you both be happy."

Esme tossed her head. "We will. Of that I have no doubt."

"Your Edmund wants to speak to me alone. Since your mind is made up, it's best you stay here. Father Aidan will come to get you."

"Then I shall await his return with interest."

He stared at her. She expected him to speak again, but instead he said nothing more, and quietly left.

29

Edmund and Eirik sat facing one another, separated by a low, square table that reached no higher than their knees.

Edmund poured himself a cup of wine from a pottery jug and began in a confidential manner. "Your ships and men are impressive. I'd like to offer you a job, reporting directly to us, rather than Sweyn or Olaf. We need leaders like you to fight on our side. We'll pay handsomely – more money than you can ever spend in a lifetime."

Eirik shrugged. "I already have that."

Edmund took a gulp of wine from his cup. "A man can never have enough. But tell me then, what else can I offer you?"

"Land," said Eirik.

Edmund smiled. "I'm sure that can be arranged. When Aethelred is deposed we'll have extensive areas at our disposal."

"There's another matter upon which we must speak," said Eirik.

Edmund raised his brows. "Do go on. I'm intrigued."

"Esme, your ward, is under my protection."

Wine spurted from Edmund's mouth and sprayed across the table. "She's what?"

"She is under my protection," Eirik repeated calmly.

"Yes, yes, I heard you, but how can that be? She's staying with friends. Her brother is there also."

"I fear you are misinformed," said Eirik. "She came here to repair a tapestry in the church and became embroiled in the outcome of the battle – most unfortunate."

Edmund's face was bright red. "And just exactly what does being under your protection mean? Is she your slave?" He sneered. "Have you enjoyed her?"

"No."

"A young woman with looks and a figure such as hers would arouse the lust in most men, and you tell me you've not touched her? I don't believe you." Edmund was apoplectic.

"She's a spirited girl and well able to defend herself," said Eirik.

Edmund guffawed. "I see, and too much for you to handle, eh? I can't say I blame you. She's always been difficult to bring into line but at least she looks after that snivelling little brother of hers. I have little time for women or the diversion of domesticity. I find the company of men more to my liking. But I want her returned. Are you intending to ransom her?"

"Is she of value to you?"

"Yes, indeed, in one respect at least. The lands under my guardianship are vast. My forests provide valuable oak for building ships."

"And provide you with a substantial profit."

"Of course, how much do you want for her?"

"There's no ransom."

Edmund huffed. "In that case, she has almost certainly been violated by someone, if not by you. A lovely young girl would never survive in a male environment such as this. Once her virtue has been defiled, she is of little value to anyone, except perhaps a whore house. She'd be no use to me if this became common knowledge. It would damage my reputation."

"She's in disguise – dressed as a monk."

"A monk!" Edmund's mirthless laughter penetrated the air. "This I must see."

"What will you do if I return her to you?" asked Eirik.

"If? What do you mean – if? You're impertinent. Let me assure you, *if* is not an option. There is no question that I shall take her home where she belongs. And I shall expect the greatest discretion on your part about anything that took place here. I would not wish it to be known that my wife – as she will be one day soon – spent time at the mercy of Viking predators."

"It will go no further," said Eirik.

"Good. I want to see her – now!"

"I shall arrange it immediately."

Esme was unable to stop trembling. She knew her guardian would be appalled by her appearance, unable to recognise the clean, tidy and well-dressed young woman he knew a week or two ago. Worst of all, she didn't feel like herself anymore. Her peaceful and joyful spirit had been smashed by recent events. She despised the Vikings, yet Eirik had aroused in her feelings which she knew she could never feel for Edmund. That worried her; she'd been flirting with the forbidden. Her friends returned to the kitchen and the three of them sat waiting, expecting the call from Aidan at any time.

"I'm horrified," said Astrid. "I've always disliked Edmund but never imagined him to be a traitor. You really must not go back with him, Esme."

"And you definitely should not marry him," added Rowena.

Tears rolled down Esme's face. "I'm scared by the thought of marriage to Edmund, but equally frightened by the thought of not marrying him. What will become of Brand? Edmund will at least keep him safe, as he's always done."

"But if Edmund is capable of betraying his king, who else might he turn against?" said Astrid.

"I must dismiss that thought. Edmund has always been distant, but we rely on him. If he is now against the king, there must be a good reason." Esme sighed. "In any case, he'll not allow me to stay."

"There will always be a home for you here," said Astrid.

Esme held out a hand to each of her friends. "Thank you, both of you. That is a comfort to me, but I suspect Brand has become accustomed to his life at Saxstow."

Rowena folded her arms across her chest. "The boy will have to do as he's told."

Esme sighed. "Let me see how Edmund behaves towards me when we go home. I have done nothing wrong. There is no reason for him to reject me."

Astrid looked askance at Rowena but neither of them said any more. They helped her comb her hair and straighten creases from her clothes. It was precious little and Esme knew she would look a frightful sight in Edmund's eyes no matter what she did. Then the moment arrived when Aidan came to fetch her.

Edmund remained seated as she ventured into the room, but Eirik crossed to the door to welcome her. She saw Edmund's eyes upon her, critical, cold – like ice. The derision on his lips said it all.

"My god! Is this her? The Viking monk?"

"You know it is, Edmund," said Esme. "How do you expect me to look after several days dressed in a monk's habit?"

"Where are your clothes, girl?" he asked.

Esme hesitated. She felt the warmth in her cheeks. "They were destroyed."

"Destroyed? And why so, what was wrong with them? The other women have managed to keep theirs on."

Esme bristled at the insinuation. "I . . . I fell," she said.

"Into what?"

"A large grave."

Edmund snorted. "Oh, come now, girl, you can't expect me to believe that. Besides, they would wash wouldn't they?"

"They were torn."

Edmund looked suspiciously at her. "Torn by whom?"

"Edmund, it was not my fault. Two of Olaf's men attacked me and—"

"Enough," he shouted. "Lord Eirik, you assured me she had not been touched."

"Neither was she."

"Eirik saved me," said Esme.

Edmund's eyes narrowed. "Oh, its *Eirik* now is it? I see you have become on most friendly terms with your captor. And he saved you?" He sneered. "And what was his reward for such a favour?"

Esme glanced at Eirik. His jaw had tensed and the muscles in his cheeks moved as he ground his teeth. His eyes glowered with dislike, his knuckles white. She became fearful, anticipating trouble between the two men. Eirik could easily kill Edmund in a fight.

She tried to remain outwardly calm despite her inner turmoil. "I see I shall not be able to persuade you with words alone, Edmund. If your distrust means that you would rather discard me, please say so now. Perhaps one of the women from the village will take me in."

"And leave you for the entertainment of the likes of your captor?" said Edmund with scorn. "Is that what would give you pleasure, my dear? You'll be damned to hell."

Esme was wounded. "Edmund, are you willing to take me back with you?" she asked again. "I know you are upset by what has happened."

"Upset! Upset!" Edmund raged. He rose from his seat and strode to where she stood. He raised a hand to strike her, but Eirik moved in a flash and caught hold of his wrist.

Edmund glared at him. "How dare you intervene? She's not just my ward but my future wife. She's mine to do with as I please."

Eirik's tone was even. "Not while she is still under my protection."

Edmund bared his teeth in a snarl. "In that case I shall ensure that she's free of your protection once and for all. I insist we are married right now. Since we have a priest to hand, we'll marry in his church. That way she'll be obliged to make her vows before God. It will ensure she keeps them. Should she be with child there'll be no gossip as to its father, and a puking infant will keep her amused."

He dismissed her with a sneer. "Go and find some decent clothing, my dear. I can hardly be expected to ride away from here with a monk on my arm."

Esme's face was ashen. "Edmund, so soon?"

"Yes. It's the only satisfactory way forward. It's how you can prove to me what you've been saying. Otherwise, I shall see to it that you never set eyes on your brother again."

Esme's lower lip quivered as she held back tears. "My friend, Rowena, may have a spare dress. I'll ask her if she has something suitable."

"Go then, and come back resembling a woman." Edmund addressed Eirik. "And while she's gone, I'd like to make a complaint to your overlord."

"By that I presume you mean King Sweyn."

"Indeed," said Edmund.

Eirik made no attempt to enlighten him on the nature of their respective relationships. He called to Father Aidan who had been waiting outside.

139

"Ahh, priest," said Edmund. "Esme and I are to be married at once – as soon as she's found some clean clothes that is. You are to perform the ceremony. We'll be leaving immediately afterwards."

30

As they walked back to the kitchen to find Rowena and Astrid, Aidan's brow was deeply furrowed. "Esme, I'm worried."

Esme thought she had never felt more wretched in her life. "I'm content, Father. Please don't be concerned about me."

Aidan huffed. "I can't believe you're to be married so soon. You remember what we talked about? How he might react? Is that what happened?"

"Yes. Exactly in the way you predicted. He thinks I've been violated."

"Dear God!"

Esme looked at the ground. "He's threatened never to allow me to see Brand again if I don't obey. When he sees that all is well, he'll change. My priority is my brother. I must fetch him home. Then all this will be put behind us."

"Edmund's treachery is in danger of discovery. You will live every day waiting for the worst."

"As you said, Father, Edmund is powerful, surrounded by powerful men. Nothing will happen. Once Brand is safe, maybe I'll be able to come and see you again. Then you'll be reassured."

The selected outfit was pale yellow. Rowena said she had made it for her own wedding day – finely woven wool, dyed using weld. She had kept the dress since slimmer days, before the children arrived. It hugged Esme's figure rather more than she would have wished. Astrid helped Esme to dress then trimmed her hair with bows. "You look beautiful. How could Edmund treat you so when he has the best-looking girl in all of England?"

"Will you come with me?"

"Of course, we wouldn't miss your wedding day," said Rowena.

Esme lowered her eyes. "It was not exactly how I planned it."

They made their way to the church. Eirik was standing in the doorway. Their eyes met. Esme knew she would never see him again. In any case, there would be no point. He was bound to Thor and she was bound to Edmund.

"Is this what you want?" he said.

"What I want has nothing to do with it. You know how it is for women. We've had this conversation before."

"But you have such wonderful skills with your sewing and tapestry work. Surely you could create an income for yourself doing that."

"I already have. But I need space and money to do it. Edmund controls everything. I have nothing of my own."

"You'll forgive me if I don't attend the ceremony," said Eirik. "Edmund is waiting in the church. I shall say farewell. I have enjoyed our talks, even those where you have berated me. I admire your spirit. Please don't allow anybody to take that away from you – man or woman. I wish you well." He turned to walk away but looked back and smiled. "By the way, you look lovely."

Esme felt unexpectedly bereft. She turned to her friends. "I feel so desperate. What shall I do?"

"There is only one thing to be done," said Astrid, "we must pray, and leave the outcome in the hands of the Lord. Let us do so now."

Rowena and Astrid each stood at Esme's side and together all three held hands. They thanked God for his mercies, asked for a strengthening of their faith and for his unswerving protection.

"Now," said Rowena, "leave it to Him. Sometimes He has plans for our lives and solutions for our problems that come in most unexpected ways."

Suddenly, Edmund came striding towards them. "Praying for forgiveness for your sins, I hope," he mocked. "Whores used to be stoned in Our Lord's day. Just be grateful we're a little more enlightened."

Rowena squeezed her hand. "I'm always here," she said, "and the Vikings may soon be gone if they are to head for Southampton for the winter. Then we'll be free."

It was a small gathering where Father Aidan performed the marriage ceremony. Rowena and Astrid were the only guests. Afterwards, when Esme mounted Kizzy ready for the journey, it was as Lord Edmund's wife.

"Won't you consider staying until morning?" asked Father Aidan. "It's already late and you'll not make it back before dark."

Edmund looked at him disdainfully. "It has nothing to do with you, priest. You've played your part. We'll camp overnight. That will be infinitely preferable to spending another hour in this despicable place." He twitched the reins of his horse; Kizzy followed, breaking into a trot.

Soon the church and Maeldun were out of sight.

31
London 1979

Emma makes an appointment to meet Matilda on Friday. Ben tells her to take the car and carry on to Norwich for the weekend.

She finds the nursing home easily. Graceful deciduous trees, with leaves unfurling, give privacy to a wide driveway until a long, white, double-storey house comes into view. Emma counts eighteen Georgian windows on the ground floor. The upper floor mirrors the one below, except each room also has its own wrought-iron balcony. A terrace, running the full length, gives way to sloping lawns with copious flower beds. Perennial plants promise a blaze of colour. Patients are sitting outside, enjoying the sunshine. Many are in wheelchairs, with a nurse or visitor seated beside them.

As instructed, Emma walks to the reception in the foyer and asks to speak to the matron. A woman, perhaps in her fifties, appears on the threshold of an office and beckons her in. "Please take a seat," she says. "When I mentioned your name, Matilda said she wants to see you because she is convinced you are related."

"Tell me about her."

Matron nods. A hair grip loosens and her white cap wobbles a little, settling slightly askew on her head. "Matilda has been with us for several years so we know her well. At first she was physically able and used to help out by talking to the residents, making them feel at home. But now, well, she tires easily."

"How is she today?"

Matron pouts, tipping her head from side to side. The gesture puts the cap in danger of slipping further; she raises a steadying hand. "Good days and bad days, like us all I suppose. Sadly, most of her friends and relatives have passed away, including her unmarried daughter. An elderly gentleman used to drop by most weeks, but he hasn't been for some time now. She was always cheered by his visits, and often spoke of some common ancestor from long ago. Even now there are times when she seems quite jubilant. I think she must re-live those visits."

Emma holds her breath as an unbidden notion pops into her mind. "Would it be inappropriate to ask the name of this gentleman?"

"Not at all. His name is Reginald. She always called him *My Reggie*."

"I don't suppose his surname is Reed by any chance?"

"Do you know, I believe it was – yes, Reginald Reed."

Emma releases the air suspended in her lungs. "It just so happens that I may know of him. I'm afraid he died recently."

Matron raises her eyebrows, clearly less concerned about the report of his death than the fact he is known to Emma. "You knew him? Well, that will explain Matilda's wish to see you. How did you know Reginald?"

"I never met him. My mother is a distant relative."

"Wonderful. Reginald must have told Matilda. She'll be delighted you're here. I'll show you to her room."

Emma is bemused. How could Reggie have known about her mother? Was he told before his death? She will have to check with Ben.

The room in which Matilda spends her time is large and south facing, overlooking the lawns and woodland. Georgian floor-to-ceiling windows fill the space with light. The old lady is sitting in an armchair with one leg perched on a foot stool. She instantly smiles. "Welcome, Esme," she says, pointing to another armchair. "Do sit down."

"My name is not . . ." begins Emma, but she hesitates. Her father's favourite novel was *The Hunchback of Notre Dame*. She had been named after the character of Esmeralda, shortened to Esme, but she changed it in later life, believing Emma sounded more professional.

"May we have an extra cup with the tea, please?" asks Matilda.

"I'll see to it straight away," is the obliging reply as matron backs out of the room, closing the door behind her.

Despite her unease at the spontaneous way in which Matilda called her Esme, Emma cannot resist a smile. At one hundred and two, she is in full command of her faculties.

"You came to ask about the story written by Esme of how she met and fell in love with a Viking called Eirik. There was another, you know, by a woman called Phoebe, who was a descendant of Esme. Now, the interesting thing is this: my gentleman friend Reggie is a descendant of Phoebe, and he found her writings among some esoteric books in his library. It had been there as long as he could remember, but he never took any notice of it because it was too difficult to read." Matilda peers at Emma. "Are you following me so far, dear?"

Emma nods.

"Good. Well, one day, a professor friend of Reggie, who was visiting him, managed to read little bits of the text. He said that Phoebe was recording what happened several years after the battle." Matilda giggles. "Do you remember King Cnut – you know the chap who tried to turn the tide?"

Emma nods again not wishing to interrupt Matilda's wandering train of thought.

"Well, he made Eirik the Earl of somewhere up north."

They are interrupted by a knock at the door and a young carer walks in with a teapot, milk, and two cups and saucers, all neatly set out on a tray. "Have you brought the biscuits, dear?" says Matilda.

The girl smiles, "Of course." She sets the tray down. "Shall I pour or will you?" she says to Emma.

"Thank you. I'll do it. How do you like your tea, Matilda?"

The next few moments are occupied with tea and biscuits before Matilda resumes. "Reggie would have liked to know all the story, but he left it too late."

Emma gulps her tea. *Does she know he's dead?*

"Reginald says Esme's story is also kept safe in his house, somewhere, along with other treasures. I'm sure you've been sent to find them. That's why I'm telling you," she says triumphantly.

What kind of treasures? Emma remembers the window latch in Reginald's bedroom, the footprints and the missing key. "Well, I must admit my mother has recently inherited a house from a man called Reginald Reed."

"That's my friend. Wait until he knows I've met one of his descendants," says Matilda rather smugly. "He'll be delighted. I shall be seeing him again fairly soon. Anyway, my dear, my job is done. I can move on peacefully now." Matilda closes her eyes and begins to doze. Her arm settles by her side, leaving the cup and saucer on her lap. Emma gently places them back on the tray. She picks up a rug folded over the arm of Matilda's chair and spreads it across the old lady's knees, then quietly leaves the room.

On her way out, she bumps into the matron. "Matilda is sleeping now. Thank you for the tea. I enjoyed the visit very much."

"I'm glad you came." Matron smiles and opens the main door. "Thank you for coming. It will have done her good. Drive carefully."

32
Maeldun 991

Overhead, trees stretched out their branches forming lush green arches. Shafts of sunlight danced through the leaves until eclipsed by evening shadows. The resultant gloom matched Esme's own depressed spirit. She tried several times to open a conversation, but Edmund resolutely refused to speak to her. Perhaps he needed time to calm down and reconsider. There was much she wanted to know and understand about his betrayal of King Aethelred, but she must allow him to believe her ignorant of his treachery. Brand's safety was much to the forefront of her mind.

Before long, Edmund selected a small clearing near a stream to camp for the night. He collected kindling in silence. Esme unpacked the blankets and watched from the corner of her eye as he took a flint from a pouch and created a spark. The dry tinder leapt into flames. Their warm glow filled her with renewed optimism as they began to share the domesticity of their first few hours as man and wife. She heated the potage provided by Rowena until it bubbled, and then cut off chunks of fresh bread.

Edmund settled himself on a log. Esme approached with trepidation and offered him a bowl. "I don't want any of your whore's soup," he said, scowling. "What kind of poison have you filled it with?"

Esme was dismayed. "Edmund, please, there is no poison. Why would I wish to do that?"

"So you can return to your heathen friends." He grimaced. "The more I think about that Viking's arrogance, the more I disbelieve you."

"I'm your wife. If I had not wished to be so, I would not have come with you."

But the comment, intended to appease, served only to enrage him. Edmund's face was a mask of hatred. In his anger he grabbed the front of Rowena's dress, tugging it apart, and threw the broth over Esme's chest. She screamed. "See if that provides your filthy breasts with warm comfort," he growled. "I trusted you. I allowed you complete freedom and this is how you repay me, by sneaking off, cavorting and fornicating. I was a respected figure amongst those Vikings. They relied on me for vital information to enable this country to gain a new king – one with strength and valour, not weakness and indecision. How can I expect them to regard me in the same way? I've become a figure of their scorn and derision since your despicable behaviour. Now any loose talk about this incident could send me straight to the executioner, and *you* are entirely to blame. You are a stupid, ignorant and feckless whore and no longer of any use to me."

He slapped her hard across the face with the back of his hand. Her head jerked sideways. Clenching his fist, he punched her cheek. She cried out as the rough edge of his diamond ring gashed her skin. He pushed her to the ground. "Like it when it hurts, do you? How many heathens have you enjoyed? Do you prefer them one at a time or all together?"

"Why did you marry me, Edmund?" said Esme in a voice hardly audible.

"That Viking friend of yours was staking a claim to what was mine. I showed him otherwise."

Her breath was short, uneven. "So you've never cared for me or Brand?"

He grunted. "Cared? What do you think? That I looked after you both out of the goodness of my heart? Caring is an overrated emotion. This is how much I care." It was as though the devil had gripped his soul; he kicked her repeatedly in the abdomen and small of her back as she lay helpless. Pain seared through her body. Finally, he stopped, panting hard, regarding her with revulsion. "That'll get rid of any Viking bastard," he said.

Esme groaned: her body broken and wretched. There was no hope for a life with this man. How could she have thought otherwise? His blurred outline stood scrutinising her. Surely he would take pity. Instead, he took hold of her arms and dragged her deeper into the undergrowth. The stream trickled nearby. She could hear it gurgling over small boulders.

"Don't think of sleeping anywhere near me," he said. "I don't want your stench under my nose." He stepped back and wiped his hands on a tussock as though even touching her had been distasteful to him. Then he gave her one final kick in the groin and walked back to the warmth of the fire, leaving her alone and in agony.

Esme was unable to move. She lay flat on her back on the ferns. The skin on her chest was inflamed and her insides felt squashed like pulp. The bruised rib cage would not support her upper body as she tried to lift herself up. If only she could reach the creek. Inch by inch she crawled closer. Each small movement racked her bones and the intensity of the pain took away her breath. Yet she was determined, and eventually slipped into the icy water, the chill ripples numbing the pain. Settling on the stony bottom, her head and shoulders resting on the bank, she prayed for healing, oblivious of time. At last her mind went blank, and registered nothing more.

33

Eirik had left the meeting with Edmund and Sweyn feeling disgruntled. He knew he could no longer countenance his current existence. Father Aidan and Esme between them had opened his eyes to a new way of life: one without constant battles and fighting. For years he had religiously kept his vow to Thor and Odin and had felt their protection; but it was no longer enough. He had seen the change that had taken place in Aidan since his days as a Viking. Although he didn't know him personally at the time, he knew what type of men stood and watched mass executions and enjoyed them. He no longer believed that the Christ was puny. This God proposed a way of life that could bring contentment, not riches, but a peace that was beyond price.

Eirik had reached a decision. He would step down as leader of the Jomsborg monks. There were plenty who were ready to take his place. Leif was one, although he doubted whether the young man was sufficiently disciplined for such a task. Nevertheless, the men would choose their own chief as they had chosen him. He would inform Sweyn how he felt, that he could no longer ask his men to follow him into fights, to kill, to maim and wreak havoc. Owning vast tracts of land in Denmark would enable him to return to farming and rearing horses as his adopted father had done before him. Maeldun had given him time to think, to consult Thor. He felt the responsibility of his pledge had been lifted, and now it was time for life to take a different direction.

He sat on a stone bench in the church grounds, looking westward towards the late afternoon sun. The soft padding of sandals on gravel broke his thoughts. The edge of Father Aidan's robe swung into view.

"You're looking contemplative this evening, Eirik. May I join you?"

"Please do."

"Have you come to any conclusions since our discussions?"

"You know I have. Did you not baptise me the other evening? What greater commitment can a man make than that?"

"Thor will not relinquish you so easily. Baptism is only the beginning. The commitment comes in how you renew your life."

"I shall continue to read your translations. The word of God will show me how to live my life from now on."

Aidan put a hand on his shoulder. "Who would have thought that the young man I saw so bravely speaking up against Earl Haakon, all those years ago, would be my first real convert."

"Who could have foreseen *your* conversion? Life takes strange turns."

"So what seems to be troubling you?" said Aidan.

Eirik frowned. "I'm worried about Esme. I'm not at all sure Edmund is in his right mind. He was greatly disturbed by her appearance and refused to believe she was still chaste, despite our efforts to persuade him otherwise. Surely, if he loved her, he would accept her back and comfort her. None of it was of her making. I feel responsible for ruining her life."

Father Aidan gave him a quizzical look. "Eirik, you ruin everyone's life when you invade their existence." He sighed. "Nevertheless, I agree. I've never quite trusted the man since he offered to become the guardian of Esme and her brother. I doubt she married Edmund because she loves him."

"All women seem to marry for material gain," said Eirik.

"Eirik, do you have no understanding of the plight of women?"

"Yes – nevertheless, I could never marry a woman who wanted me only for what I could provide."

"I see. You wish to marry for love? Eirik, I think you are in danger of being an incurable romantic. Most people marry out of necessity."

"The whole arrangement sounds extremely mundane."

"For most people that's how life is – mundane. A man must feed his family. He has little chance to make a name for himself. His life is the same each day, until the one when God claims him for Himself."

Eirik stood and paced up and down. "Edmund is going to hurt her, I'm sure of it. His resentment and anger were blatant. He'll take it out on her."

Aidan raised his eyebrows. "I think your worries are needless. It sounds to me as though you are close to being a little in love with her."

"Nonsense," said Eirik.

"What man would not be in love with her?" Aidan said calmly.

"I feel a certain responsibility for her welfare – that's all. Besides, she hates me. Have you not heard the scorn in her voice as she speaks of Vikings?"

Aidan smiled. "Yes, I'm sure you must be right. Will you join me for supper this evening?"

"Thank you, but I'm not hungry. I'll go back to the camp. Sometime soon the men must be told how I feel."

"What do you think will be their reaction?"

"Some of them will agree with me. Take Fenrir, for example, he's been loyal and a good friend. I think he may be getting tired of the continual trekking across the seas. There are others, too."

"Well, I'll leave you now, Eirik. I must go to evening prayers. I shall remember you while I'm doing so." Aidan gathered up his habit and strolled towards the church.

Eirik lay on his pallet, looking up at the sky. All around him were sounds of men enjoying the evening. But he had no peace in his heart. How could he have allowed Esme to escape from him so easily? He should have fought harder, stopped her from marrying Edmund. She had touched his heart and mind, and now he felt empty. She'd challenged him, winning his admiration. Her body was perfection and, try as he may, he could never put out of his mind what lay beneath that shapeless habit. Neither could he dismiss her lovely face, suffused with vitality. Now she was gone for good – married to a feckless traitor, a man not worthy of esteem who had no appreciation of his wife's true qualities.

Eirik sat up, thumping the soil with his fist, furious and frustrated that he lacked the courage to change his own future instead of burying himself in his old life. He strode towards the estuary. A swim would do him good – help him to forget. Stripping off his tunic, he waded into the water, black as the ink with which Father Aidan wrote his transcripts. At that moment, he wished it would swallow him up and transport him to a place where he could find rest for his soul.

His strokes were fuelled by exasperation and he soon reached a second island further up the river. The beach was silent. No cicada sang and no night birds squawked. Across the estuary, the camp fires of Olaf's warriors flickered. Eirik closed his eyes and breathed deeply, emptying his mind, concentrating on the inner strength at the core of his being. He sat meditating until the sky grew black and the moon shone on the soft waves like a silver crimped ribbon. The orange fires extinguished one by one as he drifted into sleep. Then suddenly his eyes jolted open. What unseen enemy was attacking him? Was Thor taking revenge? He was cold; his legs had turned to ice. He stood and shouted Esme's name into the emptiness, convinced she was suffering.

The first streaks of sunrise brushed the sky as he re-entered the water. With every powerful stroke he prayed for God to protect her. Arriving back at the camp he dressed quickly and called the bay stallion, which by now was familiar with his new master. The steed walked towards him, standing obediently while the heavy saddle landed on its back.

Fenrir emerged from a tent, rubbing sleep from his eyes and watched Eirik fasten the girth. "Where are you off to?"

"To help a friend."

"It wouldn't be your youthful little monk?" said Fenrir, grinning.

"There's no fooling you, is there?"

Fenrir's grey locks quivered as he shook his head. "Her touch was too caring when she stitched up my wound; her fingers too nimble when she sewed my clothes, and voice too gentle when she asked me questions. I must admit, though, the pretence was good and well conceived in the circumstances. I suspected you had more than a passing liking for her the night we sang songs."

"She's in trouble. I can feel it. I'm going after her."

"Isn't it too late for that? She's just got married to that two-faced devil. Never could abide a traitor."

"I'll have to take the risk," said Eirik, gathering the reins. "I think Esme is dying."

"Have the runes told you so?"

"I'm not sure how I know, but I can feel the pain."

"Then you'd better get going. Don't waste time talking to me." Fenrir held the bay horse while Eirik mounted. "And good luck to you, lord. Bring her back safe."

34

Eirik tracked the westward road. He had no idea where Esme and Edmund would be, but, after an hour or so, he began to look for clearings surrounded by the safety of woodland, places suitable for camping overnight. He reached the edge of a ridge and looked down into the hollow below – an ideal position. He strained his eyes through the foliage. More slowly this time he allowed the horse to pick its way down the bank. Eirik began to doubt the veracity of the call he'd felt last night. Supposing he found Edmund and Esme cuddled up, making love? That's what he would be doing if he'd just married her. How on earth would he explain his bizarre behaviour?

As he approached the bottom of the bank, Eirik was certain this was the place where they had stopped for the night. But there was no sign of either of them. He dismounted and dropped the reins of the horse. Warm, grey ash indicated the remains of a fire that had not been fed with kindling for at least an hour. A pot of soup sat over a tripod. An upturned bowl lay on the ground. A fleeting scene passed over his inner eye – hot liquid being thrown. The burning sensation whipped his chest. He removed his sword from its sheath.

The ground was freshly churned. Turf lay in clumps, newly wrenched from the earth. He stooped to examine them. At least five sets of hooves, maybe more, were clearly visible. A blanket was tossed to one side. He picked it up and slung it over his shoulder. From the indentation in the soft soil it appeared that a body had slept on the spot.

His steely gaze took in every tree, every nook of the area. He felt no fear but each fibre of his being was taut, ready for action. He stood completely still and listened for signs of life. Then he heard a familiar whinny. "Kizzy!" he whispered. The little mare trotted into view wearing neither saddle nor bridle. She walked up close to him and nudged his shoulder. He stroked her nose but she nudged him again in the same direction; then, again and again until Eirik understood the message.

"Sorry, girl," he said, "you lead the way."

Kizzy tossed her head twice and trotted away from him, pausing once to look back. Satisfied that he was following, she quickened her pace and led him to the stream.

At first Eirik could see nothing. Kizzy snorted. "Show me. Show me," pleaded Eirik. "Where is she?"

He looked beneath a bush overhanging the water. Then he saw her: a face, white as snow; wispy strands of fair hair stuck to the forehead – Esme.

Eirik waded into the stream and lifted her submerged body out of the water. Her head was lodged between two branches, saving her from drowning. But he recalled the freezing of his limbs, and guessed what she had been through the night before. He felt for a pulse; detected none.

An agonised groan vibrated in his throat as he gathered the lifeless form in his arms. He carried her to what was left of the fire and laid her down. Then he carefully removed the sodden dress. Her ribs and lower body were black with bruises: the result of a terrible beating. Her chest was red and sore. His eyes filled with tears of compassion as he wrapped her in the blanket, frantically massaging her limbs to bring back warmth. "Did Edmund do this to you?" he muttered. "I'll kill him."

He refused to believe she was dead. That could not happen. What instinct had warned him something was wrong? Had he not responded as quickly as possible? The mare nuzzled the side of

157

Esme's face; then, dropping to its knees and bringing up its haunches, it settled its warm body beside her, whickering.

"Clever girl," said Eirik. "Save your mistress for both our sakes." He found another blanket and wrapped it around Esme, then gathered moss to make a pillow for her head. Using residual heat from the charred remains among the ashes, he revived the fire, feeding the flames with kindling. Then he too snuggled close to her, talking continuously, describing what he could see: the trees; foliage; insects; birds, anything to encourage consciousness to return. But still he felt no heartbeat.

Eirik was unaware of how much time passed, but the afternoon sun had found a gap in the treetops shining a hot shaft directly upon them. He examined Esme's cheeks. Could he detect a tiny bloom of life or was it his hopeful imagination? He felt the pulse again. Yes, he was sure there was a feeble movement. He heard a slight moan and saw the smallest flicker of those wonderful long lashes. His heart leapt. Eirik beamed, hardly containing his joy. "Esme, don't worry, you're safe." Waves of relief crashed over him.

She made no reply but fell into a deep slumber.

There was still no sign of Edmund. His horse was missing. It appeared they had been attacked, by robbers perhaps? Had they left Esme for dead and taken Edmund for a ransom? Or perhaps he'd met up with some of his fellow traitors and headed off to make more devilish plans. What did he mean by leaving Esme? How had she come to be in the stream? Had he beaten her and absconded, hoping she would die? Surely her husband would not do such a thing? Eirik's thoughts ran wild. The most likely explanation seemed to be that a band of vagrants had set upon them.

"My beloved," he whispered. "What did they do to you? Please forgive me for not coming sooner." Kizzy raised her head. "If only you could speak," said Eirik. "If only you could tell me." She snorted gently.

Eirik allowed Esme to sleep. There was plenty of time to return to Maeldun and for now rest was what she needed. He lay on his back next to her. The sun was warm on his face and he dozed gently, one hand on his sword. It seemed a long time before he felt her move. Instantly he was alert. Propping his head on his elbow he stared down at her.

She opened her eyes and blinked, "Eirik."

"Yes. I'm here."

"I called you," she murmured.

"Then I believe I must have heard."

"Good," she said, before going to sleep again.

Another hour or more passed before she woke for the second time. Now there was colour in her face. She spoke to him, her words barely audible. "Eirik. Do something for me?"

"Anything."

"Kiss me."

Eirik furrowed his brow.

"Sorry. I disgust you," she said.

"No, no, I'm afraid I'll hurt you."

"Please, let me feel, just for a moment, that I'm not worthless."

"Whatever happened to you, Esme?" He placed light, tender kisses on her cheeks until he reached her mouth; then he hesitated, feeling her breath cool on his skin. He pulled away from her.

"Mother always kissed me better."

Eirik thought his heart would break. He stood, stoked up the fire and warmed what was left of the potage. Then, with a supporting arm, he lifted her head and encouraged her to take small sips. He was fearful for her recovery. "I'm taking you back," he said, clenching his jaw. "This will never happen again."

"Will you help me to my feet?"

"Do you feel strong enough to travel?"

As she stood, the blankets briefly parted, revealing the extent of her bruises.

"I'm ugly," said Esme. She hung her head.

"No. You're beautiful," he said, covering her; longing to touch, to heal, to love, to give his all. But she was not his. Instead he spoke briskly. "Come, my girl, let's get you to Maeldun. You need Astrid's help." He removed his tunic and placed it gently over Esme's head. He felt the delicate touch of a small finger trace the scar across his bare chest and his heart lurched. He folded her hand in his and leaned her against Kizzy's side while he quickly gathered more moss for a cushion.

He was worried about moving her, suspecting she might have other injuries – internal, unseen. Every jolt could damage her further, and she may not even survive the journey. There was no doubt that the safest place for her to travel was in his arms. He lifted her carefully onto the back of the great bay horse then swung smoothly into the saddle behind her. She leaned against him and he held her close.

They walked slowly back to the village while Kizzy trotted happily behind.

35

Esme continued to sleep, but Eirik could feel a reassuring heart beat. She was alive. He went straight to Astrid's cottage. She looked at the bundle in his arms and glanced up at him in alarm, "Esme? Is she...?"

"She's been badly beaten, may be bleeding in her belly. Her chest is burned. She spent a night in a cold stream. Can you help her?"

"The poor girl," said Astrid. "Whatever could have happened? We'll put her in my bed." She clicked her tongue against her teeth. "I can't imagine what she's been through."

A partition screened the sleeping quarters from view. Astrid's pallet was soft and comfortable. "What else do you need?" said Eirik.

"Go to the barn behind the monastery where I make my potions. Fetch some arnica lotion. It's labelled. It'll help the bruising." Astrid put her hand on Esme's face. "The girl's heating up. Bring aconite too. She's shaking like a leaf in a storm – the fever will get worse before it gets better. And bring honey for her skin and willow bark for pain, although I doubt she's feeling much at the moment. When you've done that, go out back and chop firewood." Astrid began to shoo Eirik from the room. "Get going. This precious girl needs rest above all."

Eirik allowed himself to be pushed gently towards the door, though he could hardly endure leaving Esme. "May I come and sit with her later? You'll need your rest too."

Astrid gave Eirik a curious sideways glance. "Of course, if you want to. But won't Edmund be arriving soon? Or has he been injured too?"

"I don't know. And I don't care. Do you want Rowena's help?"

Astrid shook her head. "She's so many chores and the children to look after."

"Then I'll help you," said Eirik. "We'll take care of Esme together."

"I'm not acquainted with the proprieties of that, but these are not times when the natural order prevails. Since you rescued her, I'm sure she would have it no other way."

Eirik went to find the needed herbs and potions and soon returned with as many as he could carry. Then he went to the back of Astrid's house and found logs and an axe. He was glad to have some physical activity to vent his anger, and berated himself with every blow for allowing Edmund to best him. He knew it was the comment about Esme being under his protection that had provoked Edmund into marrying her. He cursed the very words he'd spoken. And now she was Edmund's wife. But for the moment, all that mattered was her recovery, her health and strength. Eirik was still unable to understand the affinity he felt with Esme. This was a new experience for him; one which frightened but intrigued him at the same time. He entered the house with an armful of chopped logs and set about making a fire. Then he stacked up the remainder on the hearth. He noticed that Astrid had removed his tunic which was now slung over the back of a chair.

"You can have that back," she said. "I found something loose for Esme to wear. It's a nightgown – the one I made for my wedding night." She grimaced. "I only wore it once. It was too delicate for everyday use."

Eirik smiled. "It's perfect."

Astrid had rubbed lavender oil into Esme's brow to induce rest. The heady aroma hit his nostrils, filling him with a sense of well-being, soothing the anxiety that churned in his stomach. "Will she be . . . will she survive?"

"I don't know," said Astrid. "The fever may last several days. She'll need someone with her constantly."

Eirik squeezed Astrid's hand. "I'll leave you now but I'll come in a while. I'm going to find Father Aidan. Esme is much in need of his prayers."

Astrid tightened her lips. "Indeed she is."

Eirik found Father Aidan at his writing desk, constantly renewing the ink on his quill. Aidan looked up. "I knew it was you. I recognise your step. Fenrir told me you had a task to do today. Was it successful?"

"I went to fetch Esme," said Eirik.

"You did *what*?" Aidan put down the pen and turned round to face Eirik. "I married the child not two days ago. Have you had a fight with Edmund? What on earth possessed you to do something so rash?"

"That's the oddest thing of all. I'm not given to rash behaviour. Yet last night I had the strangest feeling . . ."

Aidan stared at him under a heavy brow. "Eirik, I hope your actions are not simply because of a strange feeling. If that were the case my indigestion would take me in all sorts of undesirable directions."

Eirik drew up a stool. "I don't understand what happened, if truth be told. Perhaps you could explain it to me. I felt a burning on my chest and a severe pain in my stomach and ribs. Then I was buried in ice, as though rolling about in the snow that covers our Danish shores in December. I was freezing and felt the life-breath ooze from my body."

"And what did you do about this strange occurrence?"

"Somehow I knew I was experiencing what Esme was feeling. She was in distress."

"Come now, were you not given to fanciful imaginings? She was no doubt safe in the arms of Edmund – it was their first night of matrimony after all."

Eirik's face soured momentarily. "I understand what you're saying. At first I tried to tell myself I was just missing her."

"*Missing her!*" said Aidan. "My dear Eirik, you go too far."

"Do you not miss her too?"

"Well, that's different. To me she is a child of God to be nurtured in the best way I can. It's my duty."

"What rubbish you speak sometimes, Father. There is nothing dutiful in the love that you have for Esme. You love her spirit, for what she is."

Father Aidan sighed. "Yes, I love her spirit. And if the good Lord sees fit to find me a place in eternity, then I would deem it a privilege to share her company there. I admit there are many whose company I would not relish forever. But tell me, what did you do about this odd feeling?"

"I went to look for her, of course."

"Goodness! I can't imagine what Edmund would have said about such a response. Did you two fight?"

Eirik shook his head. "I found their camp. There was no sign of Edmund although I saw the imprints of several hooves."

There was a sharp intake of breath from Aidan. "Do you think he's been arrested?"

"I don't know. Perhaps Esme will be able to answer that when she recovers – if she recovers." Eirik stood and paced back and forth.

Aidan frowned. "What do you mean? Is she ill?"

"I found her in a stream. She was icy cold. I couldn't find a pulse. Kizzy and I managed to warm her body, but she's still unconscious."

Aidan leapt to his feet. "What? Why was I not told immediately? Where is she?"

Eirik put a hand on his shoulder. "I'm telling you now, Father. She's in good hands. I have taken her to the home of Astrid."

Aidan nodded. "You chose wisely, Eirik. She has more healing skills than anyone else I know."

"Esme needs your prayers."

"And she shall have them. May I see her?"

"At the moment there would be little point. She knows no one," Eirik sighed. "The fever is upon her. All we can do is to wait until it breaks. Astrid believes it could be several days."

"But how do you suppose she came by this condition? Do you think the men who came for Edmund did this to her?"

Eirik paused, studying Aidan's face before continuing. "Why would they? It is my belief that Edmund did it himself."

"Come now, surely he wouldn't do such a thing to his bride? I have always had reservations about Edmund's love of money, rooted in a sin that's the basis of many evils. But I have never attributed a streak of cruelty to him. I think you must be wrong."

"I'm sure it was him. She has severe bruising to her stomach."

Aidan stroked his chin. "As though trying to abort a child from her womb," he said slowly.

"I see you understand well, Father."

"I recall the look of anger on his face even as they were being married. It's the sort of behaviour one expects from Viking marauders, but not . . ." Aidan left the comment unfinished and shook his head. "To kick the dear child when it was impossible to be her fault – that would be unforgiveable."

"Nevertheless, I suspect it's the truth."

"But why would he abandon her in a stream? That makes no sense. It is more likely to be the actions of attackers."

"Her neck and chest are reddened. It looks as though hot soup

165

was thrown over her. I think she may have dragged herself into the stream to cool the burning."

Aidan held his head in his hands. "Dear Lord in heaven; save her."

"Because of the injuries to her ribs, once she was in the water I doubt she had the strength to pull herself out. She was probably there overnight and would have remained so had I not found her. It was Kizzy who directed me to her."

"Her little mare? Yes, the horse loves her indeed. But beating your wife is one thing. Leaving her to die is quite another. Surely Edmund wouldn't leave her there on purpose?"

Eirik's lips twitched. "I believe him capable, but, I suppose if he had turned his back on her the night before, he might not have known she was in the stream. If he had an assignation in the morning with some of his fellow conspirators and couldn't find either Esme or Kizzy, he might have assumed she'd found her own way home."

"That does seem to be the most likely explanation," said Aidan, wiping his brow with the sleeve of his habit. "In that case, when he finally reaches home and finds she's not there, I suspect he'll come here looking for her. And he'll not come alone."

"If he does, I'll kill him." Eirik clenched his fist.

"Not a good idea," said Aidan, "and not an easy thing to do."

Eirik frowned. "Surely Esme wouldn't return with him if he *has* beaten her?"

Aidan sighed. "Eirik, I have never been able to get to the bottom of a woman's mind, and there is not enough time left for me on God's earth to start doing so now. It's a question I cannot answer. I know that Esme's motivation in all things is to care for her brother, and she will do nothing to jeopardise his future. She has taken the place of both his mother and father."

"In that case, I shall have to ask, Father, that you pray not just for her, but for me also, because I shall struggle to live without her. I feel an affinity with her heart and soul that I never thought possible with any other human being. It's as though I am her and she is me. Does that sound foolish?"

Aidan smiled. "No, Eirik, it sounds as though you are very much in love with her. Does she know?"

"I have tried my best to hide it from her. She still sees me as the enemy."

"Then I'd suggest you keep your emotions to yourself until we find out about Edmund. If she does reciprocate your feelings, it will do nothing more than cause her misery to know what she has lost, especially because she's now tied to Edmund. On the other hand, if she does *not* share your feelings, then nothing can be gained by telling her."

"She wouldn't have me if she did know. She thinks I'm a heathen," Eirik moaned.

"Then continue to let her think so. You must never tell her that you came to me to be baptised in the name of Christ. That information would overwhelm her. Promise me you'll keep it to yourself – at least for the moment."

"I promise, Father," said Eirik solemnly.

"And come and get me if . . . if she gets worse."

36

Eirik thought with shame how hard he had worked Esme, demanding that she be in charge of so many duties when she hardly had time to recover from the trauma of her attack by Olaf's men. He had not understood the struggle her mind endured to come to terms with it. She was right when she told him he had no idea what it was like to be a woman in a man's world. But he was learning, and learning fast.

Eirik went to find Kizzy. She nuzzled him, and he de-tangled her mane with his fingers, recalling doing the same for Esme after she'd washed in the water butt. He remembered, too, the admiration he'd felt for her at that moment.

"You know, don't you?" Eirik said to Kizzy. "You know that I love her as much as you do." The horse snorted and shook her head.

"Do you not approve either?" Kizzy turned and pushed against his shoulder.

"Not saying, eh? Well . . . I don't blame you." Kizzy placed her soft muzzle against his nose.

"You wouldn't be trying to kiss me now, would you?" Eirik laughed. Kizzy shook her head and repeated the action.

"Perhaps you think I should kiss Esme?" The horse snorted again, and pawed the ground. She walked with Eirik to the enclosure at the back of the church. He shut the gate and turned to leave. When he cast a backwards glance, she was still watching him.

Eirik returned to Astrid's cottage. "How is she?" he asked.

"Not well. Her breath is shallow. Her heartbeat is irregular."

Eirik looked towards the bed, made snug by its feather mattress and pillows that supported Esme's back and shoulders. Astrid had untied the ribbons on the nightdress which was now drenched in sweat.

"Does Rowena know?" he asked.

"Not yet. I've had no chance to tell her. She'll be in the kitchen."

"Go and tell her. Stay and give her a hand if you wish. Esme will be safe with me."

Astrid picked up her cloak. "There's water in a bowl next to the bed and lavender oil to cool her skin."

Eirik looked. "I see it."

He sat on a wooden chair next to Esme and soaked a small flannel with which to wipe her bloodless cheeks and lips. Feeling the faintness of her heartbeat, his face contorted in grief. "Esme, my love," he whispered, "don't leave me. You own the other half of me – the loving half. If you die, I shall be an empty shell doing the bidding of the dark evil controlling my heart."

He took hold of her hand, pressing it against his lips as though he could breathe life into those delicate white fingers. "Dearest Esme, I cannot bear the thought of you not being in this world. You discovered my feet of clay. Take what strength I have, drain it like sap from a tree."

He hung his head. He knew no Christian prayers even though he'd turned away from his old gods. "Thor, Odin, Freya," he murmured. "Are you jealous of my new allegiance? Is this to be my punishment? Have I not killed and maimed enough men to satisfy your appetites?" He punched the air with his fist. "I want to be released from my vow. I crave peace. Don't wreak your vengeance on this young woman. She has done nothing. What is she to you?"

Exhaustion overcame him and briefly he slept, Esme's hand still clasped against his face. When he awoke it was dark. The room was cool since August was near its end. He stood and stoked the fire. Its glow bathed the walls, but the warm light brought him no comfort.

With Astrid's permission, he sat all night by Esme's side. The day after, Esme became delirious, groaning and rolling her head from side to side. She shouted the name of Edmund, re-living her experience in a nightmare. She fought off attackers and cried out against demons. Eirik lived each moment with her. He comforted, entreated, and, in the less frantic moments, even played the panpipes. They seemed to soothe her and she would sleep like a babe while the sweet notes filled her ears.

"He's like a man possessed," Astrid remarked to Rowena one morning, as they pulled the bread from the ovens. "He really loves her. What it must be like to have a man such as him love you so passionately."

"And much good will it do him," said Rowena, pulling a face. "How long will it be before Edmund turns up? He won't let her go that easily."

"I wonder he's not turned up already," said Astrid. "I really cannot understand it, unless he no longer cares about Esme. Perhaps once they were married he became conscious of what a mistake he'd made."

"That's no help to Esme though, is it? In fact, it makes matters worse. She's in limbo – not loved by her husband but unable to take another. What a terrible situation. All I know is that he scares the life out of me."

Astrid grimaced. "I know what you mean." She inclined her head towards the pantry. "Incidentally, I've heard nothing about you-know-who, have you?"

"Not a word. It's a good thing we took him a long way into the tunnel. He must smell bad by now."

Each day Eirik read to Esme words from the scriptures that Aidan had copied for him. It was all he had, but somehow he felt it would help Esme recover if she could hear a voice. He had no evidence for this belief but did it anyway. He read a passage on love from a letter of St Paul; recited parables, stories, and poetry from the Psalms. Each word dripped into his mind, lodging its wisdom. He was amazed to find that he understood – not just the actual words, but the meaning behind them. They spoke only of kindness, joy, peace, patience and faithfulness. It was all so different from the culture in which he had previously thrived. When he played the panpipes he chose a selection of tunes which conjured up different colours, including the song for which she had composed the simple lyrics. Once he thought he detected a sign of recognition in Esme's face. But it disappeared as quickly as it came.

On the fourth day Esme's fever was at a pitch. Eirik constantly wiped her forehead and neck, trying to ease her discomfort. It was on the fifth day that he saw a change. A fresh pink haze had crept into her face. The fever had broken and her heartbeat was stronger. He smiled. "Thank you, God. Ask of me what you will and I shall oblige you." He stood and kissed Esme's forehead and took her hand in his, pressing her palm to his lips. It was time to leave. He had made a promise to Father Aidan not to let her know of his feelings. It was too late for such a revelation. She was another man's wife. Therefore it was prudent to leave her bedside before she became aware of his presence.

"Esme will recover," he said to Astrid as she walked through the door. "I must leave now."

"You've looked after her well. If you don't mind my saying so, you look exhausted. I think you need rest yourself."

"I have plenty of strength left, thank you, Astrid. I leave Esme now in your capable hands."

Astrid reached out and patted his arm. "God bless you, sir," she said.

Eirik rode back to the camp with a heavy heart.

Fenrir watched him walk to the fire, warm his hands and help himself to some food. "You've been nursing that young'un for several days," he said. "Is she better?"

"I'm hopeful she'll make a full recovery."

"You look tired, lord. You must love her a great deal."

"More than my own life, I can safely say, my old friend."

"What are you going to do about it?"

"Nothing. What can I do? She's a married woman."

"That never stopped us Vikings from taking what we wanted."

"It's not like that, Fenrir. I don't want to take her. She has to come willingly. At the moment she's *willingly* married to someone else."

"What is it with you?" said Fenrir. "When you meet a person you love you shouldn't let her slip through your fingers."

"Enough, Fenrir. Don't you think I'm aware of it?"

"Tell her then. If she feels the same, take her off to Denmark. No one will object there."

"She's a God-fearing, Christian woman and would never agree."

"Then all Christian folk are fools. Freya would tell you to do it. Our goddess of love would say there's nothing more important in life than love . . . and sex – mustn't forget about that."

Eirik shook his shoulders irritably. "I don't want to hear another word. Tell me, have you seen Sweyn?"

"He's camped across the water. Thorkel and Olaf are with him."

"Where are the men?"

"Olaf's lot are still in the village with some of Sweyn's. Thorkel's followers seem to be more like us though. Keep themselves to themselves."

"I'm going to try and get some sleep," said Eirik. "Then perhaps later I'll go across and see them. There's something we need to discuss."

"Are you not joining in the raid on Southampton?"

Eirik cast a glance at Fenrir and smiled. "Is there nothing that escapes your notice?"

Fenrir shrugged. "No. I can see the unhappiness in your eyes. Something has happened. I know change is coming. I just want to say this, lord. Whatever decision you make I shall follow you, come what may. And there's many others feel the same."

The two men looked at one another. Eirik placed his hand on Fenrir's shoulder and gripped it. "Thank you."

Fenrir wiped the back of his neck. "Felt some rain. There's hail in it. We might be in for a storm later."

"In that case, I'll sleep in the tent. Wake me in an hour or so."

37
London 1979

After visiting Matilda, Emma drives on to Norwich. During the weekend in Norwich, Emma tells her mother about the visits to Maldon with Bjorn Erikson; meeting his daughter, Greta; and the odd conversation with Matilda in Ipswich. Sonia is intrigued and delighted when she hears that Mr Erikson might be interested in buying her property. "Please invite him over, and he can bring his daughter too if he wishes. I'd love to show him the plans. I'll cook them a Danish meal."

The usual Monday morning tutorials completed, she drives straight back to London and visits the National Archives Museum in Kew, which opened a couple of years previously. She intends to check any Charters, Writs and Wills from the tenth and eleventh century; historical references from the Domesday Book within the time frame, and relevant sagas. Did Earl Eirik really exist, or is he a figment of imagination from stories based on rumour rather than fact?

Her thoughts ramble as she drives, and on one occasion she isn't sure if she's jumped a red light. After that, she opens the window, takes some deep breaths and reminds herself that all her training has been based on verifiable facts. *Stop day-dreaming, woman. Go find the truth.*

She finds a space at the museum where she is known to the staff. Emma orders documents with any reference to Eirik, Earl of Northumbria (except his name may now be spelt Erik), and handles them with care. She is intrigued by the findings, and soon believes that Eirik *could* have become a leader of the Jomsvikings, even if only for a short time. Therefore he might have been present at the Battle of Maldon.

After an hour or two, she feels thirsty and goes in search of water. The cafe is crowded. The only remaining space is at the table of a young woman she noticed earlier, studying in the same section. "Do you mind if I sit here?" says Emma. The girl looks up and smiles, "Not at all."

"Did I just see you researching the tenth and eleventh century?"

The girl nods, "Yes, although I don't think my mind is quite concentrating this afternoon." She holds out her hand. "I'm Kate."

"Emma."

"What or who are you researching?" says Kate.

"Someone called Eirik who was the Earl of Northumbria."

Kate's eyes widen. "He's one of the names on my list to study."

"Oh? Have you found out much about him?"

"Yes, I've made a start. But most of his life is taken from the sagas such as *Heimskringla* and *Jomsvikinga,* and I'm told they can be rather imaginary."

"It's true they're both semi-legendary, so they can hardly be taken as the whole truth," says Emma. "But one or two surviving official charters and diplomas have verified that Eirik was appointed the Earl of Northumbria when King Cnut acceded to the English throne. He was Cnut's brother-in-law."

Kate is thoughtful. "I know Cnut was Sweyn Forkbeard's son. So did Eirik marry Sweyn's daughter, Cnut's sister?"

"Yes."

Kate grimaces. "Nice bit of nepotism. Do you know anything about his father – Haakon Sigurdsson? He's on my list too."

"Eirik's father was a Jarl of the northern part of Norway. Apparently,

175

he was well known for sexual assaults and Eirik's mother was a woman of lowly birth. The narrative says his father had no love for the boy and Haakon gave him to another chap to bring up."

"That's a hateful thing to do," says Kate.

Emma smiles, "Eirik must have thought so too, because when he was twelve, he murdered one of his father's friends."

Kate gasps, "Really? What happened after that?"

"Eirik fled south to Denmark where he was taken in by Harald Bluetooth, the father of Sweyn Forkbeard."

"So that's how Eirik and Sweyn became friends," says Kate. "They were probably around the same age. If Eirik married his daughter, he must have been years older than his wife." She examines her notes. "Harald Bluetooth is one of the names on my list. Was he the one who formed the Jomsvikings?"

"So they say. One of their leaders was called Thorkel the Tall, who became a deputy of Sweyn Forkbeard."

"Thorkel is also on my list," says Kate. "I discovered he became Earl of Norfolk."

"Yes, he was appointed an earl at around the same time as Eirik became Earl of Northumbria. They both replaced two of King Aethelred's most senior nobles."

Kate gathers her papers. "Thank you very much for this chat."

"Actually, it is I who should thank *you*," says Emma, wishing all her students were as assiduous. "It has helped me clarify my thoughts."

38
Maeldun 991

Father Aidan had successfully completed one of his translations. He stood and stretched, thinking it was time to move the corpse out of the tunnel while the evenings were still light. He followed the steps into the crypt, yanked the altar to one side, pulled up the trap-door and climbed down into the passage. With a lighted torch in one hand and a spade in the other, he stooped and shuffled for some time searching for Snorre. He found the sack on which he had lain, but there was no sign of the corpse. It was near the end that he saw what was left of the Viking. As he approached, wild dogs raced away into the forest, leaving the debris behind: pieces of wrenched limbs; a half-eaten torso and faceless head. "What a mess," he muttered, picking up the remnants and dropping them into the sack. He carried it the short distance to the trees to bury the remains, aware that he needed to act fast. He began to dig.

Seemingly from nowhere, two of Olaf's men appeared. "Hold. What do you think you're doing?"

The tent flap opened without ceremony and Fenrir burst through. "Lord Eirik, there's trouble at the church."

Eirik roused himself. "What's going on?"

"They've found bits of Snorre."

"Who?"

"Olaf's man who went missing."

Eirik remembered. How could he forget? "What do you mean they found *bits* of him?"

"Well there's a torso and part of an arm with a hand attached to it. There's a ring on one of the fingers. That's how they identified him. It's been attacked by rats or wild dogs. They found Father Aidan burying what was left of him."

"Father Aidan?"

Fenrir's voice rose in frustration. "By Thor's teeth, has tiredness addled your brain, lord? Someone must have murdered him. Olaf's men are blaming Father Aidan. They've bound him to a tree, intent on hanging him."

Eirik jumped up, grabbing his jerkin and sword. Outside, the bay stallion stood waiting.

"I fetched him for you, lord."

"Good man," said Eirik, hurling himself up. "Get word to Thorkel. He's Aidan's friend."

"The tide's still in, lord."

"We'll cope." Eirik dug his heels into the horse's belly and took off at a gallop. A fine drizzle clung to his hair, stinging his face. The animal did not baulk for a moment as they reached the causeway, plunging into the water at speed, lifting high his hooves, creating clouds of spray, continually dousing the rider. Reaching the other side, they raced along the river bank and skirted clumps of trees, bringing the church into view. Shouts of wrath, incited by taunts, grew louder. He reined in. A ragged shaft of white heat sliced the murky sky, highlighting the scene: the tree, horse, rope and noose fastened around Father Aidan's neck, hands tied behind his back.

A burst of thunder crashed like a portent of doom.

As Eirik closed in on the group, he saw Aidan stretching up against the biting cord. Olaf's men were hurling missiles at him: leg-bones of carcases; rocks; stones; timber. Hatred oozed through their jeers, seeped into the greyness, and billowed into an evil mist of revenge. A brutal shot pitched through the air, striking Aidan full in the face. Blood poured over his features. The horse jibbed. The noose tightened.

Eirik strained his ears. The Viking scorn was penetrated by chanting, giving thanks to God. Aidan was praising his deity. Several of the warriors seemed agitated by this worship of the white divinity in the face of death. Regardless of their derision, they still feared the puny Christ, unfamiliar with His power.

Then a stone caught the young gelding on its soft muzzle. It reared and bolted, leaving Aidan hanging, his legs jerking. Eirik felt the heat of fury in his throat. He cantered forward and, raising his sword, with one fluid movement he sliced the rope. Aidan's body slumped to the ground and lay in an awkward heap. Eirik slid from the back of the bay horse and stooped to release the noose and untie Aidan's hands. Onlookers shook their fists at this ending of their sport. Deadly blades were drawn simultaneously from their scabbards. Several of the men were so drunk that the weight of heavy iron above their heads sent them careering over backwards, but eight of them, whose wits were sharper, brandished their weapons.

Eirik heard a snarling roar. "You arrogant pig – it's time we taught you a lesson."

One man leapt towards him, taking a swipe at his head. Eirik straightened and jumped back to avoid the swing, then slashed the edge of his sword into the arm of his attacker. Four more approached and engaged him on all sides. He lunged to the right. A man lost his balance and staggered. Without mercy Eirik struck him down. Another hesitated for a fatal moment, and uttered a choked cry as blood erupted from his chest. Like a well-rehearsed dance, Eirik ducked and weaved, rolling onto his shoulder, nimbly landing upright to avoid the vicious and murderous onslaught.

He used his feet as weapons, kicking one man in the groin and another in the throat. The former instinctively bent double: it cost him his life. The latter struggled for air, too late to stay the gash in his neck. Eirik's anger was such that his speed and strength outmatched any man set against him. The groans and screams of the injured and dying rent the air, masked by the spectacle of wrath overhead as the storm roared across the sky with a madness that matched Eirik's own.

The few remaining stragglers, stunned, ran into the church. Eirik threw down his sword and knelt beside Aidan, using the priest's own scapular to wipe the blood-stained face. Then, raising him up beneath the shoulders, he carried him to the well, drawing water to wash his head and revive him.

Aidan stirred. "Thank you," he whispered, his eyes too swollen to open. "The church, is it safe?"

Eirik turned to look. A pungent smell reeked through the dampness. He stood, his jaw clenched as comprehension dawned. Orange flames licked at the windows. Dried reeds which were spread around the outside of the wooden Saxon church had been set alight. Soon the greedy all-consuming inferno would scale the walls, seeking the arches of the roof. A torch, tossed into the thatch, had already taken hold.

A group of Olaf's men watched and cheered. "Your puny Christ has lost this fight," one of them shouted at Aidan. "Your prayers and singing were for nothing."

But Father Aidan did not let up, finding renewed energy in adversity. "Oh Lord God, let not the church be destroyed. Protect Your house," he cried in a loud voice. The jeers grew more raucous as the blaze gripped its prey.

And then a miracle happened. A strident boom that bruised the ears followed a zigzag of startling, brilliant intensity; with it came pitiless rainfall. Torrents lashed the earth. Water seeped into the roofing and poured through the open shutters, spitting and steaming. For some time a battle raged between the elements. The fire seethed through smoky nostrils, sensing defeat, yet unwilling to surrender until the final sparks were extinguished.

Eirik looked to the skies and allowed the welcome deluge to run down his forehead into his eyes. "Maybe there is a God after all," he said.

"I told you so," said Aidan. He squinted through swollen lids; his lips attempted a smile. Then he gave a start. "Look out."

From the shadows came Snorre's friend, his sword pointed directly at Eirik. "So, you killed him. Thought you'd got away with it. The time has come for you to die." He raised the weapon in both hands.

Eirik pitched himself protectively across Aidan. Then, with the heel of his foot, he struck the man in his gut, temporarily winding him. In response, his opponent lowered his elbows, but kept his sword in position. Eirik kicked out again, clipping the man's wrists. Incensed, the warrior made to strike. But, quite suddenly, he stopped. His mouth gaped. A grunt passed his lips. His body crumpled, sinking slowly onto the soft mud. The tip of his sword dropped from his hands, and wobbled as it stuck in the soil.

Blood bubbled from the man's gullet though he was still alive. "Thor will take revenge on you," he murmured. "You'll never reach Valhalla." His eyes glazed and remained open as he died with a knife firmly wedged in his back. Eirik removed the weapon, amazed to see it was the type of knife used in a kitchen. He shoved it in his belt. As the squall subsided, he scanned the small number of villagers who had come to observe from a distance. *Who could have thrown the weapon with such accuracy?* Then he spotted three women, two crouching beside a third who was stretched out on the ground. Their outlines were unmistakable.

Aidan saw them too. "You go," he said. "I can manage. Find out what's happened."

"Thorkel is on his way," said Eirik. "I'll be back as soon as I can." He left Aidan propped against the wall of the well and hurried across to the women.

Astrid and Rowena were holding Esme. "She's fainted," said Astrid.

Eirik lifted Esme into his arms. "Let's get her home."

Back at Astrid's house, he stoked the fire while Astrid and Rowena ministered to Esme. Eventually they emerged from behind the screen and announced that her breathing had steadied.

Eirik stood with hands on hips. He lowered his voice. "Good. Now would you mind telling me what's going on?"

Rowena wrung her hands. "Esme must have overheard us talking and followed us. We thought she was asleep."

"Why did you come at all?"

Rowena started to cry. "We had to help Father Aidan. We couldn't let him die for something that was our doing."

"Your doing?" Eirik stared at her. "How can this mayhem be your doing?"

"We killed Snorre," said Rowena.

"Not strictly true," said Astrid. "The truth is, *I* killed him. Not intentionally, you understand. I just wanted to stop him so I hit him over the head with a kitchen pan."

Eirik hesitated while this image sank into his mind. "What did he do to deserve that? Let me guess. He attacked one of you, and you were simply defending yourselves."

"Yes, me," said Rowena. Tears coursed down her cheeks. "He was about to rape me."

Eirik drew in a deep breath. "So how did Aidan get involved?"

Rowena looked at Astrid as if asking how much she should tell. Astrid smiled encouragement and Rowena continued. "Esme wanted to help us. She showed us where to hide the body. We put it in the tunnel leading from the crypt to the woods. Aidan offered to bury it when he got the chance."

"I see," said Eirik. "There wasn't much of it left. Wild dogs found it."

"In that case it's a pity Father Aidan didn't leave the rest of it to the dogs," said Astrid. "Then he wouldn't have been caught."

Rowena blew her nose. "Will Father Aidan be alright?"

"I expect so. He's a tough old raven and been through worse than that."

Rowena's mouth dropped open, not understanding what Eirik meant, but she enquired no further.

Eirik removed the knife from his belt. "So which of you threw this?"

Astrid jerked her head. "Not us. It was Esme. But the effort has exhausted her."

Eirik forced out air through tight lips. "Esme? How did she ever have the strength? She must have been in terrible pain. And the knife?"

Astrid turned to look at the bench where she prepared food. "Over there. One is missing."

Eirik followed her gaze and handed over the weapon. "Wash it thoroughly. Olaf has no idea who killed his man. He'll never assume it was a woman."

"I wonder where on earth she learned to throw a knife with such accuracy," said Rowena.

Eirik shrugged. "All I know is she saved my life and that of Father Aidan."

Esme groaned in her sleep and Astrid frowned. "I think both of you should leave now. She needs peace and quiet."

"Quite right," said Eirik. "I must go back to see to Father Aidan."

"And I must get back to the children," said Rowena. "Send someone to fetch me, Astrid, if you need help."

39

When Eirik returned, Father Aidan had gone. Olaf and Thorkel stood observing the scattered bodies while their followers attended to the bloodied wounded. "Where's the priest?"

"Some of your men took him inside. Fenrir is looking after him," said Thorkel.

"You responsible for this mess, Eirik?" demanded Olaf, waving his hand expansively.

"They attacked me."

Olaf grunted. "They should have known better."

"These men beat Father Aidan then tried to hang him," said Eirik.

Olaf shrugged. "They say he was responsible for killing Snorre."

"He was burying his remains. That's quite different from killing him. For all you know, Snorre could have even been exploring the tunnel himself and been hit by a falling beam. It's old and unsafe. Your men were their own judges and executioners without hearing any defence."

"Well, Aidan has questions to answer," said Olaf.

"No, he doesn't," said Thorkel, with a vehemence that surprised Eirik. "Aidan's a good friend of mine. He used to be one of us. Sorry, Olaf, but your louts were completely out of line. Why did they attempt to burn down the church? And risk the wrath of Aidan's Christ."

"It seems the storm was fortuitous."

Thorkel was insistent. "Or the will of their God."

Olaf looked chastened but was determined not to give in just yet. "Someone in the crowd killed Snorre's colleague. Who was it?"

Eirik shrugged. "Why are you asking me? I was about to be skewered and was too preoccupied to see who killed him. But whoever it was, they saved not only my life but Father Aidan's too, and you can't blame them for being loyal. Any one of your men would have done the same for you."

"I agree," said Thorkel. "Besides, Snorre and his friend were known bullies. They had enemies even within your own band of men. Perhaps one of them took the opportunity to murder him. I doubt anyone in the village would have such skills." The edges of his mouth twitched slightly; his glance at Eirik was one of complicity.

Olaf glared at both of them with a petulant look. "Where's the weapon?"

Thorkel sighed. "Isn't it obvious? The man who did it must have taken it with him."

Next morning Eirik went to find Esme. She was sitting beside the fire, alone, her embroidery on her knee. There was no sign of Astrid.

"How are you?" he said.

She turned her ashen face to his. "Much better. Astrid insists I rest today so I'm working on my design."

Eirik leaned over her. "May I see?"

She held it up.

"There's one of our boats and the church. I think that's you, and if I'm not mistaken that's me on a horse," Eirik observed.

"Correct," said Esme. "You're riding out to find me."

"And there's Byrhtnoth."

Esme nodded. "It started out as a tribute to the dead."

"And now it's a tribute to the living."

"I suppose it is – for those of us who've survived."

"How will it end, I wonder?"

"Either with the truth or however I wish it to be," said Esme. "Or maybe it will remain unfinished."

Eirik stood looking at her for several moments. "I must thank you, Esme. You saved my life."

"I got him, didn't I?"

"You certainly did. And you saved not only my life but also Father Aidan's."

"I'm glad."

"Where did you learn to throw a knife?"

"I once took Brand to a village fair. He loved the knife-throwers. After that, we practised together all the time."

"I expect you always won," said Eirik.

"There was luck in my aim."

"Very lucky – for me and Aidan." He grinned. "You all deserve the honours of great warriors and I shall be the first to bestow them upon you, when you are well."

Esme smiled. There was a pause before Eirik asked what he really wanted to know. "Esme, tell me what happened to you. Were you robbed?"

She shook her head.

"Did Edmund do this to you?"

Tears filled her eyes and trickled down her cheeks. "He was convinced I was with child. It ate up his reason."

"Did he . . . did he touch you?"

"You mean rape me? No. He could hardly bring himself to come near me."

Eirik felt a wave of relief, but acknowledged to himself it was unreasonable. "What's become of him?"

"What do you mean?"

"He'd gone when I found you."

"He must be at Saxstow Hall."

"There were several pairs of hoof prints. Do you remember seeing anyone arrive?"

"No. All I could think about was trying to relieve my pain in the water. Then I couldn't lift myself out. Perhaps Edmund didn't see me and thought I'd gone home."

"If that were the case he'd know by now. Would he not have come looking for you?"

She shrugged. "I'm not sure. What husband would kick his newly wedded wife in the way he did if he were not seriously displeased with her."

"Your generosity of nature does you credit, but I fear I cannot share it. The man is a rogue and deserves to be punished. You owe him nothing. He promised to care for you."

Esme frowned. "Eirik, Brand is staying with Sweyn's sister, Gunhilde."

"Yes. I remember. You told me."

"I'm worried. If Edmund is discontented with me, he may take out his frustration on my brother. I need to find him."

"You're in no fit state to be going anywhere. Not yet. Woman, you try my patience."

The merest mischievous glint flickered in her eyes. "Good."

Eirik sighed. There was a lump in his throat. Never had he anticipated his capacity for the all-encompassing passion that filled him at this moment.

After leaving Esme, Eirik went to find Father Aidan. The old monk was seated with head bowed. Eirik waited in silence until the morning prayers were completed. When eventually Aidan lifted his face, it was barely recognisable: swollen, black, distorted. An ugly bruise encircled his neck. One eye was completely constricted; the other a mere squint. He was barely able to move his lips. The words caught in his throat, restricted by the narrow flow of air from his lungs. "Eirik," he murmured in acknowledgement.

The younger man strode towards the broken figure and placed a hand on his shoulder. "I should have been there sooner."

"They were . . . angry," said Aidan.

"They had no right to treat you thus. We have principles, even in our heathen land, and rarely judge a man without evidence."

Aidan gripped Eirik's arm. "I knew."

"But you didn't kill him," said Eirik, in a soft voice.

There was a movement behind him as someone entered and closed the door. Eirik turned to see Astrid holding a bowl of steaming water wrapped in a cloth. "No, I did," she said.

Aidan held up a palm and waved it from side to side, attempting to silence her.

"It will not do, Father," said Astrid. "I must own up and exonerate you."

Eirik stepped towards her and took the bowl. "You obviously weren't aware of your own strength, Astrid."

"I didn't mean to kill him, just knock him out."

Eirik began to laugh. "That was the best day's work you women have ever done."

"Please, lord, don't joke. It's serious. I don't know whether God will forgive us."

Eirik looked down at her. "You're not a murderer and neither is Rowena. You acted in self-defence, protecting your friend. Think of the consequences if you'd failed to stop him. But tell me, how did the body get into the tunnel?"

"The three of us dragged him down there and left him to rot. It had nothing to do with Father Aidan."

"I knew," repeated Aidan, "promised to bury—"

"Never mind that," said Eirik, carrying the water to the priest's side, inhaling its astringent aroma. "Olaf has other things on his mind now."

Astrid bent down, squeezed out the cloth soaking in the basin and gently dabbed Aidan's inflamed wounds. "Nevertheless, Father, you didn't deserve this."

"Nor you, Astrid," he whispered.

Eirik pursed his lips. "No, but Snorre did. I nearly strangled him myself when I used a rope to yank him away from Esme. I'll take care of this, and I want both of you to put it behind you."

Astrid raised her head. "What about Rowena and Esme?"

"None of you must speak of it again," said Eirik.

After a pause, Astrid conceded. "What do you plan to do?"

Eirik hesitated before answering. "It's time I put an end to my old way of life. Time to break away from Olaf."

"Be careful," said Aidan. "Olaf is not a man who takes well to being crossed."

40

Olaf and his men had retreated to the encampment close by their ships. He had summoned a meeting mid-morning to include himself, Eirik, Sweyn and Thorkel. Eirik was the last to arrive. The flaps of the spacious tent were tied back. The guards glared at him as he entered but allowed him to pass.

Olaf wore a bear skin over his shoulder to emphasise his warrior status. The four men sat round a trestle. Olaf stood as Eirik walked in. "So you deigned to come. Several of my men are dead thanks to you. I thought we were on the same side."

Eirik took the remaining seat and, picking up a pitcher of water, filled the mug in front of him. "I have served you faithfully, and you Sweyn," he said, inclining his head towards the King of Denmark, "but I can no longer approve of your aims. This is the end of our alliance, and I must insist on a parting of the ways."

"Because of some insignificant old monk?" Olaf's voice roared.

Eirik looked at him with a hard gaze. "He is not insignificant to me. The methods used by your oafs were insupportable."

"He murdered my faithful follower, Snorre."

"He did no such thing. If anyone is to blame for Snorre's death, it is I. A week ago I found him interfering with one of my women, yet again. I hit him and he fell to the ground. He must have died later, and wild dogs carried him to their lair in the tunnel."

Olaf slumped back in his chair. "I accept what you're saying. But an incident such as this is as nothing compared to a friendship that's been forged over many years. Why destroy that?"

Sweyn nodded vigorously. "I agree. It doesn't have to end."

"I am beyond negotiation," said Eirik. "My mind is made up."

Unexpectedly, Thorkel banged his fist on the table. "I'm with Eirik," he said. Jaws dropped and the assembled company turned to stare at him.

"What can this possibly have to do with you?" said Olaf.

"Father Aidan is a close friend, a Viking from old. He's brought respect to our culture. Times have changed. Many of us have settled here permanently and are raising children. The old brutish ways are outmoded."

Sweyn gave a hollow laugh, yet his voice faltered. "So, you both intend to betray us. What will you do now, Eirik?"

"I'm not betraying you, sire. I'm being honest with you. For my part, I shall seek out your sister, Gunhilde. She's looking after the ward of Lord Edmund, a boy called Brand. His safety may be compromised."

Sweyn snorted. "Surely you cannot believe my sister would harm him?"

"No. But if Lord Edmund's treachery has been discovered, then the boy may be at risk. Furthermore, your own sister, lord, may need protection, since her husband, Pallig, is also a close adviser to Aethelred. Being Danish, his support for your claim to the throne may mirror Edmund's."

Sweyn frowned, coolly calculating the probabilities of Eirik's idea. "By Thor's thunder, you're right. The consequences could be dire. Aethelred would show no mercy to those he believed to be traitors, or their offspring. Why don't you and Thorkel take some men and find out what's happened."

"I'm willing to go," said Thorkel.

"Then do it," said the king. "Seek out my sister. If she's been harmed ... there'll be war." He sighed then upturned his palms in a gesture of conciliation. "Let us presume for the time being that this venture is but another in our partnership. Emotions are running high after last night. Perhaps a few days' respite will clarify all our thoughts."

"My self-respect forbids me to be anything but frank, lord," said Eirik. "I shall not be returning to your service or Olaf's, though I cannot speak for my men."

"You always were a stubborn mule," said Olaf, "a man after my own heart. Very well, so be it – for the time being. But there is one more task you could both carry out for me. Lord Edmund indicated that Aethelred – in his weakness – is offering to pay a substantial amount of silver for us to stop attacking his shipping. I have written to the king to say I accept his terms, and that I'll be sending representatives to finalise the treaty. Once you've confirmed that Sweyn's sister is safe, I'd be grateful if you'd ride to Lunden. The king will be expecting you."

Thorkel glanced at Eirik who gave a slight nod. "Yes," said Thorkel, "we agree to see the king on your behalf."

The next day Astrid was chopping logs as Eirik approached. "Here, let me help you with that," he said, claiming the axe.

"It's kind of you, but I've been doing this for many years and will continue to do so long after you have left these shores."

"I'm not so sure I shall leave," said Eirik. "I think your weather has some advantages over the cold winds of Denmark."

He took hold of a log and placed it on the sawn-off tree trunk in front of him. "The incident with Olaf's warrior has been dealt with. You may forgive yourself and forget."

Astrid's eyes darted to his face. "What do you mean?"

"I mean the matter is now closed."

Astrid massaged the back of her neck. "I'm grateful."

Eirik picked up an armful of logs. "Is Esme inside?"

"She is, and feeling stronger. She's preparing our meal. Why don't you take those in? I have eggs to collect."

Esme was chopping carrots when Eirik stood on the threshold. "I've brought more wood for the fire," he said, placing the logs in a neat pile. He stood to face her. "You're looking much better."

"Thank you. I feel it."

Eirik shuffled his feet. "I've come to tell you I'm going away."

Esme stopped cutting but continued to look down at the knife. "I knew you'd all go away someday soon." Her lips parted as she glanced at him. "Will you return to your lands in Denmark?"

"Perhaps, but not before I've completed something I must do. I shall make sure Gunhilde and your brother, Brand, are both safe."

Esme stiffened. "My brother is not your responsibility."

"They've both become my duty."

"I don't understand," said Esme.

Eirik stared at the thin flames licking around the logs, slowly heating a pan full of water. "By following Sweyn's orders, I became complicit in the plan to dethrone your king. Sweyn is now concerned about his sister." He grasped her hand. It felt cold but she made no move to pull it away. He longed to kiss her. Instead he said, "Can you forgive me for putting you in danger?"

"Do you need my forgiveness?"

"More than anything in this world."

"Then you have it, but on one condition only."

"Name it," said Eirik.

"That you take me with you when you leave."

41
London 1979

That evening Emma fetches fish and chips from the local shops in Notting Hill, and, clearing the clutter from the old kitchen table, she unlocks the clips of her portable typewriter and begins recording as much detail as possible. A couple of hours later she becomes aware of the telephone ringing down the hallway. "Hello," she says, slightly out of breath.

"I haven't disturbed you, have I?" says the familiar Danish lilt.

"Bjorn? No, not at all. What a nice surprise."

There's a pause at the end of the line. "Do you mean it? Is it a nice surprise?"

Emma is taken aback – a sensation of warmth passes over her and she feels vaguely faint. "Yes. Yes, of course."

"That's good, because I've missed our conversations – very much."

Emma is lost for words, and Bjorn speaks again, perhaps sensing her embarrassment. "Have you seen Matilda?"

"Yes. Apparently she knew Reginald Reed."

"The previous owner of your mother's newly acquired property?"

"Yes. He wrote to our firm of genealogists and asked them to find a next-of-kin. But he died before the job was completed. I also found out about Eirik. He was the son of Haakon Sigurdsson." She pauses, allowing Bjorn to absorb the information before announcing her denouement. "And he became Earl of Northumbria, courtesy of King Cnut."

"Cnut – the son of Sweyn Forkbeard."

"Yes, Eirik married Forkbeard's daughter, Gytha, around AD 997.

They had one son, but Gytha died soon after so they weren't married long."

"And is Eirik connected to the Jomsvikings?"

"Possibly. Eirik and his father didn't get on, to say the least, but he was certainly close to Harald Bluetooth, who is credited with establishing the Jomsvikings. There was a battle between Haakon Sigurdsson and Harald Bluetooth in AD 986. Norway against Denmark."

"The Battle of Hjorungavagr," says Bjorn. "Bernard Johnson mentioned that in his talk."

Emma was thoughtful. "That's right, he did. Now this is the interesting bit. Bluetooth allegedly enlisted the Jomsvikings to help him. A warrior called Eirik took part in the battle. One saga supposes he fought on the side of his father, Haakon Sigurdsson – but that means they would have had to be reconciled by then."

"It seems more likely Eirik would have fought for Harald, supporting the Danes against his father," says Bjorn. "Bernard seemed to think that a young Eirik became leader afterwards because of his bravery."

"I met a student who's studying Earl Eirik's life. She made the point that the account is legendary only and may be pure fantasy."

"Perhaps," says Bjorn. "Nevertheless, the battle did take place, so like all sagas it will be a combination of fact and fiction. And the fact is this; in order to be awarded a position as high as an Earl of England our man must have been a faithful supporter of Cnut and Forkbeard."

"That's what I thought. Although when his father was murdered Eirik took over his lands in the north of Norway, and ruled them with his half-brother."

"Maybe by that time they *were* reconciled or maybe Eirik felt compelled to help his brother. But there's just one question," says Bjorn.

"What's that?"

"If he is married to Gytha for only a few years and has only one son, how did he also have a son called Edgar, and a grandson called Magnus – the names on my whetstone?"

Emma is silent for several moments. "He must have married someone else."

"Before or after?"

"I don't know. There's one other thing that Matilda told me. Reginald said there are things hidden in his house that might give us answers. One of them is Esme's story, but there's another script by a woman called Phoebe. We should make a search."

"I'll be on a late flight Thursday night."

"I had a word with my mother about you being interested in her house and land. She's delighted, and wants to meet you. She's invited you over."

Bjorn sighs. "I promised to spend the weekend with Greta as I've been away."

"Mother says you can bring her too."

"That's extremely generous of her. I accept, of course. Will you give me her number so I can speak to her personally first, when I'm back."

"A good idea, she'll probably practise her Danish."

Bjorn laughs. "Do you think she'll mind if we search her new house?"

"To be honest, I don't think she'll mind at all. She seemed singularly unimpressed with the whole place."

Bjorn is pleased. "Wonderful. If all is well, I'll see you in Norwich on Saturday morning at around 10 a.m."

"Excellent. See you then, I hope. Goodbye. Sleep well."

Emma hangs up, then picks up the receiver again and dials her mother's number. "Hi, Mum. Hope I didn't get you out of bed."

Her mother snorts. "I'm not so doddery that I have to go to bed this early."

Emma laughs. "That's good because I've something to ask you. Bjorn would like to come over with his daughter on Saturday. With your permission, we would like to search your house. It's possible we may find something that will help him discover more about his ancestors. He's going to telephone you when he's back in London."

"Of course he can come. He can stay the night if he likes. The spare room is already made up. It has twin beds."

"Mum, would *you* mind inviting him when he calls you? I'm sure he'll feel more comfortable if the invitation comes straight from the horse's mouth, so to speak."

"So I'm a horse now, am I? Okay. I suppose you're right. Best not for you to appear too forward."

Emma sighs. "*That* has nothing to do with it, Mum."

"Of course it hasn't," says Sonia with irony.

42
Maeldun 991

It was a further week or more before the select party headed off in search of Gunhilde's residence. Fenrir stayed loyal to Eirik, as did several of the men whose tastes had turned against the Viking mode of life. Some accepted Leif as their leader, albeit temporarily, happy that his leanings were for further exploration of the unknown world. Thorkel found a few of his men were similarly divided, and he enlisted a couple to go with him.

When they gathered outside the church, Esme was all set to go, dressed in leather trousers, laced boots, tunic and jerkin. Kizzy was saddled. Aidan came to see them off. The bruising on his face had turned from black to a pale shade of green, but his ebullient self still shone through his smile. "I never thanked you, Esme, for what you did. I shall be eternally grateful. Please take care."

"I will, Father."

Aidan looked doubtful. "Just be warned. *Feeling* better does not mean that you *are*. The body takes time to heal."

"I'm still reluctant to take you with us," said Eirik. "It could be a dangerous venture."

Esme's response was to sheath a knife at her waist. "Please help me mount my horse."

"She's a determined young woman," commented Thorkel. "If I were you, Eirik, I'd give in now."

Fenrir winked. "I agree. Prolonging the argument could mean we're here 'til noon."

Eirik conceded and lifted her onto Kizzy's back.

Rowena and Astrid also came to say their farewells with unrestrained tears. "Take care of her, lord," said Astrid.

"What makes you think it is *I* who will need looking after?" said Esme, teasing her. "Don't worry about me. I'm well supplied with arnica."

Astrid jutted out her chin. "Indeed. It's best for those bruises. And, don't forget, plenty of bark of the willow tree for relief of your pain."

Saxstow Hall was to the west of Maeldun. It was agreed they should go there first in case Brand had already returned home, although there'd been no word from Edmund to confirm it. They rode at a slow pace, conscious of Esme's injuries. Eirik glanced often at Esme, aware she would still be in pain and anxious for her to take frequent breaks. "I applaud your bravery, but can I not persuade you to rest a while?"

She shook her head. "I'm concerned for Brand above anything. I'll never forgive myself if something has happened to him. I hope by now Edmund's anger has subsided and he's gone to fetch him."

Eirik could think of no reason why Edmund would bother doing so, but refrained from voicing his opinion.

Sometime after midday the group sought a place to rest and take refreshments. Eirik helped Esme dismount. Her body had little vigour and discomfort was etched on her face, reflecting in her eyes. "I'll ride on a little to patrol the area," he said. "I'll not be long."

He'd travelled no more than half a mile when the sound of voices rose from over a ridge. He dismounted and, crouching low, wriggled silently to the top. A company of ten to fifteen men were spread about in a clearing: drinking, eating, snoozing or engaged in conversation. By the volume of their voices, he judged their cups and bellies had been filled already with their daily ration of ale. They wore black tunics with no markings to indicate their allegiance, but their weapons were those of highly skilled warriors. A hissing sound beyond some bushes forced Eirik to shrink back. The aroma of sweet urine filled the air, and steam emerged where the warm liquid hit the cool ground.

"I'll be glad when we're in Lunden again," Eirik heard one man say. "I want a soft bed."

"Yeah," said the other, "and a soft wench."

"I reckon I've earned enough to pay for two soft wenches," retorted the first man.

The other laughed. "What, both together?"

"Why not?"

"You'll do yourself no good with dreams like that. The abbot will have your manhood with a paring knife."

"You're not telling me he hasn't sowed some oats in his time. None of us is perfect."

The first man sighed. "We signed up for poverty, chastity and obedience. Didn't we?"

"Yes, but it's the chastity that worries me."

There was a throaty chuckle. "You'd better ask for extra rations of saltpetre. That'll dampen your ardour."

The voices faded as they made their way back to camp. Eirik observed them for a minute or two longer, trying to assess their provenance. Who would a band of warrior monks fight for in Lunden? There was only one possible answer: the king. They were moving south and if his small group continued west they would cross paths. He crawled down the ridge and rode back to report what he'd seen.

Thorkel listened intently then offered his opinion. "Men with no identifiable colours are bound to be up to no good. We should stay here longer and give them time to move on. We don't want to be seen."

"It's my belief they're working for the king," said Eirik. "They'll be on an assignment."

"Perhaps they're looking for spies," Fenrir suggested.

Eirik raised his eyebrows. "Precisely!" He turned to Esme. "How far are we from Saxstow Hall?"

"About another five miles," she said. "We should be there within the hour even at this pace."

When they reached the outskirts of the Hall Esme insisted that she should go in alone. "I have to find out if Brand is here with Edmund. The overseer of the estate is a man called Stephan. I trust him with my life. I'll send word to you should all be well."

"And if it isn't . . .?" said Eirik. "If Edmund dares to attack you I'll—"

Esme held up her hand. "I promise I'll send Stephan." Then she added, "Or come myself."

The main part of the building was made of stone but there was an extension built of split wooden trunks similar to the church. It was a fine-looking establishment and one Eirik could believe any woman would be content to be mistress of.

Fenrir echoed his own thoughts as he watched Esme ride away. "We'll be lucky to see her again, lord."

Esme rode past the familiar tree-lined pathway, fence work and outbuildings to the main door. Stephan greeted her as she reined Kizzy to a halt. He held a pitchfork in his hand and thrust it into the ground, grasping the bridle. She leaned forward to speak, wincing with pain. Stephen puckered his brows, stepping forward to offer assistance. "I'm pleased to see you, my lady. But, if I may say so, you look in need of rest."

Esme waved a dismissive hand. "I'm just a little tired from the ride. Is Brand here?"

"No. I presumed he was safe at the home of Gunhilde. I've heard nothing to the contrary."

Esme's shoulders slumped. She bit the inside of her cheek. "I was hoping he'd be here. Has Lord Edmund returned?"

Stephan shook his head. "He's been away nearly four weeks. Some men came asking your whereabouts. They didn't say who they were, but gave me the impression they were from Edmund, and he wanted you and your brother to join him in Lunden."

"When was this?"

"About ten days ago."

"What did you tell them?"

"Nothing, it was not my place to do so. I merely said we'd not heard from either you or Lord Edmund."

"You did well."

Stephan reached for the handle of the fork and pulled the prongs from the soil. "Are you intending to stay, my lady? I note the group of men escorting you are still waiting beside the lower copse."

Esme smiled. "You miss nothing, Stephan."

He jerked his head to one side. "It's my duty to watch over the land and the people who work upon it, and also . . ." He didn't finish the sentence but Esme knew what he meant. He had always looked after her and Brand. He'd been employed by her father, who regarded him as one of the most trustworthy and reliable people he knew. When Edmund took over her parents' forests, he had no quarrel with keeping Stephan in his service and left him totally in charge of overseeing both estates.

"I'm going to ride to Gunhilde's place and collect Brand. I'm worried about him. The men waiting will come with me."

"Who are they? Are they able bodyguards? If you're in any doubt, I'd prefer to travel with you myself. At least then I shall be certain you're safe."

Esme briefly touched his arm. "Thank you, Stephan. But I know these men. I shall be safe."

Stephan placed a hand to his forehead, squinting into the distance. "I don't like it," he said, his voice growling in his throat. "I don't know them."

"But *I* do," said Esme. "After we've fetched Brand we'll go to meet Lord Edmund."

Stephan searched her face. Then he bowed. "Take care, my lady."

"If those other men return, tell them you haven't seen me."

"I will, my lady. I haven't set eyes upon you. God speed."

43

Esme tightened her calves around Kizzy's belly and the little horse headed off to join the waiting men. Her stomach churned at the thought of Stephan's news and she felt more anxious than ever. She'd been certain that Edmund would have returned home after their dreadful argument. Why would he not do so?

"What have you learned?" asked Eirik, as she approached.

"Edmund has not been home, neither has Brand. But some men have been looking for us. Stephan says they came ten days ago."

"Does he know who they were?"

"No. But he thinks they were sent by Edmund asking that Brand and I join him in Lunden. We must go to visit Gunhilde," she said. "I need to know my brother is safe. I won't rest tonight until I find out."

"How much further?" said Thorkel.

"Less than an hour," said Esme. "She and her husband rent a lodge on our land in a forest where my father's boundary abuts Edmund's estate."

Eirik rubbed his hand across his face with the uncomfortable realisation of the extent of Edmund's control.

Thorkel looked at the sky. "We'll be there by late afternoon. But, my dear girl, should you not stay here for the night in your own bed? Have you not travelled far enough for one day?"

She shook her head. "You have no need to ask me that. Let's be away."

The lodge was a beautifully crafted timber building reached by a twisted bridle path through oak and beech trees. Although Esme found the setting peaceful during the day, by night she sensed an unsettling and sinister ghostliness that shrouded the woods.

Gunhilde was a handsome young woman with a fulsome figure. Standing on the door step, she beamed when she saw Esme, and ran forward to greet her. "What an unexpected pleasure," she said. "I'm delighted to see you again, Esme." She glanced up at Eirik and Thorkel. "And pleased to see you have protection. I've never understood why you take off on your own."

"These men are from Denmark. Thorkel is your brother's lieutenant."

"Yes. I'm acquainted with him. Is Sweyn here, too?"

"He's in Maeldun with his men."

Gunhilde lowered her eyes in understanding. "I see. I hope he's not come to cause further trouble. I have so many Danish friends who've settled here and married. I fear there may be reprisals from Aethelred if my brother creates unrest."

A young boy raced towards them brandishing a bow and arrow. Gunhilde smiled endearingly. "Please excuse my son's exuberance."

"Is Brand still with you?" asked Esme anxiously.

Gunhilde looked surprised. "No. Why?"

"He hasn't returned home and—"

Gunhilde interrupted her. "He's been taken to Lord Edmund."

Esme's voice quivered. "What do you mean by *been taken?*"

Gunhilde wiped her hands down her brown linen dress. "A band of the king's men came to collect him and took him to Lunden to join his guardian."

"The king's men?"

"Most certainly. I asked for proof of who they were and was shown a letter bearing the seal of Aethelred asking me to release Brand into their safekeeping. They were to accompany him to Thorn Island where the king is presently residing at the monastery."

"Did it specify why?"

"Edmund has a job for him, so I understand. I'm sure there's nothing to worry about."

"How were the king's men dressed?" asked Eirik.

"Dressed?" repeated Gunhilde. "Well I don't—"

"They were all in black," said the boy at her side.

"When did they come?" Eirik persisted.

"It was over a week ago. Yes, I remember hearing the horn of a hunt on the same day. I thought at first they were members of the chase needing water. They were most courteous. I had no reason to suspect they had any ulterior motive. Brand was happy and excited to go."

"What boy would not be eager to ride out with the king's men," said Fenrir. "If indeed that was who they were."

Gunhilde twitched her mouth and shook her head. "Who else could they be? Don't make me out to be a fool. I told you, I saw an official letter. Have I done something wrong?"

Esme hesitated, not wishing to blame her friend for letting Brand go. "You've done nothing wrong, Gunhilde." She ran her fingers through her hair. "I'm sorry, you've been most kind and I trust your judgement. It has been a shock to find Brand is not here, that's all. I'm pleased to hear he's in good hands."

Gunhilde looked relieved. She turned to Thorkel. "At least you'll be able to reassure Sweyn that his sister and nephew are both safe."

"The King of Denmark will be delighted to know that," said Thorkel graciously.

Esme felt sick with the sharp stabbing pain in her ribs. She needed to take some of Astrid's concoction. Her vision blurred. Fenrir jumped off his horse and stepped forward to help her down.

"Come in, all of you," said Gunhilde. "Welcome to my home. We'll be serving our evening meal shortly. There's a water pump at the back of the lodge if you wish to refresh yourselves. You must all stay the night."

"I really don't think we can," said Esme. "We should ride on."

"That's nonsense, woman," interrupted Fenrir. "You're tired. Besides, we must think of the horses. They've gone far enough for one day."

Esme nodded. "Yes, of course, I'm being thoughtless."

"No. You're behaving like a worried sister," said Thorkel, kindly. "But in any case, we'll never make Lunden before nightfall. It will be much too dangerous. Do as your friend suggests. Rest now and eat. Tomorrow we'll leave at dawn."

"They speak good sense," said Gunhilde. "Please try not to worry about Brand. There is no reason why anyone should wish to harm him. He'll be safe with Edmund."

Esme disagreed, but was not about to reveal Edmund's treachery to Gunhilde. She could think of no reason why Edmund would call for Brand's company. He had always seemed jealous of the boy or, at best, dismissive of him. Her anxiety remained. However, she allowed herself to be ushered to the ladies' bower which adjoined the main lodge. A servant brought her a bowl of water, fresh towels and a simple dress of delightful blue – one which Gunhilde assured her was now too small for her own figure. When she joined the men for dinner Esme had changed from her leather riding gear. Her hair was brushed and shone with health, although her cheeks remained pale.

She noted that Gunhilde's husband was not present. Instead there was another man at her side, swarthy in appearance. His eyes never left Esme as she entered the room and took her place at the table. Pork stew and dumplings had already been served on a polished wooden plate in front of her. Normally Esme would have set to with gusto but her stomach was in turmoil. She glanced at Eirik. His face was thunderous, eyes narrowed and his mouth hardened into a thin line. Then she noticed the stranger lift his hands to the table. Esme stifled a gasp. The lower part of one arm was missing.

44

Gunhilde was cheerful, flushed and clearly fulfilled in her role as hostess. "Allow me to introduce you to a friend of ours from Denmark. He brings me delightful goods at such low prices." She pointed to a large amber brooch pinned to her bosom. "Just look at this, Esme. Isn't it beautiful? After dinner you must ask him to show you his wares. They are safely hidden in his wagon in the stable."

Esme glanced towards Gunnar who passed his tongue slowly over his top lip as he gazed at her with a lascivious leer. Her insides lurched with disgust and she turned away, briefly wondering why Gunhilde seemed so fond of him. Was Pallig, her husband, away as often as Edmund? Did Gunnar fulfil her need for male companionship, or was she genuinely enthralled by the baubles he brought her?

She pushed away those thoughts and allowed her mind to dwell on how Eirik must be feeling. Gunnar was the man who lost his arm, inadvertently saving Eirik from execution. Father Aidan said he'd seen him in the area, and warned that the man would not rest until he had witnessed Eirik's demise. Her attention was drawn back to Gunhilde who was now talking loudly to Thorkel after he'd made an inquiry about the men dressed in black.

"One of them mentioned my husband and asked me to give him his regards. That amused me. I said he could give them to him himself since he was in Lunden."

"Have you heard from Pallig?" Esme asked.

Gunhilde lost a little of her buoyancy. "No . . . not for a few weeks. But his work is important and often keeps him away for long periods."

Esme cast a fleeting look towards Eirik. He was staring at her and their eyes met. He frowned, rubbing his chin.

Gunhilde's comment confused Esme even more. Was *her* husband part of the conspiracy too? Surely he would know if Edmund was a traitor, so perhaps they both were. They had worked together for a long time. After all, Pallig was Sweyn's brother-in-law and it would be natural for him to be his supporter. Did Gunnar know of these relationships? Is that why he spent time here? She had little appetite and noticed that, while Fenrir and Thorkel both tucked into their meal with relish, Eirik was moving the food around his plate. His mood was dark and brooding.

Gunnar, however, was cheerful. He addressed most of his remarks to Thorkel. "Have we not met before, Lord Thorkel?"

"I don't believe I've had the pleasure."

"Were you not once a member of the Jomsborg Vikings?"

Thorkel placed his knife on the wooden platter before replying. "That was a long time ago," he said slowly.

"Can I tempt you to more of this excellent wine?" said Gunnar, his voice jovial. "I know you have a discerning palate for a good alcoholic beverage."

Thorkel's brows knitted over the bridge of his nose. "In that case, you have been misinformed. My capacity for such is limited."

"Come now," said Gunnar with a smirk, "it's in the Viking blood to be inebriated, particularly before battle. I'm sure you remember how it provides the edge of courage. One just has to make sure not to lose one's head."

Fenrir, who had remained silent so far, suddenly interjected, "*Or* one's arm."

This time it was Gunnar's turn to be disquieted. He glared at Fenrir, who merely lifted his mug by way of a triumphant salutation. The tension around the table was palpable. The only one who seemed not to notice was Gunhilde. She was animated by the unexpected surfeit of company, and it struck Esme that she must be lonely living here in the middle of a forest with a husband, who, like Edmund, was constantly called to duty.

After her son was bundled off to bed at the end of the meal, Gunhilde encouraged Gunnar to his feet. "Come, Esme, see what he has to offer while there's still a little light."

"I really do not feel up to—" Esme began.

"Nonsense," Gunhilde interrupted, taking hold of Esme's hand and pulling her from the seat. "It's such an exciting treasure trove. I'll fetch a torch."

She reluctantly gave in since Gunhilde was so insistent, and followed the two of them to the barn at the back. The large doors stood wide open. Inside was a covered wagon. Gunnar parted the flaps and pulled out a tray of jewellery. Gunhilde held each item against Esme's cheek to determine which trinket best suited her colouring.

Esme noted how frequently her friend touched Gunnar and he responded by patting her bottom. He knew how to charm his lady clients. A servant ran into the barn, breathless. "My lady, can you come please. Your son needs you. He refuses to sleep until he has spoken to you."

Gunhilde sighed. "Alright, I'm coming. Gunnar, you must show Esme your kirtles and gowns from France. She'll be delighted."

Esme turned to follow Gunhilde but Gunnar grabbed her by the wrist. "Why in such a hurry? Taste some of my delights first." He pulled her towards him. "What harm can I do to you with only one arm?"

"Don't touch me," shouted Esme.

"Let her go!" Eirik stood in the doorway.

Gunnar immediately released her. "There really is no need for this," he said. "The little lady can hardly have anything to fear from me, a man crippled by the misfortunes of battle. Why don't you take a look yourself, my lord? I have goods to interest everyone."

"Nothing you have would interest me," said Eirik. "Esme, leave us please."

Esme left but retreated only a little way so she could still hear their conversation. She peeped through a gap in the wooden slats.

"I've seen the way you look at her," said Gunnar. "Don't pretend to me that you're not lusting for her body and enjoying a dalliance with a married woman."

Eirik's hand found the sheath of his knife. Gunnar observed without concern. "I see my words disturb you. The depth of your desire is more than I imagined. Don't tell me you fancy yourself to be in love with her. Loving unobtainable women is such a wasteful emotion. Why not just take them? They rarely object. Some of them positively cry out for it."

Eirik raised his fist.

Gunnar's mouth curled into a sneer. "You wouldn't dare touch me in these circumstances. I am a peaceful trader and work under the law of Aethelred." He laughed. "This has turned out to be a very good day. I have sought you from country to country for many years, and, lo, I have found you in a most unexpected place."

Eirik dropped his clenched hand, struggling to control his anger. "And what is the purpose of your seeking?"

"That's a stupid question. It's your fault that I'm only half a man. I shall never be satisfied until revenge is mine."

"The loss of your arm was not of my doing."

"There I must beg to differ. It was the jolt of your head that caused my arm to be severed."

"I was not the one to put your arm there in the first place."

Gunnar's voice expressed agitation and the derision fell from his face. "You encouraged me to grab your hair. Don't pretend you didn't know what you were doing. You had been defeated. As a prisoner of war you deserved your punishment. I, however, did not deserve mine."

"What is it you want?" asked Eirik.

"Your death."

"It would not be a fair fight."

"No contest between us can be fair, until your arm has been severed also. You treated me unjustly, so naturally you cannot expect any such consideration. I advise you to be on guard at all times. Be assured, as soon as you are unwary I shall be there, like a spectre, to make the cut."

"You've become a phantom already. I feel sorry for you." Eirik turned his back, demonstrating disdain.

Gunnar compressed his jaw, grinding his teeth. Barely opening his mouth he said, "I've warned you. You may be contemptuous of me now, but it will not always be so. I have money aplenty to engage the best fighters."

"So be it," said Eirik, taking his leave.

Eager not to be seen, Esme scurried into the main hall and sat down, her heart pumping in her chest. Gunhilde returned from settling her child. "You've not been long, Esme. Did you agree to buy anything?"

"Not tonight. I shall look again tomorrow, if there's time."

Eirik lay on his back, both arms folded beneath his head, while Thorkel and Fenrir snored on either side of him. The pallet was made comfortable with a straw mattress but sleep eluded him, and he watched as strips of white moonlight bent around the ceiling beams. He was angry with himself. Gunnar, who slept in the barn, had been right to mock him. How could he have allowed himself to fall in love with Esme, yet stand by while she married Edmund? Why was he still here helping to look for her brother? If Father Aidan had not instilled in him a belief in the puny Christ, he would now be back in Denmark. But in truth, he was not the same as he had once been. Aidan had used the same words to describe himself. Eirik had to admit that he preferred to stay in England with his newly found faith. He would negotiate with Aethelred and agree to cease harrowing the English in exchange for land. Then perhaps he could put Esme and Edmund behind him; find another woman with whom to share his life. In the past he had easily buried any emotions that did not fit with the life he desired. He would do so again.

Esme was in the ladies' bower, her thoughts a whirl of conflicting emotions. Was Gunnar correct in his assessment of Eirik's feelings for her? He had always treated her like a servant, keeping her busy with chores. It was true that she had experienced a spiritual bond with him, but that was not the same as the link between a husband and wife. Such a union could never be with a heathen whose values opposed her own. He had tried to dissuade her from marrying Edmund and had saved her – twice. But that was no more than an owner would do for a valued servant. So why was there an aching in her heart at the anticipated loss of his company once Brand had been safely recovered, and Edmund had taken his rightful place by her side? Life was no longer normal since the invasion of the Vikings. Perhaps once routine returned she would feel differently.

45
Norwich 1979

Bjorn pulls into the driveway at the back of Emma's house. He and Greta walk through the garden to the terrace where her mother is sitting. Sonia springs to her feet. "How lovely to meet you both."

If Emma had any unease about this meeting, it is quickly dispelled. Soon her mother and Bjorn are speaking in the language of their birth. Jack is clearly taken with Greta. She has brought a guitar with her, and in no time the two are exchanging ideas about their preferred music. Sonia brings out a choice of sandwiches and cake for lunch. "What a lovely conservatory," says Bjorn. "It's a beautiful Gloriosa you've got there." That comment opens up a wide-ranging conversation about plants and flowers.

The children take their food upstairs. The haunting strains of 'Summer Time' drift from above. Emma notices that Bjorn closes his eyes and wonders if he, too, is visualising the colours that hover and soar with the haunting strains, telling their own dramatic story.

"Amazing," says Bjorn. "Is that your son playing, Emma? He's going to be the next Bix Beiderbecke." He listens entranced as Jack begins the melody of 'Nobody Knows the Trouble I've Seen'.

"I understand you wish to take a look at my recently inherited property," says Sonia, finally getting around to the purpose of the visit.

"Yes, I would," says Bjorn. "I'm a horse breeder and trainer and am looking to buy somewhere not too far from Newmarket."

"Come with me and I'll show you the plans."

Bjorn and Sonia disappear into the front room and Emma can hear various murmurings and guffaws as she washes the dishes in the kitchen. *They are getting along well. So are Jack and Greta. Just like a family.*

Emma, Bjorn and the children head off to the sixteenth-century cottage. Sonia stays behind to prepare crispy pork and apple sauce for dinner. The children bounce up and down as they pull into the drive of the farmhouse. "Can I take Greta and show her the outhouses?" asks Jack. "I promise we'll be careful."

Bjorn fetches two large torches from the boot of the car and gives one to Jack. He and Emma enter the front door and walk into the living room. Emma looks around. "Things have been moved. There was a glass and ashtray on this small table. Mum and I thought someone had broken in through a window in Reginald's bedroom. There's no key to the French doors. Matilda talked about treasures being here. Do you think they've been stolen already?"

"I think there would be more sign of movement. I'll take a look and make it more secure," says Bjorn.

Emma indicates the door that leads upstairs but suggests they first examine the library. "Matilda said Reggie found Phoebe's narrative in there."

Between them they inspect all the shelves but find nothing relating to the Battle of Maldon.

"I think this used to be two cottages," says Bjorn. "There could be a space behind this wall if a staircase was removed. I've been looking for a possible way in."

"Do you think there might be a secret passage?" says Emma a little breathlessly.

"If there is I haven't found it, I'm afraid. There must be an attic. Let's go and see."

Upstairs, a door at the back of a cupboard clicks and swings open, exposing wooden steps. "This looks promising," says Bjorn, climbing up and pushing open a trap door. It crashes onto the floorboards. Years of choking dust fly into the air. He waits for it to settle then swings his flashlight around the room.

Emma gasps. "It's huge. It must run the whole length of the building. And look at all those trunks. I think we may have found something. She begins enthusiastically rummaging in chests but they are filled with nothing more than old curtains and blankets. She sighs in frustration.

"Don't despair," says Bjorn. "We've not finished yet."

At that moment, they hear Greta shouting, "Help, Papa, help. Come quickly."

46
Lunden 991

A grey mist cloaked the morning. Esme was ready, so were Eirik and Thorkel. Fenrir appeared dishevelled and whinged about the untimely hour. There was no sign of Gunnar. Gunhilde provided water and fruit for the journey and the address of an inn at Sydenham where they could stay for the night, if necessary. She had drawn a map of the Thames indicating ancient Londinium, built and abandoned by the Romans, now a busy Saxon enclave known as Lundenburgh, one of several communities. To the west was Lundenwic, a trading area, and further round was their destination: Thorn Island, where an abbey provided safe accommodation for the king when in Lunden, and where Esme would meet her husband and brother.

Esme's first glimpse of Lunden was from a northern eminence that provided a view of all the independent settlements, interspersed with woodland and fields, on either side of the broad, winding river. To her left, she could see the walls surrounding the old town. On her right, barges bulging with cargo rocked gently on the water, waiting patiently like beasts of burden, to be loaded and unloaded.

She marvelled at the number of dwellings squashed into such a small space. Smoke from open fires curled into the air, shrouding the whole area with a gloomy pall. Yet it was no corpse that laboured beneath. Even from a distance, life and hope prevailed; the affairs of common humanity breathed expectation and continuity. Somewhere in the jumble was Brand, fit and thriving. She was filled with a sudden optimism that all would be well. Soon they would meet, and the nagging anxiety of the past weeks and days would dissipate.

The small party broke into a gallop, reining in as they approached the northern entrance of Londinium. The narrow streets bustled and hummed. Stalls clothed in vegetables, fruit, cheese, herbs, pottery, jewellery and leatherwork offered vibrant regalia of opportunity. Vendors shouted heartening words of profitable deals for would-be punters. Strips of meat and fish sizzled on braziers, emitting aromas to stir hunger pangs. Assorted live poultry, trussed in nets giving freedom only to their confused, twitching heads, clucked and squawked as an exchange of coins sealed their fate.

The horses trotted through the old streets then turned west, following an early Roman road that crossed the bridge of the river Fleet, which ran into the Thames. Along the embankment, homes and establishments of trade and commerce flourished. The muscular frame of a blacksmith glistened with the sweat of labour and the heat of the forge as he hammered a glowing horseshoe into shape. Narrow lanes led away to the left, channelled by streams of sewage spilling towards the river. A sickly stench wafted in the air.

The road curved southwards. The sounds of civilisation gradually faded. Stretched out in front of them was an eyot formed by two branches of a northern tributary. It was the size of a Saxon village, surrounded by a steep earth bank, some twenty- or thirty-feet high, topped by dense wooden stakes. On one side, the bank arced out into the river to form a docking area. At intervals within the palisade, watchtowers stood as reminders of the fragility of peace.

As if from nowhere, a band of riders dressed in black surged towards them with weapons drawn. Eirik instinctively tugged the hilt of his sword but then shoved his blade firmly back into place. "Do nothing and wait," he said. "They'll not attack if we don't provoke them."

Esme's heart quickened with the anticipation of what was to come. "These must be the men who took Brand and came looking for me.

Have they come to arrest us?" she murmured.

"We'll soon find out," said Fenrir, squinting against the sun.

The pounding slowed to a stop. Snorting beasts, as black as their riders' clothes, hemmed them in. One of the men addressed Eirik. "What is your purpose here?"

"We seek the presence of King Aethelred." Eirik spoke with authority. "We have a message from King Sweyn of Denmark."

The leader eyed Esme beneath heavy brows. "And the woman?"

"Lady Esme of Saxstow Hall. She's looking for her brother, who we understand was brought here."

The fellow nodded. Pulling on the reins, he turned his horse's head. "Follow me."

The island was fordable from the north bank. There was a causeway of planks supported by crossbars and piles driven into the river bed, but this was largely ignored. Instead, water sprayed from sixty hooves as the horses galloped their way through the swampy river bed. Midges besieged them in swarms, eager for fresh blood. No extent of flurried swipes deterred their intention.

Two solid gates, opened by unseen hands, permitted their entry and clanged shut behind them. Echoes reverberated around the spacious courtyard.

"Wait here," said the leader. "I'll be back shortly."

Esme chewed her lip, her earlier optimism evaporating in the dismal obscurity of their situation. She dismounted. Eirik moved to her side and, more than ever, she was aware of her weakness as a woman in this world of male power. Yet she had some rights under the law and would make sure the king acknowledged them. She was guilty of no wrong doing, neither was her brother.

Two habit-clad monks scurried through an archway on the left and entered the door of a church. At least they were in a house of God.

Facing her was a walkway lined with bushes leading to a tall, elegant hall, finished in oak, the size of Saxstow. She assumed this must be the king's residence. Attached to it was a separate ladies' bower. A gate led to clusters of identical, rectangular houses separated by pathways; others led she knew not where, but must surely reach the river.

The group leader returned. "The abbot is at prayers. The king is indisposed. You men, come with me." He turned to Esme. "The housekeeper will see to your comfort."

A middle-aged woman of ample proportions bustled forward and beckoned Esme. She led the way to a beautifully appointed room in the ladies' bower. Deep upholstery cushioned wide chairs; colourful tapestries adorned the walls; a thick, soft mattress topped the bed.

The housekeeper appraised her. "You cannot expect to enter the presence of the king looking and smelling like that."

Esme was undeterred. "There is no need for discourtesy. What's your name?" she said tartly.

The woman puckered her lips, "Mildryth."

Two young women entered the room carrying a copper tub and emptied buckets of steaming water into its bulbous shape. "There's soap and perfume," said Mildryth. "The servants will wash and dry your hair. Then we'll see what fits you."

An hour later Esme sat on the bed wearing undergarments of smooth linen. Her hair hung freely down her back, but was partly braided on top and decorated with pearls. A range of exquisite outfits were paraded before her, embroidered and trimmed with silk. Mildryth made it quite clear that these were on loan and the final choice would be hers, not Esme's. As it happened, she selected a fitted gown of rich green with an under-dress of deep purple which felt wonderful against Esme's skin. Amber stones studded the neckline. A woollen cloak revealed matching colours below the sleeve and hem.

Mildryth scrutinised the final effect. "Yes, fit for a king. He'll be pleased with you."

Esme tried to push away undesirable thoughts, but they persisted. She assumed she was to be reunited with Brand and Edmund. Now doubts grew like spectres, unsettling and disturbing.

"Dinner is served, my lady," said Mildryth. "You are to eat with your companions. The king dislikes eating with strangers. He'll grant you an audience afterwards."

The men rose from their seats as Esme stood on the threshold of the dining hall in the main building. Eirik's eyes scarcely left her. "Never have I seen such a vision of loveliness," he said.

Thorkel, who was nearest the door, reached for her hand and escorted her in. "It seems we have all been treated with civility," he said. A lamp hung low over the table. Eirik was dressed in a white silk shirt with a royal-blue linen tunic, black hose and high leather boots. She thought how handsome he looked. Even Fenrir had been scrubbed and trimmed, sporting a red tunic. Pork, chicken and beef were laid before them. Esme prayed they were not fatted calves before the slaughter.

After the meal, Thorkel, Eirik and Fenrir were the first to be summoned into the king's presence.

"My friends," the king began. "On the advice of my government, I agree to our drawing up a treaty. In return for provisions and a large sum of money, you shall undertake to keep the peace towards me and my subjects, and agree to join in our defence against any hostile Viking host that descends on English soil."

"We are agreed . . . in principle," said Thorkel.

"Excellent," said Aethelred. He signalled to Mildryth who was awaiting orders. "Bring in the wine. We'll celebrate our alliance."

The king made the toast. "In two days Archbishop Sigeric of Canterbury will be with us, together with Elfric and Ethelweard, respected ealdormen of our West Saxon provinces. We will all meet again in the evening and the details of the deal will be signed and sealed. The silver will be brought up from our vaults on the following day. May I suggest that you transport it back by cargo boat? That will be less conspicuous and less vulnerable to attack. Now let us drink to our preliminary agreement." Each man raised his goblet.

47

Esme had returned to her room. A knock was followed by the entrance of Mildryth.

"The king has called for you," she said with no hint of servitude. "You are to come now."

The king's chamber was furnished with comfortable armchairs. Esme curtsied low and awaited his response.

"My lady Esme, welcome. I've been expecting you."

Esme regarded him with wide eyes, "Sire?"

"I knew you'd come looking for your brother. I hear you have nurtured him since infancy and he looks upon you as a mother."

"That's true, but why the subterfuge to gain my attention? You are my king. You had only to ask and I would have come."

Aethelred grinned and Esme observed that the description of his *fair face* was accurate. He was handsome and only a few years older than she. The king was attentive and guided her to a seat. "My dear lady, forgive my abruptness. I had rehearsed how I should impart the news I have for you, but my manner is terse. I see that you are a loyal subject. However, you may feel less disposed to be so once you've learned of my actions."

Esme's heart sank. "What actions, Sire?"

"I have been obliged to undertake the execution of Lord Edmund, your erstwhile husband."

She could feel blood draining from her face, even though she was aware that this had been one of the options of her dread. Despite his treatment of her, Esme had never dared to seriously contemplate

Edmund's death. Now she had to acknowledge the reality. The future, no matter how bad it may have seemed, was shattered; her way of life taken away. She sincerely hoped the execution had been carried out in secret. Regardless of Edmund's faults, as a thegn of England surely he deserved privacy. Aware of the urgency to give the king no inkling of her suspicions about Edmund's treachery, she said, "But why? Why would you feel it necessary to do such a thing? I thought he was one of your closest advisers."

Aethelred sighed. "So did I – that is what makes his treachery unforgiveable. He was a traitor of the worst kind. I acquired the throne when barely more than a boy. I depended on certain individuals, and believed they were my friends. Lord Edmund was one such. He was a thorough Saxon with no Danish blood." Aethelred shook his head sadly. "I thought he of all people would be true to me. But of late I have learned that it was not so, that in truth he was plotting my demise and the installation of the King of Denmark on my throne. Therefore retribution was necessarily harsh."

"How did you find out?"

"I've had my eye on him for some time. He has a Danish friend who kept me informed."

Esme supposed he was referring to Pallig – Gunhilde's husband. That means Brand would have been under no threat from Aethelred while staying with them, but what of Sweyn? Did he know that his brother-in-law was against a change of ruler? That he was a spy for the king? Or was Pallig merely protecting himself by exposing Edmund? Perhaps he played for both sides too. She gently massaged her forehead unable to rationalise these complicated dilemmas. "When, when did this *execution* take place?"

"Last week. My men captured him in the forest. He was afforded a trial, I'm not a monster, but the evidence was unequivocal. He told me that he'd married his ward only a few hours before his arrest. My men sought you at Saxstow Hall to no avail. But we knew where to find Brand. Bringing him back to Lunden was a sure way of attracting you here."

"When may I see him?"

"Tomorrow morning."

The knot in Esme's gut relaxed a little. "I'm grateful to you, Sire. When may we leave?"

Aethelred pursed his lips, stood and paced the floor two or three times with his hands folded behind his back. "I'm afraid I cannot let either of you go just yet. There is something I want you to do for me. I need you now to serve your country."

"I don't understand. What business could you have with me?"

The king sat down again and leaned forward, resting his elbows on his knees. "Your father's estate was considerable, awarded by charter to your Danish predecessors for loyalty to the crown. Under your father's will, the land was left to you and your mother. Since your mother died at the same time as your father, the land is ostensibly yours. The estate provides a handsome income."

Esme couldn't believe what she was hearing. "Indeed, Sire, you are mistaken. The land is willed to my brother Brand."

"I have studied the documents and assure you I am correct. It seems we were both deceived by Lord Edmund. He had much to gain by your marriage." The king raised an eyebrow. "Although I doubt it would have been a union in the traditional sense of the word."

"But we were married only a few hours."

"Good. I assume the marriage was not consummated?"

"No."

Aethelred seemed greatly unsettled by the conversation they were having. He rose yet again from his seat, crossed to the fireplace and stood with his back to the fire. "Forgive me for saying so, but your purity makes you even more valuable. I have a role for you – that of a peace-weaver."

Esme's lips parted as she struggled to absorb this latest blow. "You mean you want me to marry an enemy for the sake of keeping amity?"

"Precisely! I can reclaim your land, should I choose to do so, under the terms of the charter. I have already reasserted title over Edmund's. However, I am prepared to overlook the nature of the tenure if you agree to marry according to my wishes."

Shock numbed her senses. "So this was to be her fate – married to a stranger for the sake of England's defence. She tensed, unable to keep the hostility from her voice. "And who is it you wish me to marry?"

"I confess I hope it will be a man of your liking. His name is Roger de Caen, a Norman count."

Esme could feel the pulse in her throat. Not only was she to marry a man of the king's choosing but he was a foreigner who lived across the sea. She tried to keep her voice even. "May I ask why a Norman?"

Aethelred paused. He turned towards the fire and continued to gaze into the flames as he answered. "Esme, I have to admit to you that my throne is insecure. I became king after Edward, my step-brother, was murdered whilst visiting me and Aelfthryth, my mother. I was too young to have any knowledge of the plan, yet it was carried out by members of my household. No one was held to blame and I was crowned a month later in the midst of intense suspicion, which damaged the good reputation of the Crown in the eyes of the people." He turned to look at her. "Furthermore, miracles began to happen where the body of my brother was taken, and he came to be regarded as a saint – at my expense. Within two years of my reign the raids began. It was in one such attack on Thanet that your parents were killed."

Esme's throat tightened. "Why are you telling me this?"

"Please, allow me to continue. I'm trying to explain the importance of my decision. Renewed raids, a few years later, brought us into open conflict with Richard, Duke of Normandy. He and most of the aristocrats have Viking heritage, and they willingly opened their ports to protect marauders, storing the spoils of their invasions. Hostilities were so bad between us that Pope John intervened. We agreed that neither party would support the other's enemies. If we did, then reparation would be made."

"It sounds a perfect solution," said Esme. "You have made peace with Normandy already, so can have no need of my assistance."

"The peace is fragile, and now the attacks have begun again, one of which you have just experienced. I need the Normans as allies, but I also need bargaining tools."

Esme spoke with feigned poise which at this moment she lacked. "Sire, I shall be no one's bargaining tool."

Aethelred sighed. "Come now, Esme, I'm sure you will appreciate that you are a valuable asset with which to negotiate a pact for the peace of this country. Forgive me, I have been blunt, but I have no desire to insult your intelligence by pretending this is not the reason you are here."

"And what does Count Roger de Caen think of this bargain."

"He's most amenable to the idea."

"How noble of him," said Esme wincing as she heard her own scorn.

Aethelred raised both hands in the air. "Goodness, Esme, you are such a beautiful and wealthy woman that I would have married you myself if any good would come of it. The count is the youngest man I can offer you. I believe you will find him to be a pleasing husband."

"Sire, you turn marriage into horse-trading."

"Well, since you put it that way, I suppose it is. Do not entertain the idea that I, as the king, am permitted to marry for love. My unions are planned for the greater good of England."

Esme held both hands to the sides of her face. "I have just learned that I've been widowed. Am I to have time to consider your proposition? Am I even to meet my suitor?"

"Indeed you are," said Aethelred, walking to the window and looking out across the yard to the stables. "I fancy myself as something of a horse breeder. I always allow a filly to spend time with the stallion I have selected for stud. Once they have become accustomed to each other, copulation follows naturally and without stress."

Esme clenched her fists; rage boiled up from within. "So, I'm allowed to sniff the odour of my stallion before making the inevitable choice?"

Aethelred turned to look at her, but was unmoved. "My, you do not mince your words, but, yes, that about sums it up. The count will be arriving tomorrow. You will both stay here as my guests to give you time to get to know one another. But I warn you, Esme, I cannot allow an opportunity like this to slip through my fingers. You should be honoured that you've been asked to serve your country."

"I can see no honour in serving it on my back for the satisfaction of a foreigner," said Esme.

Aethelred blew out breath through his lips. "There are many women – most, I venture to say – who do just that for a great deal less reward. Go now and rest. Don't reject the proposition out of hand. I confess I rather presumed you might have readily agreed to my proposal. After all, marrying Edmund was hardly a love match.

You must have considered it one of convenience, particularly if its purpose was to ensure the inheritance which you considered to be your brother's. Am I wrong in that assumption?"

Esme stared at the king and then at the fire. The beginnings of tears filled her eyes and she blinked rapidly, admitting to herself that there was truth in his words.

Aethelred noticed her distress and, taking a step towards her, he reached for her hands, holding them outstretched in front of him. "Come now, I am of a generous nature. I am sure you will agree with me when you've had time to weigh your options."

"Do I have any other option?" asked Esme.

The king shrugged. "I confess I cannot think of one at the moment, unless you wish to become a nun. I cannot allow you to retain such valuable lands alone. You must have a man at your side. And I prefer that you choose one who will be good for England. You may find that the count is just the man for you."

Esme slumped into the sumptuous pillows on her bed. The green dress lay stretched out beside her. How could she marry a man unknown to her under such circumstances? Of course the Norman would agree to Aethelred's suggestion. He had everything to gain by doing so: land and a wife. Any protestations of love would have alternative implications.

Her mind wandered to Eirik. What had the king demanded of him? She touched her hair, remembering the night they first met, and the morning on the beach when it seemed their spirits connected. He had protected her and come in search of Brand. She ran her fingers across the sleek dress. How would it feel to have him next to her, to feel his touch? A fire lit in her veins at the thought.

She sat up and swung her legs onto the floor. Tomorrow she would see Brand. Perhaps his presence would help her to decide, if indeed there was a decision to be made; but for now she must sleep. Removing the rest of the borrowed clothes, she snuggled under the soft covers. Yes, tomorrow she would think about it.

48

Esme was woken by a wild banging. She opened the door and Brand burst into the room, a broad smile on his face. He threw both arms round her waist and she held him close. "I was so worried about you," she said.

Brand took a step back, gripping his sister's hands. "I was safe at Gunhilde's. But I didn't know where you were."

"I was taken prisoner in Maeldun and had no chance to tell you."

Brand frowned but asked no further questions. "Black riders came. They said I was to meet you here with Lord Edmund."

Esme sat her brother down. "Brand, I have bad news. Edmund is . . ."

Brand's eyes filled with a vague curiosity, "Dead?"

Esme caught her breath, astonished by the boy's matter-of-fact manner. "Yes. He did some bad things. The king was angry."

Brand nodded with understanding. "He was a traitor. The king executes traitors. It's their punishment. My tutor told me."

"Your tutor!"

"It's Latin this morning." Brand pulled a face.

"You're not upset about Edmund?"

The boy thought for a moment. "No. I didn't much like him." He smiled. "Can we stay here now?"

"Don't you want to go home?"

Brand shook his head. "I like it here."

Esme was surprised by his fervour. "The king wishes me to marry."

Brand bounced up and down. "Is he nicer than Edmund?"

Esme considered for a moment how life was so simple to the

young. "And what sort of man would be nicer than Edmund?"

"Someone to teach me how to fight."

Esme pouted. "But you've already practised your knife and axe throwing with me."

Brand sniffed. "I know. You're very good – for a girl." He stood and pretended to thrust and parry with a sword. "But I want to be a warrior."

There was a knock at the door and Mildryth appeared. "Forgive me. I've come to take the boy to his lessons."

"Then I'll detain you no longer." Esme kissed his forehead. "We shall see each other later."

As she dressed in her riding clothes, she heard the hooves of several horses on the courtyard below. She watched through a half-open shutter as a well-dressed man with a neatly trimmed beard brought up the rear. He was riding a beautiful chestnut steed. Too good for you, she thought, as the newcomer carelessly spurred on his mount through the entourage of servants and bodyguards. She judged him to be only a few years younger than Edmund.

The horses jostled and the chestnut jerked his head, rearing in the mêlée. The man slipped sideways in his saddle and a servant quickly helped him dismount. Incensed, he indicated the servant should hold the bridle while he whipped his horse's flanks. The horse whinnied, flung its head in the air and sidestepped to avoid the lash until the servant was no longer strong enough to control it. A groom from the king's stables ran forward and breathed into the animal's nostrils, calming it with softly spoken words. The action reminded Esme of Eirik.

"Give him no hay or water for two days," said the man with the whip. "I'll not be thrown from my own horse. He must learn total obedience."

The groom bowed and led the animal away.

The man turned to the waiting servant. "Tell the king that Count Roger de Caen has arrived."

"My lord, the king is away hunting today. He promises to be back before sunset."

"Sunset! I rose early this morning simply because he told me to come today. This is an outrage. How am I now expected to be kept entertained for the rest of the day?"

"Our servants will make you comfortable, my lord. There are walks in the grounds of the abbey that lead down to the river."

"Walks! Walks! I don't want to walk. I can do that on my own estates. I shall rest. Take me to my quarters and bring me food with plenty of your best wine. I shall be speaking most sternly with your king about this lack of civility." He cast his eyes around the yard and then, unexpectedly, looked up at the windows of the ladies' bower.

Esme darted back, fearing he had already spotted her. So this was to be her suitor. She took a deep breath and let air pass slowly through her lips, briefly wondering whether it was the king's intention for her to live in Normandy, or whether the Norman was to live in England. It made no matter, she'd already seen enough. Even the thought of meeting him was abhorrent to her.

Feeling low in spirit, she made her way along an adjoining corridor to the hall where she supposed Eirik and Thorkel might be having breakfast. But only Fenrir sat at the table, tucking into meat, eggs and bread. "Where is everyone?" she said.

Fenrir stumbled to his feet as she entered. "Thorkel left for the hunt today. Didn't fancy it myself. Apparently the king rides out several times a week. Don't know about Eirik. Haven't seen him. I expect he's practising, as usual." He lowered his tone. "Esme, I'm very sorry to hear about your husband."

Esme tightened her lips and tweaked them to one side of her face. "The traitor? Really? I believe you are alone in that sentiment, Fenrir."

Fenrir pouted. "I don't doubt it. I'm sorry not for him but for the position you might now find yourself in."

Esme helped herself to fresh bread, honey and juice. "It would seem that full advantage of the situation has been taken already."

Fenrir resumed his seat and continued his breakfast. "What do you mean?"

"A man arrived this morning. Has he been in here?"

"I've seen no one. Why do you ask?"

"His name is Roger de Caen."

"Who?"

"The man the king would have me marry. A Norman count. The plot has been well hatched. The king has likened me to a mare. I am to be permitted time together with his chosen stallion to assess whether we are desirous of mating."

"What has the king proposed?"

"I'm to be a peace-weaver."

Fenrir stared at her and frowned, not comprehending the term.

"Aethelred needs to make a pact with the Normans. They provide protection for the Vikings along their shores, thus making it easier for them to raid our southern coast. My suitor is from Normandy. Our marriage would ensure the Vikings were denied such shelter."

236

Fenrir swallowed a lump of bread. "I assume you're not keen on the idea."

"What do you think, Fenrir? A man I don't know, who will whisk me away across the water? What future for me or my brother?"

Fenrir nodded wisely. "Perhaps it may not turn out to be as ill as you presume."

Esme lifted her eyes and stared at him without raising her chin. "Unlikely. Aethelred has already taken back Edmund's lands."

"We spent time with the king last evening," said Fenrir.

"What does he want of you?"

"Peace."

"And what do you want of him?"

"Danegeld."

"More Danegeld? More silver. More money to protect our land."

Fenrir sighed. "Thorkel offered him a treaty. In exchange for the silver, Sweyn promises to maintain peace for the king."

"Has he accepted?"

"Yes. His advisers and signatories will be arriving in two days."

Esme was curious. "It's all very well for Sweyn to make promises, but how long can he contain Olaf's natural aggression, or anyone else's come to that? Haven't Norway and Denmark been enemies for years? Wasn't it in just such a battle that Eirik nearly lost his head and Gunnar lost his arm?"

"Yes. It's as you say. But Eirik and Thorkel have always been a formidable force."

Esme smiled. "Well, at least you would be on our side – even if for a price."

"Everything comes at a price, Esme."

She sighed. "So it would seem."

237

Fenrir couldn't face going back to his dwelling, reserved for visitors. Unused to being alone, he missed the camaraderie of his fellow warriors. He needed to be surrounded by people, so he headed for town. Striding out, he mused over what Esme had told him. He gritted his teeth feeling anger on her behalf. She was free of Edmund but now the king expected her to marry again – to someone she'd never met. He wanted to do something to help her – but what? An idea started to creep into his head. Yes, it was a good idea. And suddenly, amidst the hustle and bustle of Lunden's commerce, he found just the place to mull it over – a tavern. He went inside, bought a beer and chose a seat.

A man was propped on his elbows at a nearby table – a mug of ale positioned in front of him. He took several large swigs. Ale spilled down his beard, dripping onto his tunic. A second man entered and strode towards him. "Hello, Ulf. How are you? Seen that woman of yours?"

Ulf pulled a face and pointed to a seat on the opposite side of the bench. "I'm heading over to see her when I've finished my jar." He grimaced. "I need it before I can face her."

His companion laughed. "Has she kissed you yet?"

"That she has – and some."

"Lucky you."

"You think so? I have to shut my eyes."

"What have you promised her?"

Ulf lowered his voice as though the very word distressed him, "Marriage."

"And she believes you?"

"She loves me."

His companion laughed again. "So, have you got some . . . trade for me?"

"Plenty. I've got some deliveries. I just needed a drink first."

"Take these by way of encouragement." Ulf's companion shoved a few coins across the table. It was then that Fenrir recognised him – a man with half an arm.

At that moment, a jug flew close to Fenrir's ear. Two or three men on the other side of the room had started a fight and stools were upended. Gunnar stood. "I don't want to get involved in this. Report back tomorrow. And Ulf, try to stay sober."

Fenrir would have loved a fight. His fists were itching to hit someone's jaw, but he knew how unwise that would be. Reluctantly, he took one last gulp of his beer and headed back. Gunnar must have followed them from Gunhilde's house and was bound to be up to no good.

49

After her conversation with Fenrir, Esme strolled out into the morning sunlight and headed for the stables where a young groom, the one she had seen earlier, was brushing a horse until its coat gleamed. She was surprised and delighted to see that it was Kizzy. The little mare was standing quite still, enjoying the attention. "Thank you," said Esme. "I've had very little time to do that lately."

"It's my job, my lady. Lord Eirik asked specially for it to be done."

"Will you obey the command about denying food and water to the chestnut horse?"

The groom inclined his head towards the stable. "The animal is well fed and watered. Its coat is shining. Creatures behave well if you treat them well."

"You're not worried about incurring the wrath of Roger de Caen?"

He shook his head. "I take my orders from King Aethelred. He instructs me to look after the horses, not starve them."

Esme smiled. "When can I take Kizzy for a ride?"

"Kizzy? Nice name. Now, if you wish. I've just finished."

He was about to help Esme mount up when they both turned to see Mildryth hurrying towards them. "Sorry, the king has left orders that you are not to leave the island."

Esme tightened her mouth, her breath laboured by indignation at the audacity of the king to keep her locked away until she made the decision that pleased him. "Am I then to be a prisoner?"

"No, my lady, but you must be accompanied at all times."

"This is not to be endured." She fought back unwanted tears.

Mildryth was indifferent. "You are free to walk the grounds, which are extensive. The monks have worked hard to clear away the brambles, and there are many pleasant groves. Follow me, I'll show you where to go."

Esme decided that arguing would get her nowhere. She made a fuss of Kizzy and then followed Mildryth without enthusiasm, determined to speak to Aethelred about this imposition on her freedom.

Mildryth led the way through a side door which Esme had seen the monks using the evening before. "You can come and go through here," she said.

They entered a quadrangle where the monks were practising sword fighting, just as the Vikings had done on the banks of Northey Island. Her heart beat faster as she spotted Eirik among them, but he was too absorbed to notice her.

"They're warriors," explained Mildryth, "the king's personal bodyguards. They dress in black. Their leader, the abbot, is an important personage in affairs of the government." She opened another gate and allowed Esme to pass. "You're free to walk around the abbey buildings and down to the river. As I said, the monks have cleared wide tracts of land, but the perimeters are still thick with brambles to deter trespassers. You'll find some lovely clusters of trees where you can sit and rest."

Strolling through the grounds, Esme had to admit that the gardens were beautiful, their layout complemented nature. Bees buzzed around an area of wild flowers filled with daisies, cornflowers, poppies and campion – a colourful mass of white and yellow, blue, pink and red. Two monks, heads covered by hoods, tended hives nestling comfortably among the trees in an orchard. Seating, shaded by trellises of bright orange rose hips, gave the opportunity to sit and admire.

She followed an avenue of newly planted trees to the river where three ships were moored. One was rounder than the others – a cargo boat for deliveries to the abbey. Despite the freedom of her wanderings, she felt trapped. Without the king's support she had no house, no land and no money. What of Eirik? She recalled once again the times when he made her feel special in a way Edmund never had. He had protected her, sat beside her bed until she was well, and helped her find Brand. But she also knew she could never be yoked with a follower of Thor.

She was tired of being told what to do by powerful men. In Maeldun she had friends. She had her sewing skills. No one had more understanding of medicine than Astrid. No one could best Rowena's knowledge of dyes. She clenched her hands into tight balls and held them against her thighs. Let Aethelred reclaim the land that once belonged to her family. She would work hard and earn enough to keep her and Brand starting right now. Holding her head high, she made her way back to the abbey.

Mildryth was in the kitchen where a man was sitting close-by with a mug in his hand; she was giggling like a young girl – obviously enjoying her companion's attention. Fresh eggs and vegetables were spread over the trestle.

As Esme entered Mildryth stood, smoothing her hair and then her apron. "Good day, my lady. Have you enjoyed your walk?"

"Yes, thank you. Can you tell me if it's possible to buy embroidery materials nearby?"

"There's all a person could desire in the old city," said the man.

Mildryth frowned at him. "This is Ulf. He delivers our goods and can bring in anything you want."

"I prefer to see for myself," said Esme. Then, with a glance at Mildryth, she added, "If possible."

"I'm not sure . . ." began Mildryth.

Esme knew quite well what Mildryth was about to say and interrupted her. "I'll pay you for your trouble."

Mildryth bowed her head. "Very well, I'll see what I can do." She turned to Ulf. "Go now. I must prepare refreshments for when the king and his companions return from the hunt."

Ulf looked at Esme. "I'll come back with some samples of threads," he said, "or I'll take you to see them for yourself." He winked at Mildryth. "You can be a bit lax, can't you?"

Mildryth sighed. "I suppose so."

Fenrir knew that Eirik would be training with the warrior monks until late afternoon. Having spent some time poking around the stalls in town, he returned at a leisurely pace to the exercise area. Just as he was passing the kitchen, he saw a man emerging through the low door, ducking his head as he did so. Fenrir stepped into the shadows and watched him climb aboard his wagon. There was no mistaking who it was. Eirik must be told. He waited.

One last lunge and Eirik's opponent lost his sword. The monk wiped his brow. "It's no good. You're too fast for me. In fact, our abbot is due to retire soon. How about taking over?"

There were general murmurings of approval.

"You're the best I've ever met. Are all the Jomsborgs like you?"

Eirik grinned, donned his jerkin and raised a hand. "I'll see you all tomorrow. Thank you for the practice."

Fenrir moved to greet him. "I need a word with you. It's of the utmost importance."

Eirik sensed his urgency. "Come now to my quarters."

As they walked back in silence, riders were returning from the hunt. Judging by the sounds of raucous laughter resonating from the stables, Fenrir guessed the day had been a success. Eirik opened the door to one of the small homes, threw down his sword and invited Fenrir inside. "What's happened?"

Fenrir sighed. "This morning I went into the town and found a tavern."

Eirik looked at him expectantly, "And . . .?"

"I saw Gunnar."

"Gunnar?" Eirik narrowed his eyes. "What's he doing here?"

Fenrir sank into a chair. "Trade, so it seems. That's what he does for a living, but I think he's followed us."

Eirik perched on the end of the bed. "Did he recognise you?"

"No. He never looked at me. Doubt he'd remember me anyway. But he was talking to a man called Ulf who I've just see him coming out of the kitchen. He's a delivery man."

Eirik was quiet for several moments, running his hand across his chin. "It may, of course, be totally unrelated, but we can't take the risk. The treaty is due to be signed tomorrow night, and the day after we'll be taking the silver up the Thames."

"You'd best change the plans – just in case. Will you tell Aethelred?"

"Yes, and Thorkel. I must speak to them both, and decide the best course of action to keep everyone safe."

"Particularly that lass of yours," said Fenrir, raising his brows.

"If by that you mean the Lady Esme, then yes, although she should be safe enough within these walls. By the way, she is not my lass."

Fenrir grunted. "I feel sorry for her. She's being treated very badly."

Eirik was immediately alert. "What do you mean?"

Fenrir sniffed. "She's only just lost her husband – not that it's much of a loss – and already the king is making her marry some

Norman lord, who then promises not to allow Vikings to winter on his coastline. She's deeply unhappy about it, but the king threatened to take her lands. He's forcing her to be what's called a peace-weaver – that's a woman who's married off for the sake of alliances with her country."

Eirik's knuckles were white.

"You can't go on pretending," said Fenrir. "I know you love her. Why don't you tell her?"

"Because I have nothing to offer that she wants."

"How do you know unless you ask?"

"I know she wants land and status, even if only for her brother."

"Edmund's lands have already been taken by the king. Where's your courage, man? Is it all in your sword? Little good will it do you. What's the worst that can happen? She might turn you down."

"How can I compete with a Normandy lord?" Eirik stood and paced the floor.

"There are very few men who can compare favourably with you."

Eirik's laughter was stilted. "Oh yes. And I suppose you would know, being such an expert on women."

"I've seen the way she looks at you."

"I'll think about it. There are more important issues to deal with first."

Fenrir got to his feet. "Well, don't think too long, because if you're not going to do something about it, then I will." He smiled, knowing that Eirik didn't believe him.

50
Norwich 1979

Reginald's coat and cap are lying in a heap on the floor. A tearful Greta is standing beside an open panel exposing stone stairs to a basement. "Jack thought he would try on these clothes as a joke. When he took them off the hook, it lifted up, and this door slid open. There's a light switch. We went to investigate. Jack was with me but now I can't find him anywhere."

"Have you looked outside?" says Emma.

"Yes."

Bjorn hurries down the steps followed closely by Emma and Greta. There is plenty of headroom. The space below is about six-feet square. The back wall is filled with wine racks. The wall to their right is a combination of bricks interspersed with vertical wooden beams. "Clearly, a staircase was removed from here to build a cellar. It seems to have been used regularly."

"Jack was here with me," Greta wails. "I was looking in this cardboard box and when I turned round he'd gone. I'm sure he didn't go back upstairs. I'd have seen him, or at least heard him." Tears trickle down her cheeks.

"Jack," shouts Bjorn. There is no reply.

Emma is beginning to feel Greta's panic. "Let's all shout together."

This time they hear a faint reply. "In here."

"Where?" his mother yells.

"Behind the wall. Just a minute, I'll see if I can get this thing working from the inside."

"Are you trapped?" shouts Bjorn.

"I don't think so. People must have been able to get out as well as in."

After several anxious moments, they hear a clunk and a timber beam swings outwards. Emma jumps aside to avoid its trajectory. Jack wriggles out on his hands and knees. He stands, calmly wiping his hands on his trousers. "It's a bit stuffy and cobwebby in there."

"How did you get in?" says Emma incredulous, giving him a relieved hug.

"We studied the Reformation in class last year. I remembered our teacher told us about priest holes. Vertical timbers like these were fixed to the wall so they swivelled in and out. I had a torch."

"Congratulations, Jack," says Bjorn. "What did you find?"

"There are some pieces of silver – a chalice and candlesticks. They look like they belonged to a church. I'm afraid you'll never get in there though, sir. You're much too big. People were smaller in those days."

Bjorn kneels down and props open the beam. His flashlight illuminates the area beyond. "This is underneath the library. Jack's right. There are items used for the sacrament. They seem undisturbed. Perhaps even Reginald didn't know they were here. I can see a chest. Can you reach it, Jack?"

The boy shuffles back inside and pushes the chest through the gap. It is secured with straps, pulled tightly. Bjorn carries it upstairs. "Let's take a look."

51
Lunden 991

Esme was awakened by the clatter and shouts of the hunt moving out once again. From the window she noticed Roger de Caen among the riders, and heaved a sigh of relief. Yesterday, she had deliberately taken the evening meal in her chambers to avoid him. Already she'd seen enough to know he could never be the man for her. She had hoped to have an audience with the king today to express her view. Clearly that would now be impossible, but it did give her freedom to go outside. Being cooped up in the room gave her a headache.

A young maid brought in a bowl of water and some fresh clothes – a simple red dress which tied with a cord around the waist – unlike the elaborate green silk which she wore to meet the king. But Esme shunned them, preferring her riding clothes. At least they were her own.

She left the room and hurried down to the kitchen. Mildryth was nowhere to be seen, so Esme helped herself to milk and a fresh crust. From the open door she heard the sound of clashing wood and then a voice – it was Brand. She took the bread and hurried to the gate leading into the courtyard. There was her young brother. With him was Eirik, who was teaching him the preliminary moves of defence. Esme stood watching from the shade of a young oak tree.

Brand was eager to strike, but Eirik constantly sidestepped his blows and swiftly brought the wooden sword gently onto the boy's shoulder or chest. Brand was frustrated. "Why can't I do it?"

Eirik dropped the end of his weapon to the ground. "Because you're in too much haste. Wait. Lull your enemy into a false sense of security. Let him think he's getting the better of you. Then, when he attacks, you make your move."

Brand listened intently. He practised again and again, obtaining more control over the weapon. Esme smiled, feeling proud of her little brother.

Eirik stripped off his shirt; Brand did the same. After half an hour, Eirik stopped and wiped his brow. "Enough for one day."

Brand could hardly contain his excitement. "Please, let's stay longer."

"No. Your muscles are unused to the moves you've been making. Time to rest. We'll try again tomorrow."

Esme stepped forward from the shadow and Brand noticed her for the first time. "Esme, did you see me? Did you see me fighting? I've had such a wonderful time. Lord Eirik has been teaching me."

Esme put her arm around her brother's shoulder. "Yes, I saw. You were trying very hard."

"He's done well," said Eirik, pulling his shirt over his head. "This brother of yours has plenty of energy, I'll give him that."

Brand still had a sword in his hand and he waved it at his sister. "Eirik says my sword skills are improving. I have no lessons until tomorrow and he says he'll go for a ride with me. It won't be for long because he has things to do today. Will you come?"

Esme was surprised and pleased by the familiar way in which her brother referred to the Viking, as though they were friends. "I'd love to. But I'm not sure it's permitted. I was refused yesterday."

"I expect the king is anxious to protect you," said Eirik, with a slight hint of sarcasm. "But I'm sure there'll be no problem with two men to look after you."

Brand beamed with pride. "It's true. We'll protect you."

They walked to the stables. Esme asked the groom to saddle Kizzy. The young man looked at his feet. "I beg your pardon, my lady, but I have express orders not to allow you out alone."

Eirik took her arm. "I shall accompany Lady Esme and see she is safe. Saddle our horses," he said.

Esme took a deep breath, swallowed her indignation and said nothing.

The groom hesitated, then nodded and returned to the dimness inside.

Taking advantage of the low tide, they headed west, cantering along the banks of the river. Brand pulled up his pony on a wooden bridge and jumped down. "Come on, you two. Let's see whose stick can ride the stream the fastest."

Eirik frowned and looked bemused. "This is a game I've never played before."

"We all take a stick, drop it into the water on one side of the bridge then run across to the opposite side and see who's won. It's a race."

"Sounds like fun," said Eirik.

Brand dismounted, sought and found three sticks of roughly equal size, and leaned over the edge of the bridge. "Are we ready? Everyone drop their sticks . . . now."

The three of them raced across.

"I win," said Brand.

"No, you don't," said Esme. "That one in front is mine."

"It doesn't belong to either of you," said Eirik with a grin. "It's mine."

Brand pulled a face. "We'll have to do it again. I'll find some different shaped sticks."

This time Esme won. She gazed at Eirik with a triumphant glint in her eye. Her cheeks were flushed and she smiled with delight. The air was warm and the horses ambled. As the morning wore on, Esme was glad to see Brand so happy. She wondered whether Eirik had ever experienced such camaraderie with a child before. His behaviour towards her brother gave her an intensely warm feeling. She wanted so much to trust him, and pushed aside the underlying doubt about his possible motive.

They travelled a little further then stopped to rest on a stony shore hidden from the road by trees. Eirik waded into the softly lapping waves, scooping up a handful of water and splashing his face.

Esme picked up a couple of round, flat pebbles. "I bet I can skim these further than you. I've been doing it all my life."

Eirik bowed his head and raised his hand. "I accept the challenge."

Brand wandered away, searching for suitable pieces of shingle.

The stones bounced across the surface of the water one after the other. "You're good, wench," said Eirik, "but still have much to learn."

"Rubbish," said Esme, scowling, "just watch this one." She bent her knees and lobbed the missile with such force that her foot slipped on the unstable river bed and she lost her balance. Landing on her backside, she jolted her ribs and shrieked with annoyance at her own foolishness. The shooting pains reminded her that healing was not complete. Forcing a laugh at her predicament, she tried to gain a foothold, but each time she fell again. Eirik offered a hand but she refused, determined not to give in. Finally, she had no choice.

"Get me out of here," she yelled at a grinning Eirik.

"Since when do I take orders from a wench?"

Esme inclined her head. "Please."

Eirik reached down and hauled her out, but as he did so she splashed him, soaking his shirt and jerkin.

"Serves you right," she said.

"So that's how it is. This time you've gone too far." He gathered her up and drew her towards him. Then, taking a sharp breath, he released her immediately, seemingly surprised by his own actions. Her face remained close to his even after they parted. She could feel his breath on her cheek. Esme glanced at Brand, but he had his back to them, too busy testing how far he could throw his selected pebbles. She placed a cool palm over her warm cheeks, raking her fingers through the tumble of curls falling about her face.

Eirik stared at her. "You're so beautiful," he whispered. "You could seduce a stone statue."

Esme sensed the strong pumping of his heart. But still he waited, and ran his hand across his face, struggling to control the tension built up inside him, now threatening to explode. She understood.

At last Eirik spoke. "I hear the king intends to use you as a peace-weaver and you are to marry a Norman nobleman."

Esme tossed her hair. "That's what he wants, but it's not what he's getting."

Eirik furrowed his brows. "If you don't comply, you'll lose your land and Brand will inherit nothing."

"I shall rely on my skills and wits to make a living. I'm not sure Brand wants his inheritance anyway."

"Have you told Aethelred?"

"Not yet."

"You don't know what he might do."

Esme stretched. "Do you remember that moment outside the church before my marriage when you told me to never let any man break my spirit?"

Eirik nodded. "How could I ever forget? I blamed myself for allowing Edmund to take you."

"Be assured, no man shall ever do that to me again. Besides, it was you who always thought a woman should never marry for material gain alone."

"This is different. It's the king's orders."

The moment was interrupted by Brand running back towards them. "Hey, you two, what are you doing? Have you given up?"

Eirik turned towards Brand. "Right, young man, do your worst."

"Don't you mean my best?"

Eirik ruffled his hair. "Right. Let's see who can throw the furthest."

Brand sat in Esme's lodging eating supper. His talk was all of Eirik, what he'd taught him and the fun they'd had together that afternoon. "I like him. Can you marry him so he can be my father?"

"No, certainly not."

"Why not?"

"He's a heathen. Besides, he hasn't asked me."

"But he's promised to teach me how to play tafl. It's a Viking board game with battles." Brand thought for a moment. "I know, I'll ask him to ask you."

Esme laughed and threw a cushion at him. "Don't you dare!"

52

While Esme and Brand ate supper, Eirik, Thorkel and Fenrir met the king and Archbishop Sigeric of Canterbury, who was to sign the treaty with Aethelred. The ealdormen of two other West Saxon provinces, Elfric and Ethelweard, were to be witnesses. They all assembled in the king's quarters.

"Remember," said Thorkel, "this formal agreement means we have a truce which does not include any compensation for damage done before now, and we are not promising to defend England against other hordes which may descend upon it."

"I understand the terms," said Aethelred. "I'm expecting this to ensure protection from attack for English ships abroad, and we agree similar immunity for your merchants. For this peace we will give you a down payment of 10,000 pounds of silver with continuing payments up to 22,000 pounds."

Elfric gasped at the amount. "Outrageous," murmured Ethelweard.

The king gave each of his ealdormen a warning look. He turned to Thorkel. "I trust that will stop your onslaught for some time to come. I understand we are agreed that we shall continue with our plan to deliver it by boat tomorrow afternoon and may God protect you."

"Before we finish, there is another matter which I wish to discuss," said Eirik.

Fenrir knew he'd be unable to sleep. A life inside walls, sleeping in a bed of goose down, was not his way. He thought about what Esme had told him. Feeling restless, he strolled through to a sitting room hoping to find something to drink that might make him drowsy.

An elegantly dressed man sat absent-mindedly examining his finger nails. Fenrir scrutinised him. Was this Esme's intended husband?

"Good evening," said Fenrir entering the room. "Mind if I join you?"

The man merely raised his brows. "Please yourself," he said with a heavy Frankish accent. "There's wine, but no one to serve it – a quite scandalous lack of hospitality!"

Fenrir noticed a silver pitcher with matching goblets sitting on a side table next to the man's chair. He approached and helped himself. The man gestured with a languid wrist. "Fill mine up too."

Fenrir bristled at the man's lack of manners, but determined not to allow his growing dislike to interfere with his mission. He slumped onto a nearby couch, as though he could no longer take the strain of standing, and took a swig. "This wine is excellent and strong. Allow me to introduce myself. I'm Lord Fenrir. I don't believe we've met."

Finally, the man looked his way. "Count Roger de Caen."

"Pleased to meet you," said Fenrir. "Did you enjoy the hunt?"

The Norman snorted. "I have finer sport in my forests at home."

"You've been let down and I'm sorry to hear it. I hope your disappointment has been recompensed in other ways."

The count sighed. "Well, it has not. It's all most unsatisfactory." He took several large gulps, emptying his goblet.

Fenrir stood and reached for the pitcher. "Here, allow me," he said, topping up the man's wine once again. "Where is your home?"

"Normandy."

"Indeed? A lovely country. And, if you don't mind my asking, what is it that brought you to the abbey?"

The Norman's head wobbled slightly. Fenrir guessed the wine was taking effect. "An arrangement. Although it has yet to be fulfilled."

"Oh?" said Fenrir, relaxing in his seat once more.

"I'm here to meet a lady. It's for the benefit of the king, not for me, you understand."

"Of course," said Fenrir. "He must need your help."

"Yes, he does. To stop Viking raids on his south coast. They're making heavy demands on his purse. It happened in my own land. My grandfather told me how Charles, our Frankish king, offered large tracts of land to Vikings in an attempt to stop their raids."

"And did they?"

The count shrugged. "Their leader, Rollo, paid lip service to the crown. But over the last few generations they've integrated so much into our society that we've even adopted their name."

"Norsemen," said Fenrir.

"Normans. Yes, precisely."

"The same has happened here," said Fenrir. "So the king has offered you a wife in exchange for your help?"

"He has. The Lady Esme."

Fenrir smiled. "A fine filly."

The count bridled. "Sir, I would ask you to mind your language. You are speaking of the woman I shall marry."

"My apologies."

"I have yet to meet the lady, but I believe I glimpsed her from a window. She seems to be everything a man can desire."

"That depends on what you desire, I suppose," said Fenrir, twirling the wine in his goblet. "When I first met her she was dressed as a monk." He took a sip. "I think she likes to dress as a man."

"I beg your pardon?"

"Well, you know how it is with some women. They would like to be men, if they could."

Roger de Caen's mouth dropped open. "Explain yourself, sir."

"She was a prisoner of the Vikings for some time after the battle of Maeldun. Olaf's men were, let us say, fond of the ladies. She had to be rescued from their clutches."

"That's shocking." He was silent for several moments. "Do you think they damaged her?"

"It's my belief they certainly tried. But her late husband, Lord Edmund, believed it without a doubt."

"The king tells me the marriage was never consummated. He was arrested before he had the chance."

Fenrir sniffed. "Not before he had the chance to beat her half to death. He kicked her stomach so hard that it was many days before she recovered."

"Why would he do that? Why would a man kick his wife in the stomach?"

"Because he believed she was pregnant."

The count gasped. "Pregnant? By whom?"

"Come, sir, does it matter?"

The Norman looked aghast.

Fenrir shook his head slowly. "In fact, her husband kicked her stomach so hard I doubt she will ever be able to conceive."

Roger's eyes widened in disbelief. "No longer able to conceive?" He opened his palms. "Producing an heir is all important to my family's succession."

Fenrir shrugged. "Then if I were you, my lord, I'd look to the young fillies in your own court. Besides, I hear they're not as frigid as those from England."

"So you're telling me that this woman is frigid, has probably been raped, is unlikely to bear children, and prefers to dress as a member of the opposite sex?"

Fenrir adopted his most serious expression. "Forgive me for speaking so frankly."

Roger de Caen leaned forward and held out his arm. "Lord Fenrir, my friend, let me shake your hand. I think you may have done me a great service."

"How come, my lord?" said Fenrir, with innocence painted all over his hairy face.

"I must think very seriously about what you've told me. It seems I may have been duped into a very unwise choice of marriage."

Fenrir went to bed happy and, for the first time since arriving at the abbey, he slept extremely well.

53

Next morning, Mildryth knocked on Esme's door. "Did you peruse the threads, my lady?"

"I did. They are fine indeed."

"Put on this brown cloak and no one will know who you are. The stalls open early so we could go soon if you wish to look for yourself."

"Has my brother been taken to his lessons already?"

"He left a short time ago."

Esme's face lit up with a smile. "You are kind, Mildryth. I hate being confined. I'll come now."

Outside, a cart was harnessed. Mildryth pointed to the back. "Hide in there. I'll tell you when it's safe."

They passed the old wall and rode into the labyrinthine streets. Esme had no idea where they were, but was surrounded by the sounds of trade and longed to look. Eventually, Mildryth stopped and told her they'd arrived. They pulled up outside a wooden-fronted shop. Esme threw back her hood.

"You can get everything you need here. Go in and look around," said Mildryth. "I need to select a few items from the merchant across the road. I'll follow in a few minutes."

Esme shaded her eyes as she approached the entrance. Inside, the gloom enveloped her. Dimly, she could see a man seated at a table. He stood to greet her. Then she identified his voice. "Come in, my lady. I have waited a long time for a moment such as this," said Gunnar.

Esme's arms were pinned to her side by someone standing behind her. Gunnar sidled forwards and slipped her cloak from her shoulders. His fingers slid down her throat. "Lord Eirik has good taste in women. That's one matter on which we agree. It's a shame for him that he'll never taste you again. That is now to be my privilege."

"I would rather die first," said Esme.

Gunnar smirked. "That would be a dreadful waste. Besides, once you've experienced me, you may decide you prefer it."

There was a protest from the man behind her. "What about me? You promised I could take a turn after enduring that old cow."

"Indeed I did. And so you can, one day, when I've finished with her. She'll not feel the same once your dirty hands have pawed her."

Esme's knees were shaking. "You can't keep me here. I'm being accompanied by a member of the king's household. She'll be here soon and will report what's happened."

"You mean that obnoxious woman who works in the kitchens? Now believe it or not she's in love with Ulf here. She has no discernment in my view, but beggars can't be choosers."

Suddenly, all became clear. It was Ulf restraining her. Esme began to shake, realising the trap she'd fallen into and recognising the danger. She spat in Gunnar's face. He responded with a hard slap to her cheek and smirked. "I like a woman who puts up a fight. What other decadent skills do you have to excite a red-blooded male?"

"Do you not fear hell?"

"I went there many years ago, but, rest assured, I shall make absolutely sure that you join me there."

Esme struggled and kicked back at Ulf. Her boot caught his shin and he let out a yell.

"Quite the little vixen," said Gunnar. "However, I have something that will calm you down. Bring in the boy."

A henchman dragged in Brand. His mouth was stuffed with a cotton cloth and his hands were tied. Esme stifled a cry. "Let him go, he's only a child. He can serve no purpose in your plan."

"In that you are mistaken. He is my insurance you'll not try to run away, and that you'll do my every bidding. If not, he dies, and I shall take my time about it. First, I shall chop off his right hand, and then his left." He grabbed a tuft of Brand's hair and pulled back his head. The boy looked at him with revulsion. Gunnar grinned. "I do so enjoy hatred. It's such a stimulating emotion, more satisfying than lust."

Esme was breathing hard. "What do you want with us?"

"Surely you cannot be so ignorant? It's your Lord Eirik that I want, his arm and then his death."

"Then you are mistaken," said Esme. "Lord Eirik has no interest in me or my brother."

Gunnar observed her from under his heavy brow. "My, my, you're even more stupid than I thought. Lord Eirik will want to enjoy your body, the same as any man. Marriage allows a man unconditional rights. Your Bible says that as a wife you must not deny your husband. I quite like some bits of advice from your puny Christ."

"You are not worthy of even breathing the name of Our Lord."

Gunnar rocked back his head and laughed out loud. "If I had the time, my lady, I'd show you here and now what I think of the morality of your God. However, I have more pressing matters. But I promise tonight you will feel the full force of my violation, and you *will* please me. You'll have no time to think of other men." Gunnar barked an order to Ulf. "Bind her hand and foot. We'll collect the others and prepare our attack."

"Attack? What attack?" said Esme, the words tremulous.

Gunnar huffed. "Ah, I see you're interested after all. Your Viking thinks he's so clever carrying silver by river, but I can assure you he'll feel my blade before Grenewic."

At that moment Mildryth arrived. "I trust you've made all the appropriate excuses," said Gunnar, "buying provisions, taking my lady to her brother's oratory lessons and listening to some edifying musical entertainment this evening?"

Mildryth smiled and curtsied. "I have, lord." The woman looked coyly at Ulf expecting some approbation, but none was forthcoming. There was a sneer on his lips. The joy fell from her face. She glanced briefly at Esme and Brand, both trussed.

"Well now, Mildryth," said Gunnar, "we have an important job for you to do until tonight. Keep guard over the woman. Make sure she doesn't escape." He turned once more to Esme. "I look forward to seeing you this evening, my sweet. I shall come back a wealthy man, able to offer you anything your little heart desires. Perhaps you'll change your tune then."

"Never!"

"Dear me, I shall have great fun taming that temper of yours in our years together."

To Mildryth there was a veiled threat that she and Ulf would never live together as man and wife if their plans were thwarted. The older woman looked terrified and wrung her hands. "Here, Mildryth," said Gunnar, "I'm leaving you a dagger. I sharpened it myself this morning. If she's any trouble, stab her."

"Oh, sir—"

"No need to kill her, woman. Stab her in a place where it hurts – shoulder, thigh. But keep her alive. She's no good to me dead."

Mildryth looked sceptical. "Alright, sir. I'll do it."

Gunnar turned to Esme. "You'll forgive me if I take your little brother with us as warranty. Should Mildryth report any attempt by you to escape, you can be sure you will never see him again. Ulf, blindfold the boy and take him outside."

Esme pleaded. "Take me instead. I'm guilty in your eyes but the boy has done you no harm. He's innocent."

Gunnar scoffed. "You really don't know the teachings of your God. In *His* eyes, we are all born into sin, shackled by guilt."

Esme wriggled and kicked out. But Ulf was ready and her efforts were futile.

54

The men left, taking Brand with them. Esme was seated on the floor with her hands tied behind her back; her feet bound in front of her. She glanced around the room. It was full of cotton, linens and even silk with threads of different colours. The array was perfect, and under different circumstances she would love to examine the goods. But her situation was dire – trussed up, unable to move, and with Brand in immense danger. She knew it would be useless to try appealing to Mildryth. The woman was besotted. She needed a different approach. Mildryth sat at a table on the other side of the room, her thighs drooping over the edges of the seat. She took up some sewing.

"What are you making?" Esme asked her.

"A nice new shirt for my Ulf. I'm embroidering it too." A look of serenity crossed her face. "It's for our wedding."

"He's lucky to have you."

A hint of a smile crossed Mildryth's lips. "Not as lucky as I am to have him."

Esme nodded. "I agree. A woman is fortunate to have a loving man to marry."

Mildryth rested her needlework on her knees. "He does love me. He's always telling me so. When he asked me to marry him, well, my happiness was complete."

"When is the wedding?"

"Once Ulf has made his money. It shouldn't be long now. He and Gunnar have plans."

"Sounds exciting. Do the plans involve you?"

Mildryth sniffed disdainfully. "Of course they do. I'm involved right now by keeping you here all day, so they can get on with what they've got to do."

"Heavens! That's a responsibility for you. Will you also be part of what they're doing tonight?"

Mildryth frowned. "I'm not quite sure what will happen later." She grinned. "I just know we'll all be very wealthy."

"Wealthy? It must be a clever plan."

"Yes, it is." She stretched from the waist and sat up straight. "And I was the one who gave them the idea."

"No wonder Ulf loves you so much. He must think he'll have the best and cleverest wife in England."

"Well, I hear a lot of confidential information working for the king. I'm in a unique position because he trusts me."

Esme hesitated, enlightenment dawning. "Have you been disloyal to him?"

Mildryth shook her head so that wisps of grey hair fell from their pins. "I wouldn't let him down. I've known Aethelred for a long time."

Esme remained silent, allowing the older woman to contemplate what she'd just said. Eventually Mildryth looked up, jutting out her chin. "I told my Ulf about the money Aethelred has been forced to give to those despicable Vikings. The king was advised to sign a treaty with those marauders by our archbishop – the old fool. This afternoon they're taking silver to those wicked men by boat. My Ulf is helping to steal it back." She gave Esme a look of self-satisfaction. "Now then, that's not being disloyal, is it? My Ulf says I'm doing the country a service."

"But how can that be if Ulf intends to keep the money? When the Vikings see it's been stolen, they'll just demand more."

"But the king won't have to give it again, will he? After all, he's given it once. It's up to them as received it to look after it." So saying, she resumed her needlework.

Esme could understand the misguided logic of her thinking. She almost felt sorry for this woman who'd been duped by her so-called lover – a man who would no doubt take off like an arrow once he got what he wanted. "Mildryth, how long have you known the king?"

"All his life. I raised him. I'm sorry I shall have to leave him once I'm a married woman. I was rather hoping Aethelred might find a position for my Ulf at the abbey so we could both live there."

"Do you really think the king will do that once he knows what you've done? Won't he be more inclined to think you've betrayed him?"

Mildryth's face reddened. She stood, causing the sewing to slip off her lap onto the floor, and shook an index finger at Esme. "You, girl, don't you go suggesting such a thing. The king will know what I'm trying to do." She scooped up the shirt and slumped back onto the chair.

Esme knew her tactic was failing; the woman had been totally convinced by Ulf's argument. She would have to escape by means other than Mildryth's guilty conscience. A sewing basket was sitting on the table. Surely it contained a pair of scissors – an essential tool for the seamstress. "Do you mind if I come and sit with you and watch what you're doing? It's very uncomfortable on the floor."

The old woman thought for a moment. "Can't see any harm in it, so long as you're tied up."

Esme rolled onto her knees. "Can you take a moment to help me stand? It's difficult with my ankles tied."

Mildryth walked over and helped Esme to her feet. Esme hopped to another chair by the table and sat down. She looked with feigned interest at the garment Mildryth was making, praying for some distraction. At that moment, as luck would have it, they heard the tinkle of a small bell at the front of the store. Mildryth was startled, "Is that a customer? Ulf must have forgotten to lock the door." She was about to bustle through to greet the punter but then remembered the dagger. She grabbed it and put it in her pocket. "Don't want you getting hold of this," she said, as if speaking to a small child in danger of cutting herself.

As soon as Mildryth was out of the room, Esme stood and turned her back to the sewing basket. She fumbled inside, relieved to find some scissors – sharp ones at that judging by the feel of the blades. She took hold of them, but with numb fingers it was difficult to manoeuvre them into position.

She had made little progress when Mildryth suddenly returned. "You can put those down as soon as you like, my girl. Thought you'd get one over on me, did you?" She snatched the scissors away. "I see now what you were doing. Get back over there on the floor. Go on." She took Esme by the shoulder and pushed her across the room.

"You can't blame me for trying," said Esme. "My brother is in danger. I need to save him."

"Don't you worry none about him. My Ulf will see he's treated well."

Despair began to paralyse Esme's thinking. Time was ticking by. She had to escape and warn the king so they could save Brand. *Concentrate, woman*, she told herself, *try to stay calm*. On her right was a set of shelves, standing a foot or two into the room, each one piled high with rolls of cloth and reels of cotton. It wobbled precariously as she leaned against it. A rusty nail, sticking out from the bottom of the wall, indicated the place where the unit had once been secured before splitting away under its own weight. A quick glance showed that Mildryth was still engrossed in her sewing.

Holding out her wrist at an awkward angle, Esme shuffled closer

267

to the spike, testing its strength. It was firmly embedded. She gently moved the rope back and forth. After a while, her back and arms ached, her neck was stiff, but she continued. Mildryth appeared to be asleep, eyes closed, chin hanging on her chest, breathing rhythmical. Gradually, the hemp began to fray. Then, suddenly, it snapped and Esme was free. She sat for a moment massaging her wrists, allowing the blood to flow back into her hands.

She began to untie her ankles. Just at that moment, Mildryth woke with a start and looked at her. "What have you done?" she screeched, grabbing the dagger and approaching with it held out in front of her. Esme gave the unstable shelves a push. They rocked and began to shed their load. Materials unwound. Skeins of wool rolled away into every crevice. Mildryth tripped on a spool of thread, stumbled backwards and fell heavily, hitting her head. The whole contraption teetered becoming more and more unbalanced, until finally it toppled forwards, pinning Mildryth's legs underneath. Esme shuffled across the floor to examine her; the woman was unconscious but her breathing was regular. She stuffed a small piece of Ulf's new shirt into Mildryth's mouth, just enough to stop her crying out. Then, scrambling to her feet, she shoved the dagger in her belt and escaped into the street.

55

It appeared to be market day. Folk milled around stalls selling everything from fresh vegetables to intricately designed buckles. The sun had moved south and sparkled on the river. Water was the quickest way back, Esme reasoned, if only she could find a boat. She ran down a side street. It ended in a warehouse. Tense and frustrated, she retraced her steps and tried another. After zigzagging through a maze of turns she finally reached the shore. There were docks to the right and left, but no towpath by which she could reach either.

She stood with arms on hips, angry and in despair. Then, from a narrow inlet, came a boy rowing a small boat. Esme waved frantically at him. At first he looked confused, but then he began to pull towards her. "Can you help me?" she shouted.

"Where do you want to go?"

"To the abbey."

"Where the king lives sometimes?"

"Yes."

The boy frowned. "I'm not supposed to—"

"I'll pay you," said Esme.

"How much?"

"How much do you want?"

"Silver."

"Done," said Esme, pulling from her pocket the coins with which she'd intended to buy threads that morning. "Here, will these do?"

The boy grinned and, leaping into the shallow water, he pulled his tiny craft ashore to allow Esme to climb into it. He took the proffered money. "Thank you," he said, as she lowered herself onto a bench.

"What's your name?"

"Esme," she said, spreading out her arms to steady herself as he pushed the boat back into the river. "What's yours?"

"Caesar," he said with pride. "Like the Roman general."

"Well, Caesar, are you any good in battles?"

"Yes, Esme, very good. You want me to fight for you?"

"Yes, please. Start by rowing as hard as you can."

And the boy did. It seemed a very short time before Esme spotted the landing stage where she stood on that first day. Had she been here only three days? As she climbed onto the shingle, Caesar said, "Would you like me to wait for you, Esme?"

"What about your parents?"

Caesar shrugged. "They're dead. I live among the homeless. We do well. I catch fish. We cook. Market traders give us old vegetables."

"Where do you sleep?"

Caesar pursed his lips as though it was a stupid question. "Under my upturned boat."

She looked at him. He couldn't be more than fourteen. Life had turned him into a strong and self-reliant young man. "Please wait then. But I don't know how long I'll be."

He nodded. "I'll not be far away. I have fish to catch. Wave if you need me. I never miss a good fight."

Esme ran through the gardens. Some of the warriors were practising, being observed by the abbot. "I must see the king," she said to him, breathlessly.

The abbot regarded her with suspicion. "What's wrong?"

"His money – the Danegeld – there are plans to steal it. I was kidnapped. My brother is in danger. Please help me."

"He's busy in talks with Lord Eirik and Thorkel."

"So much the better," she said. "It's a matter of life or death."

The abbot decided to act. "Come with me. I'll interrupt the meeting. But you'd better be speaking the truth—"

"I am. And thank you."

After a short wait, she was summoned into the king's chamber. All three men stared as she walked in. Eirik stepped forward to greet her.

"What's the matter, Esme," asked Aethelred.

"There's a plot to capture the silver being taken to Olaf Tryggvason later today."

"How do you know this?"

"I was kidnapped this morning by Gunnar." She glanced at Eirik. "A delivery man called Ulf sweet-talked Mildryth, offering marriage. She took me to a shop selling materials. I escaped. Brand was there too. They've taken him with them. Threatened to cut off his hands. Sire, please, help me."

Esme was aware that her account was garbled but Aethelred understood. "It's as you feared, Eirik," he said. "Gunnar is out for revenge. Go ahead with your revised plan."

Esme looked on in horror. "If you change the arrangement they'll kill my brother. He's expecting you to take the silver by river, but assured me you would never reach Grenewic. He intends killing you."

Eirik put his arm around her shoulder. "Don't worry, Esme. Gunnar won't harm Brand until he meets with us. All he wants is the money. Your information is most valuable. At least we now know roughly where his attack will be."

"There are three small tributaries before Grenewic," said Aethelred. "The first is not far beyond the old Roman town and traders may still be unloading. I suspect it will be the second to Stybbanhype. It's on a bend making it easier to hide."

"But then what will happen?" said Esme. A prickly heat at the back of her eyes was threatening tears.

"Then he will feel the full force of our anger."

"I must come with you."

"I absolutely forbid it, Esme," said the king. "Your life has been in enough danger already. You did well to get away. I'll hear more about it later – once your brother has been rescued."

By mid-afternoon the plans were underway. Aethelred's monks made trips to the river using a cart loaded with sacks, which they humped into the bottom of the cargo boat. They had also sewn a number of small pouches onto a belt which Eirik ostentatiously lifted over his head, settling it across his chest and under his arm. He noticed two men in a vessel moored on the other side of the river who had been watching for some time. Eirik grimaced, satisfied.

Soon they were ready to leave. Clouds began to gather, covering the sun. "Sky's as black as Freya's cauldron over yonder," said Fenrir. "Looks like rain."

Two monks, proficient in sailing, stayed on board: one in charge of the tiller, the other tending to the rigging. "The wind's getting up," said one. "Let's stow the oars for later. The sail will be enough for now."

"Where do you think they'll strike?" asked Fenrir.

"Beyond the old walled town of Lundenburgh. There's very little trading activity after that, and there are two or three tributaries before Grenewic where they can hide and then strike. The king suspects it will be the second. It's wider."

"Except we'll be ready for them," said Fenrir.

"I hope so," said Thorkel. "This had better work for all our sakes, and for the boy's life."

Eirik was as taut as the string on a lyre. His eyes glimpsed this way and that, observing everything, missing nothing. Esme had watched as they pushed away from the jetty, like any other cargo boat going about its everyday dealings. But she couldn't simply wait in the abbey while Brand was in danger. She looked around for Caesar. Wave, he'd said, so she did just that.

Within moments he appeared, grinning. "Are we going to fight now? I have a sharp dagger. Use it for gutting fish."

"Can you keep up with a cargo boat? I need to rescue someone."

"Where's it going?"

"Down river. Towards Grenewic."

"Hop in. I'll fetch my brother. He's expecting us."

They pulled into a dock where another boy sat waiting in a sailing dinghy. Except for one having slightly lighter-coloured hair, both boys had identical features. "This is my brother Julius," said Caesar. "His boat is bigger and faster than mine."

Caesar held Esme's hand while she alighted onto the quay and stepped into Julius' craft causing it to sway. It lurched once again as the boy jumped in and sat down beside his brother. Julius smiled at her, and despite her churning stomach she couldn't help but smile back. Who better than Julius and Caesar to take into battle?

56
Norwich 1979

Bjorn puts the chest on the floor in the living room and opens up the lid.

Emma peers inside. "There are two tubular-shaped packages. The one on top is much smaller than the one below." She carefully unravels the top few layers of leather, uncovering the cherished pages enclosed within its folds. "It's a manuscript, penned on vellum."

"Can you read it?" asks Bjorn.

"Yes. It's in Old English."

Bjorn shakes his head, "What an amazing woman you are."

"It must have been copied once or twice since the tenth century. It's called 'Where Ravens Circle'. She looks up with moist eyes. "It's written by Esme herself."

Bjorn gives Emma's shoulders a squeeze. "That's terrific."

"What's in the larger parcel?" asks Greta.

Emma unties the bundle to reveal the needlework. She gasps. "It's exquisite. The embroidery illustrates the tale. Each square represents a scene."

"It's so beautiful," Greta breathes.

"And to think that Reggie used to hang his coat on the very hook that opened the panel." Emma hugs Jack and Greta, one in each arm, and Bjorn puts his arms round all of them.

Jack screws up his face, embarrassed, but Greta revels in her father's approval. "Do we deserve a reward now, Papa?"

"I must admit we would never have found this without you both. So, we might think of something for each of you in the future."

"May we keep the silver?" Jack says hopefully.

"Certainly not," says his mother. "I know who to contact about moving it to somewhere safe."

"Okay," he says with resignation. Then his face brightens. "Perhaps the cathedral will give us a reward. After all, they didn't know their treasure was here."

"Jack, don't be so mercenary."

Greta springs to his defence. "If you don't ask, you never get."

Her father's sigh is emphatic. "You are like two peas in a pod. Whatever are we to do with you?"

Bjorn goes back down the stairs to the cellar, secures the beam and closes the panel, replacing the cap and coat. Then he searches the outbuildings for plywood and nails to board up the window in Reginald's bedroom.

Emma is still uneasy about who might have been in the house. While Bjorn is busy she replaces the manuscript and embroidery and takes the chest to the car. As she turns back to the house, a tall, grey-haired man, about sixty years of age, walks down the drive. "Hello," he says. "I'm sorry to disturb you. My name is Charles Burbridge. I live just up the road. Are you the new owners?"

Emma nods and introduces herself.

"My wife looked after Mr Reed for several years. When he went into hospital, he accidentally took all the keys with him, and we never saw him again. I must apologise but I broke in through a window with a loose catch and took the one belonging to the French windows. I've come to return it. My wife came yesterday to clean. Mr Reed always paid in advance."

"Ah, that solves a mystery," says Emma. "I saw things had been moved."

"Mr Reed also asked her to keep any mail that came while he was away." He hands her a letter. "This arrived last week."

"Thank you," says Emma.

"Will you be moving in?" says Charles.

"The house actually belongs to my mother. I think she's undecided as yet."

"Well, we're at Number 46 if you need anything."

"Thank you."

Emma is overjoyed to read the contents of the letter as all becomes clear.

Dear Mr Reed,

This is to let you know that the translation of 'Phoebe's Story' is ready for collection. We can arrange postal delivery if you wish. We await your instructions. I am attaching an invoice for your convenience.

Yours faithfully,

Harold Makepeace-Brown

Fleet Street

57
Lunden 991

The sky darkened. The cargo boat pitched and rolled under increasingly strong gusts; the rain was torrential by the time they reached the first tributary on their right. As predicted, it was at the second when the longboat suddenly appeared, bearing down on them – narrower, sleeker and faster. Eirik counted twelve men on board, including Gunnar. All held spears except the steersman and one other, who was holding a knife at Brand's throat. Eirik sucked in breath through his teeth. Even though he'd been expecting this, the sight still perturbed him.

"Thor's hammer," Fenrir bellowed. "The poor little fellow must be frightened out of his wits."

"Do nothing until I give the order," said Eirik. "We must see the boy safe."

A crack louder than thunder pierced the air as the longboat collided with their hull. Two grappling hooks clawed the bulwark. Gunnar and Ulf climbed aboard and stood facing Eirik. Gunnar was smiling. "I see you're being sensible. You're outnumbered."

Eirik clenched his fist around the hilt of his sword.

"Don't move," said Gunnar, jerking his thumb behind him, "or the boy dies. My man will not hesitate to kill him. You wouldn't want to upset his sister, would you?" He smirked. "By the way, you may like to hear she's safely tucked up and looking forward to my visit tonight. I don't intend to disappoint her."

"What do you want?" hissed Eirik.

"Don't underestimate my intelligence. I know the king has paid you handsomely." He eyed the belt that Eirik was wearing. "How much is in there?"

"Half the amount."

Gunnar's eyes glistened. "Half of 22,000 pounds? Prove it. Open one of those pouches."

Eirik suddenly realised that Mildryth must have misheard the idea of the 10,000 pounds down payment. Or perhaps she simply misunderstood. All she'd taken note of was the total due, which Gunnar was now expecting. "They're stitched," he said. "I'd have to cut it. See for yourself."

At that moment the boat lurched. Gunnar wrapped the stump of his arm around the rigging to stop himself from falling. He growled and narrowed his eyes, weighing up his options for several moments. Then he said, "No. Don't bother. Coins are useful to me. None must be lost."

He cast his eye around the sacks, "And the rest?"

"Hack-silver," said Eirik.

Gunnar sneered. "That stuff will need melting down – most inconvenient. I'll take charge of the money-belt. I wouldn't want you accidentally lobbing it over the side while I kill you. Ulf, secure it across my chest." He wriggled his shoulders as Ulf did as he was asked. Gunnar smiled. "That tasty whore of yours will be pleased. I understand she likes wealthy men."

Eirik's body tensed. "If you've touched her—"

"You'll what? Cut off my other arm? We'll soon see who'll be losing an arm today."

"You've got what you want. Release the boy."

Gunnar laughed. "You didn't really think I'd give either of them back, did you? How naïve of you, my friend. I'm not finished yet. I have more to do – an arm for an arm."

"Have mine. Let them go."

"My, my, you've just confirmed what I always thought. It's so much worse seeing someone you love being hurt. I think a lady's arm, plus that of a boy, might make up for a man's, don't you?"

Eirik bristled but restrained himself, biding his time.

Gunnar spoke to his men. "Heave those sacks on board."

There was a moment's confusion. The men paused, looked at each other, then all started simultaneously to make a move towards the cargo boat.

"Now," Eirik yelled.

In a heartbeat, the sacks stirred. Fifteen of the king's best trained monks sprang up, bearing weapons. An axe whipped through the air; its sharp edge split open the ribcage of an astonished raider, who tottered on the rim before falling into the water. A spear landed in the neck of another. Eirik threw a dagger into the man who was holding Brand and saw him crumple to the deck. Then he leapt onto the longboat, recovered his knife and began cutting the rope binding Brand's wrists.

Gunnar followed, first slicing through the grapnel ropes with his sword. Brand shouted a warning and Eirik swung round a moment too late as the blade dug into his upper arm. The boat reeled and he stumbled backwards, clutching his wound. Gunnar gave a triumphant cry. "See, I promised revenge – an arm for an arm."

*

Esme was impressed by the brothers' agility. They handled the oars with long, powerful strokes, and made good headway, pulling in harmony with speed until they were beyond the edge of the old town. It was there that she saw the cargo vessel; a longboat had drawn alongside. The scene was chaotic. Men were fighting. Several hurtled overboard. She gasped as she glimpsed Brand, tied to the mast. Then she saw Eirik, who seemed to be freeing her brother. But the man climbing awkwardly into the longboat had released the grapnel ropes. The two vessels floated apart. Gunnar! She screamed in abject fear as he raised his sword and she could no longer see Eirik. Where was he? Then Brand reappeared, standing on the edge of the bulwark.

She shouted at the top of her voice, frantically waving her arms. "Brand! Jump! I'm here." For a second the boy hesitated, staring at the row boat. Then he dived into the choppy waters. The waves consumed his body. For several moments she lost sight of him. Panic ensued. She knew he could swim, she had taught him herself, but these conditions were grave. Could he survive them?

She scanned the area where he entered the river until she spotted him. His head bobbed out of the water. "Over there," she yelled to Caesar, pointing. The two boys pulled on the oars, swinging the boat around time and time again, until they reached Brand. Esme seized his shoulders, holding onto him with all her strength until Julius heaved him aboard.

"Thank God you're safe," she said, hugging her brother close.

Brand took several deep breaths, water running down his face, until he recovered sufficiently to sit up. "Eirik – he's injured. I think that man Gunnar cut off his arm."

Esme shouted through the squall. "Caesar, Julius, can you get closer? A friend needs our help."

They fought the wind and the rain, but the longboat had already drifted into the middle of the Thames. Caesar shook his head. "Someone needs to get control of it – fast."

Brand pointed. "Look, there they are."

Esme watched, horrified. Brand was right. Eirik and Gunnar were wrestling; neither of them had a weapon. One of Eirik's arms seemed to be hanging useless at his side. They were evenly matched. Gunnar heaved himself up onto the edge of the boat and Eirik pursued him. Then a violent gust sent the craft listing steeply to one side and they both slid into the swell.

Caesar and Julius grabbed the oars and tugged with all their strength while Esme and Brand looked out for Eirik. The blackness had swallowed both men together.

Then she heard a voice through the wind. An unmistakable, gruff voice: Fenrir. The cargo ship was pulling closer to them; sail furled; oars in position. Fenrir was waving his arms. Esme squinted in the direction he was indicating and there, through the squall, she saw Eirik, dipping in and out of the waves, tossed about like driftwood as he struggled to stay afloat. The row boat was nearest, and the first to reach him.

"Here, Esme, take the oars," said Caesar. "Keep it steady while we save your man."

58

Early next day, Aethelred asked to see Esme. He stood and took hold of both her hands as she entered. "Esme, my dear, how are you after such a dreadful ordeal?"

"I am much recovered, Sire."

"Good. Good. And is Brand fully recovered too?"

"He is. He's resilient and seems to have no ill effects. In fact, last night, after a hot bath, he could talk of nothing else except what he chose to see as his adventure."

Aethelred smiled. "It seems he has the making of a great warrior."

"Have you heard how Eirik is?" asked Esme.

"The doctor has been with him. He's lost blood and has a fever. His arm is stitched and swathed in bandages, but the doctor is fairly certain it will heal despite the severity of the wound. Fortunately it's not his fighting arm. That's as strong as ever. Meanwhile, he's been given a sedative. There was no other way of forcing him to rest. He's strong. I'm sure time and sleep will cure him. Fenrir is with him. He's in the hands of God."

But which god? Esme thought, heaving a sigh. "When can I see him?" she said, adding, "I must thank him."

"The doctor asks that we wait until tomorrow. I promise I'll let you know. I need to speak to him myself first." He patted a place next to him on a couch in the window. "Please, sit and tell me what happened."

"There's not much to tell, Sire. I thought Mildryth was being kind to me at first. I wanted some threads. Her friend Ulf provided some. She offered to take me to a shop where I could select my own. Instead she lured me to a man called Gunnar." She stopped. "What happened to him?"

"His body was washed up at low tide this morning. Lord Eirik's money-belt must have slipped off his shoulder. He was clutching it in his hand. Perhaps if he'd let go he could have survived. Who knows? No doubt his intention was to sail back to Denmark with a hoard of silver, but there is no honour in the way he died. He'll not be sitting today in the Hall of Valhalla."

"All that silver lost," Esme mused.

"No need to worry. The pouches were full of lead and there was no hack-silver – just some of my best fighters hiding beneath the sacks."

She opened her eyes wide. "Lead? But I saw the monks loading up the cargo boat."

"Eirik suspected his old enemy would be watching from the river. Fenrir saw Gunnar in a local hostelry with the man we now know as Ulf. Lord Eirik became suspicious."

"So that's what he meant by a change of plans – men and lead instead of silver."

"Yes. He assumed Gunnar would be out for revenge. I understand he lost his arm during Eirik's apparent execution." Aethelred grinned. "It's a good story."

"Yes. Fenrir told me."

"Eirik convinced me to take some precautions. He's a good man, a capable warrior."

Esme hesitated. "I cannot disagree with you there, Sire."

The king raised an eyebrow. "Do I sense a hint of liking?"

Esme's cheeks grew warm. "Well, yes, he saved Brand." She changed the subject quickly – perhaps too quickly. She hoped the king hadn't noticed. "So, what happened to the silver?"

"It'll be safely on its way to the King of Denmark tomorrow."

"Does that mean the fighting will stop?"

"I think it may cease for a while. But, to be truthful, as I told you, my present power and control is insufficient to keep the peace. It won't be long before there's further trouble. Then more money will be demanded." He sighed. "But tell me, how did Mildryth learn of our plans?"

Esme shrugged. "She must have been serving wine at table while they were being discussed."

"Of course, I remember now, she was there. I hardly took any notice." The king shook his head sadly. "She's been with me since I was a child when I first came to the throne. She practically raised me. How is it I seem to be surrounded by people I once trusted who have now turned against me?"

"In Mildryth's defence I believe she was duped. Ulf was working for Gunnar. He wormed his way into Mildryth's affections and promised her marriage and wealth if she would help him. She was in love."

"Ah yes – love – a faultless emotion that lands us in all sorts of trouble. But this is treason, and I must deal with it as such. Still, I can't help feeling sorry for the poor, deluded woman. She was in a very distressed state when we recovered her. The man she thought to marry is dead. Instead, she is now homeless with no source of income."

Esme looked thoughtful. "Like Caesar and Julius."

"Those young men who helped you seem particularly resourceful. I shall see to it they are well rewarded. Now, tell me how Brand came to be kidnapped."

"Mildryth told his tutor she was taking him to oratory lessons, followed by a musical performance."

"I must deal with that man for not checking more carefully." Aethelred sat back in his chair. "One thing interests me. Why did you go with Mildryth when I gave specific orders that you were not to leave the grounds?"

"I'm not used to idleness. I use my embroidery skills to renew tapestries."

"Edmund allowed this?"

"I must be honest with you, Sire, I'm not sure he knew, or even cared."

"Nevertheless, you disobeyed me."

"I'm sorry." Esme bowed her head and folded her hands in her lap.

The king leaned forward and lifted her chin. "Were you hoping to escape?"

"Yes. I confess I was."

"Why, when you have everything you need?"

"The thought of being married to Roger de Caen was unbearable. He was an insufferable prig."

Aethelred laughed. "Frankly, I don't blame you. I was most unimpressed with his hunting skills. His incompetence cost me a shot at a magnificent stag."

Esme looked at him, pleased that he agreed with her but dismayed by his reason. "With respect, Sire, you cannot compare hunting skills with those of a husband."

The king laughed again, "Why not? An incompetent hunter is bound to be an incompetent husband. But you scarcely had occasion to meet him since you were recovering in your room."

"I saw how he treated his horse and servant from my window. That was enough for me to know I could never be his wife."

Aethelred stroked his chin. "I can see you will be difficult to please."

Esme saw her chance to persuade the king. "Then why not release me, Sire? I want nothing except to be allowed to go back to Maeldun, to live with my friends and continue my craft. I'm sure I can earn enough to keep myself and my brother. We don't mind about the land or the house. Please take them both."

"You have no desire for a suitable husband?"

Esme hesitated. "Yes, but only one of my own choosing. Someone I can love and respect."

Aethelred leaned forward and patted her hand. "In that case, Esme, I have some very good news for you. I thought you might be disappointed, but now I see I have no need to let you down gently. Count Roger has decided he doesn't want you. In fact, he's gone home."

Esme's eyes lit up, unable to hide her delight. "There, you see, we were not meant for one another."

"So it would seem."

"Did he give you a reason?"

Aethelred peered at her from under his brows. "I see you are interested in your desirability after all."

"No. Not my desirability. It's just idle curiosity about what changed his mind since we never met."

"Well, if you must know, he had some concerns about your ability to provide heirs for his dynasty."

"Heirs!" Esme raised her eyes to the ceiling. "You see, I'm not suitable as a peace-weaver after all. Any man who wishes to maintain his line will discard me."

The king pursed his lips. "I very much regret that may be the truth – brutal as it seems. Would you like me to search for another who has no such qualms?" He grinned. "Perhaps one who is also good at hunting?"

Esme hastened to answer. "No. Please, Sire, I beg you."

Aethelred grew serious. "In that case, Esme, I have another proposition. You may keep the land that was always intended for you and you may keep the income. Furthermore, you can engage in whatever skills you choose. However, I would like first claim on the wood from your estate, since the crown will need ships. You may marry whomever you choose. Or remain unmarried if that is your preference. If you wish to leave your lands to your brother, likewise, the decision is yours. And may God go with you."

Tears rolled down Esme's cheeks, small channels of happiness. "Thank you, Sire. Thank you."

59

The following day, Eirik was stronger. He'd moved from the bed to a chair and stood when Aethelred called upon him. The king indicated he was to remain in his seat and chose another for himself. "How are you?"

"Fully recovered," said Eirik, "and confess I'm unused to this indulgent treatment."

"Well, you'll have to live with it for a while. You're my guest. I hear your arm has survived."

"I don't think the injury was ever severe."

"That's not what my doctor said. But you must now be sensible. I need you to be fit."

Eirik wondered what he meant but refused to inquire. No doubt he would be told in the fullness of time.

The king stretched out his legs. "A pity you didn't come hunting the other day. I arrowed the most beautiful stag. His head will grace my walls for years to come."

"I think his head would look rather better on his body, Sire."

Aethelred twitched his lips. "I see you're not a hunting man."

"Only of men."

"And it is on that account that I wish to speak to you. I'll come straight to the point. Continued taxation of my people in order to pay Danegeld will send us into bankruptcy in time. I prefer to strengthen my ability to defend this country."

"I understand."

"I've heard tell of the prowess of your mercenaries, Lord Eirik. I know they are fighters par excellence. I would take great comfort in having them on my side. Furthermore, it has not escaped my notice how well you deal with my warrior monks. They need someone strong to lead them. They've been most complimentary about your skills and techniques, and already have great respect for you."

"That's most gratifying."

"Yes – and, unlike so many of my advisers, they are loyal to the crown." Aethelred pulled down his mouth to one side. "Not an attribute I am accustomed to these days. So, I'm offering you the position of commander of my warriors. The abbot takes care of their spiritual needs, but I want someone to turn my men into the very best fighting force they can be. For that, I need someone I can trust. Are you interested?"

Eirik wasn't sure whether he was expecting this proposition or not – maybe something of the sort – but hearing it put into words was worth serious consideration, especially as it was exactly what he hoped for, providing the conditions were acceptable. He shrugged. "I might be."

"Naturally, it depends on what I'm offering. But before we discuss terms, I'd like to know how you feel about defending my coastlines. Despite our treaty, I have no guarantee that Olaf will keep his word, or any other Viking army who fancies attacking these shores. And as far as Sweyn Forkbeard is concerned, he wishes to be king of this land. I know that. And one day he will try to take it from me. I am determined to prolong that from happening."

"I cannot be everywhere at once – both here and there."

"If the men are well trained the responsibilities can be delegated. Some need to be able to act as spies, to keep watch on the southern coast where the Normans may allow my enemies to shelter for the winter, ready to attack. I'd like you to make plans to protect the city. We need to maintain central control. If Lunden falls, the country falls. Would your followers be interested?"

Eirik was thoughtful. "My men may be monks but they are also mercenaries, and do not bend to the will of Denmark, Norway or England. They will go to the highest bidder. It has always been so."

"I'm prepared to pay well."

"I can talk to them and ask how many would wish to accept such terms. There are some who now want to return to their homeland. They've been away for a long time, but many of the younger ones will remain true to whoever pays the most."

"And what of you, Eirik? What is it you're demanding?"

Eirik took a deep breath, "My demands are simple. I want Lady Esme."

Aethelred's face puckered into a grin. "I think most men in England would care to be married to Esme. But I seriously doubt Esme would be prepared to marry a heathen."

"Well, I intend to ask her, but I'd like something to offer her – land, in England. Personally I have no need of your silver."

A small smirk played around the king's lips as though he was taking part in a game. "I have recently sequestrated the estates that belonged to her erstwhile husband – Lord Edmund. I'm prepared to pass the title to you, should Lady Esme be prepared to marry you. After all, it is no more than I would have offered the Norman."

"Could you ever have trusted a Norman?"

The king smiled. "You are correct. I have never trusted them. But at least that one was a Christian. I'm not sure Esme would want to marry a follower of Thor."

"You need have no worry on that account."

The king placed his hands behind his head. "Are you sure you can cope with a determined young lady such as Esme? I couldn't possibly let her go to anyone for whom she has no respect, or to anyone who is unable to withstand the lash of her tongue."

"Would you have me deny her bread and water?"

The king laughed. "I like you, Eirik. Oh that we men could take such an attitude towards our ladies. Alas, it was never to be so for me, starting with my influential mother."

"So do we have an agreement?" said Eirik. "Lady Esme and land in return for the defence of your realm?"

Aethelred stood. "We have an agreement." He grinned. "I wish you good luck."

When the door closed behind him, Eirik turned to Fenrir. "Help me get dressed, Fenrir. There's someone I must see, regardless of what the doctor says."

Fenrir tipped his head from side to side. "Doctors know nothing about human hearts."

Esme was anxious to see Eirik but waited patiently, praying and keeping vigil. Meanwhile, she continued her sewing. A particularly rich red colour, which she had seen in the shop where she was imprisoned, now provided splendid robes for the king. A dark blue denoted the waves that had nearly claimed the lives of Brand and Eirik.

There was an unexpected, insistent knock on the door. She opened it to see Eirik standing on the threshold. He strode into the room uninvited, slamming it behind him.

"Eirik!" she said, taking a step back, concerned by his apparent urgency. "What's the matter? Is it your arm? Has anything happened to Brand?"

"There is nothing wrong with my arm and there is nothing wrong with Brand, but there is something wrong with me, something only you can cure."

He pulled her towards him and covered her mouth with his. At first, she resisted, but he held her there. The kiss was soft but passionate, sweet but exciting. Her lips parted beneath his and eagerly she responded to the increased intimacy, bringing her hand to the nape of his neck, revelling in his nearness. A shaft of awakening beat through Esme's body the like of which she had never experienced, and she felt overcome, as though not of this world. She rejoiced in the strength of his hand passing down her spine, but then became conscious of how near she was to being out of control. The unleashed power frightened her to the core. She pushed gently against him with the palm of her hand. He refused to budge for several seconds but, when she persisted, he let go and backed away from her.

He rubbed his hand across his face. His breathing steadied. "Sorry, I didn't mean to alarm you."

"How is your arm?" she said, anxiously. "Is it badly injured? It appeared to simply hang by your side."

"It would have been an unfair fight otherwise."

"You mean you deliberately refused to raise it against him?"

Eirik nodded. "Gunnar once accused me of challenging him unfairly. He said there would be no honour in killing a one-armed man."

"Is that not the way in which ealdorman Byrhtnoth was duped? Did Olaf not accuse him of an unfair battle? And did the Saxon not agree that his fight with the Viking hordes should be fairly fought?"

"Yes. That's true."

"And look where that got him." She smiled. "We seem to have come full circle discussing Byrhtnoth's foolishness. That was one of our conversations when you first forced your way into the church."

He gently took hold of her stray wisps of hair and tucked them behind her ears. "I remember." He ran his finger under her chin. "I think I loved you from that moment on." He leaned forward to kiss her cheek with tenderness. "I can't live without you, Esme."

"If only things could have been different," she murmured.

"Esme, is your only objection to me that I am not a follower of your God?"

She frowned, confused. Was it true? Was this her only objection? Or had they been enemies for so long that she no longer knew the difference between love and hate? When had the two emotions become blurred? "All I know is that my faith is important to me. I would never be able to accept Thor as my guide as you have done."

Eirik glanced down at the floor for several moments then lifted his head to face hers. "I have something to confess. Do you remember the evening I came to find Father Aidan?"

Esme grimaced. "How could I forget?"

"Do you recall that I spoke to him late into the night?"

"I recollect there was a lot of coming and going. At one time you were both in the church. I thought that you and he might be designing some scheme together, that he was also a . . ."

"Traitor?"

She nodded slowly.

"Aidan could never be that. He is a true man of God. I asked him to baptise me. I knew at that moment I could no longer engage with my old life. It was a fresh beginning."

"Is that the truth?" Esme sounded incredulous.

"You are the one person in the world I could never lie to. You would identify any falsehood in me immediately."

"You truly believe?"

"Aidan experienced transformation from one conviction to

another. He says it takes time. But I intend to keep working at it, reading and understanding your scriptures."

Esme was silent.

Eirik ran his hand over his face again. "I want you to be my wife more than anything. Marry me."

"Eirik, I may not be able to give you an heir after my injuries."

He moved nearer. "I don't care. We have Brand. He will be my son."

She smiled. "Brand would be pleased."

"Then what's to prevent us?"

Esme nestled her head onto his chest, feeling and hearing the beating of his heart. His body stirred, every fibre tense, but he remained controlled, waiting. "Yes, Eirik," she said. "I would love to be your wife."

He kissed her with a passion that took her breath away. "My loveliest Esme, nothing will stop me now."

"I have something to admit to you," said Esme. "The king has released me. He no longer wants me to be a peace-weaver. He's returned my land and Saxstow Hall. All he needs is the wood from the forests."

Eirik laughed. "I thought he was light-hearted when we spoke. In return for training his warriors and protecting his shores, he has given me ownership of Edmund's land."

Esme took a sharp intake of breath, astonished. "I can hardly believe it."

"Neither can I, but at least I now have something to offer you here in England."

"So we are equal," she said. "This must be the work of God."

"If that is so, then perhaps we can be sure that everything will work out for us as He would wish it."

She laughed. "Spoken like a true believer in what you once deemed to be our puny Christ."

"I won't let it be otherwise." Eirik took the tips of her fingers and kissed each one. "I love you, Esme."

"And I you," she whispered.

He held her close. "Can we go back to Maeldun to be married?" she said. "I think Father Aidan would like to perform the ceremony."

"I wouldn't have it any other way. I promise I'll never leave you again."

Esme understood pure happiness and now knew how her embroidery would end.

60
London 1979

The silver treasure safely transferred to a place of security, Emma, Greta and Bjorn return to London with Esme's manuscript and embroidery. After calling at the office to update Ben, and then visiting Mr Makepeace-Brown, Emma returns to her flat in Notting Hill where Bjorn joins her.

"Esme's story finished with love and optimism," says Emma. "Yet, a few years later, Eirik marries Gytha. So what happened?" She removes the translation of Phoebe's account from the brown envelope and begins to read.

To whom it may concern,

Herein are diary entries and a letter dating originally from the late tenth century, presented to the Holy Trinity Church in Norwich by Phoebe Barnett, the great-great-granddaughter of Lady Christina Redman. The articles were kept in good repair by the monks until the church was demolished to make way for the Norman cathedral, at which time they were transferred to the Benedictine monastery occupying the same site. During the Dissolution, they were removed by the bishop, together with a number of other objects of the sacrament.

Signed: Brother Josephus

In the year of Our Lord 1534

"That explains a lot," says Bjorn. "Please go on, Emma."

Esme's Diary, Durham

August 995

Yesterday I was thrilled to meet Father Aidan here at The White Church – the Alba Ecclesia – in Durham, which is the final resting place of our beloved Saint, Aidan Cuthbert. He has joined the Benedictine monastery. I have joined the Community of St Cuthbert. This is now to be my home.

My beloved husband has returned to the lands of his birth. I can hardly express the pain I feel at this moment. I understand the loss he feels with the murder of his father. After so many years, Eirik was reconciled to him and also to his half-brother. They are determined to avenge their father's death. Somehow I feel he loves me still, but Thor and Odin refuse to release him from their grip. If only Edmund had not treated me so cruelly perhaps I could have borne a son.

My brother Brand has grown so. He remains great friends with the son of Swyen Forkbeard's sister, Gunhilde. I shall sign over the land to him. Stephan will continue to manage it. I confess the journey caused me constant sickness, but the women here have shown me great kindness.

October 995

The sickness I feel each morning is beginning to pass. Edith, the young woman with whom I share a room, believes I am pregnant. If so, it must be a miracle. St Cuthbert will have answered my prayers.

There are stories of how my husband plunders and burns lands in the east of this world. I fear his soul may be lost and can only trust that his gods will protect him.

April 996

Today is the most joyous of days. I have given birth to twins, a boy and a girl – Edgar and Christina – and thank our blessed Saint for the safe delivery of two wonderful new lives.

October 998

I hear that Eirik has married Gytha, the sixteen-year-old daughter of Sweyn Forkbeard. My husband is no longer my husband. Never again shall I be directed by mortal man. Only closeness to Our Lord can bring peace. Thankfully my children are a constant delight to me. I am truly glad they are without the influence of their heathen father, nor ever will be.

November 1000

Eirik's wife Gytha has given birth to a son, Haakon, named after his grandfather. I thank God that St Cuthbert gives me constant resilience.

November 1002: St Brice's Day

Devasting news! My beloved brother Brand has been sadistically murdered, together with Gunhilde and her son. They were in Oxford enjoying athletics. All those present were struck down. This monstrous command – to slaughter all Danes – was given by our once admired King Aethelred. My heart is broken. Gunhilde was Forkbeard's sister. Retribution will be swift and vicious.

August 1004

A friend from a monastic house in Norwich tells me that Sweyn Forkbeard has attacked the town and torched all its homesteads.

He ravages at will. The Archbishop of York says the Vikings are an instrument of God's punishment on the people of this land. He condemns the lack of Christian observance.

February 1012

Father Aidan, my dearest friend and mentor, has passed away. I shall miss his gentle advice and kindness, but I know that he is now at peace with God, a reward well deserved. Christina suffers his loss greatly since he taught her much.

April 1016

Today is the anniversary of the birth of Edgar and Christina. They are both twenty. Edgar is the gentlest of men. He tends the gardens of the monastery and works in the stables. Untamed horses calm at the sound of his voice. Christina is an excellent embroiderer. I believe she may yet make an income from the skill.

May 1017

Cnut is now the undisputed King of England. I hear he has divided the kingdom into four parts. One is Northumbria, of which I understand Eirik has been appointed the earl. His friend Thorkel is Earl of Norfolk. Until now Eirik has remained ignorant of our existence, but Christina has written and told him. I wait with trepidation in case he should pursue this information and wish to visit. On the other hand, I cannot deny him access to his children if he and they so wish.

June 1017

Today I received this letter from Eirik, the Earl of Northumbria:

My Dearest Esme,

Forgive me for addressing you as such but it is what I still feel in my heart. Although I know that I deserve no pardon or forgiveness.

In the year I left you to return to Norway, not only had my father been murdered, but Olaf Tryggvason had seized power. Because of this, my brother and I were forced into exile. We needed the protection of King Olof of Sweden and that of Sweyn Forkbeard. Tryggvason proceeded to force Christianity on the country using the most violent and cruel of methods. I became convinced that the Christian God was no different from Thor and Odin to whom I once made a powerful commitment.

To my eternal shame, I believed that our Christian marriage was now meaningless, and was persuaded to cement the alliance with Forkbeard by marrying Gytha, his daughter. Gytha bore me a son, Haakon, but she died not long afterwards. My life was full of continuous raids and plundering until Tryggvason was overpowered, and drowned in battle.

After that, we returned to Norway and ruled jointly for a further twelve years. We enforced the law and for a time there was peace. But my soul was not at peace. Your lovely face entered my imagination often and I envied the quiet calm I first glimpsed in your eyes. Father Aidan had written out the Lord's Prayer for me and I recited it over and over in my head, trying to find the Holy Spirit that you told me of, but which I had never succeeded in finding. Then one day I was unable to concentrate on my surroundings. It was as though my head was in a bubble and all I could see was you. It reminded me of that fateful morning when we met beside the river in Maeldun.

At that moment, I began to tremble. I wept and was filled with the desire to re-read all those scripts which Aidan had so carefully prepared for me. I knew then that your God had not left me. He had simply been waiting patiently for me to come back to Him. And that is what I did.

I had been made an adviser to Cnut, Forkbeard's son, and joined his campaign in England, aware that was where I needed to be. I am not proud of the destruction in the months that followed. I tried to find you and paid a visit to our old home. But it was overgrown and in a bad state of repair. The land had been taken over and divided into strips. There was no sign of your manager, Stephan, and no one was able to tell me what had happened to you. I assumed you were re-married or even dead. It was not until Cnut became king and made me Earl of Northumbria that I finally received news from our daughter, Christina. Imagine my joy.

I am longing to see you, but after all the pain I have caused I understand the decision must be yours. For my part I can only beg your forgiveness.

Yours forever,

Eirik

Having read this letter, I do believe I must forgive him and agree to meet.

July 1017

Today, I met my one-time husband – still a tall, handsome man, though no longer young. Edgar is the image of him. The earl seemed greatly moved, and stared at all of us for some time. His eyes were moist and his emotions ill-disguised. I'm ashamed to say my heart pounded so much at the sight of him that I momentarily fainted. But he carried me inside and placed a pillow most tenderly beneath my head. I saw tears coursing down his cheeks, and he made no attempt to hide his love and, above all, his need for redemption.

August 1017

A few days ago Eirik brought with him his friend Thorkel, Earl of Norfolk, who had once helped me find my brother. Thorkel was most courteous and was accompanied by a young man of rank named Ralf Redman who, I scarcely dare say it, paid much attention to my daughter, taking a great interest in her embroidery.

September 1017

Today an invitation has arrived for Christina from Lady Redman, Ralf's mother, to undertake a wall-covering for Holy Trinity Church in Norwich. She's delighted with Christina's designs and is prepared to pay generously for her work. She has extended a welcome to stay at her home while assessing what is to be done. I notice that her son Ralf continues to be attentive to my daughter. I suspect he may be in love. Christina seems fond of him, too.

Meanwhile, Earl Thorkel has invited Edgar to spend time learning how to manage his large estate in Norfolk. I am delighted for them both.

June 1018

I have received a letter from Edgar saying that Earl Thorkel's estate is very fine indeed. The climate in Norwich is warmer than Northumbria and supports a wider range of plants. He is learning fast. Eirik comes to see me daily and we have become close. I have forgiven him and enjoy his company very much. We walk and talk and read the Bible. He holds my hand and kisses me tenderly. These precious times are healing the rift of so many wasted years.

Christina's Diary

August 1018

Ralf has asked me to marry him. I have grown to love him more and more, and have accepted. I can hardly believe my good fortune. Mother, father and Edgar are all delighted for me.

January 1020

My joy is complete. I now have a beautiful baby daughter and shall call her Phoebe. Mother and father are both thrilled by the birth of their grandchild.

October 1020

My tears soak the page and feather the ink as I write this. Mother has been unwell for some months and today the tumours claimed her life. My one consolation is that father was with her. She died in his arms. For a while he was inconsolable. I reassured him that the precious hours they spent together in the last three years had transformed my mother and given her great happiness. Life will go on because of the love he shared with my mother.

Edgar is to visit the farm in Denmark that once belonged to his adoptive grandfather where they raise horses. I am sure he will love it.

December 1023

I am greatly saddened by the death of my father, but glad I had the opportunity to share his remaining years. I believe at heart he was a good man.

*

As the story ends, Bjorn and Emma remain still for some time, sitting side by side, gazing straight ahead through the windows of this graceful, if well-worn living room. The sun is low in the sky. Its rays highlight the newly unwound leaves of early May, which overhang the narrow balcony outside.

At last Bjorn breaks the silence. "So, that explains how Edgar came to be in Denmark and had a son called Magnus. I must find out who he married." He hesitates. "You know, don't you, that this means you and I are distantly related?"

"Yes, I do. I am descended from Lady Christina Redman, Esme's daughter, and you from her son Edgar – twins fathered by Eirik."

Once again they are silent for a few moments, deep in their own thoughts. Then Emma says, "May I ask you something?"

"Of course. Go ahead."

"Do you see colours when you hear music?"

"Yes, it's called synaesthesia. You too?"

Emma nods.

Bjorn perks up and slaps his knees. "Well, my newly discovered cousin, we must celebrate. I'm taking you to dinner."

"And what if I'm not hungry?"

"Then let's go out anyway because it's a nice evening." He takes her hand in his and turns to look at her. "Emma, I very much hope we will see more of each other. Is there a chance of that?"

She smiles. "I think so."

Bjorn relaxes a little. "Do you believe history repeats itself?"

"Perhaps."

"But we won't know unless we try." He stands and pulls her up beside him. "Come and spend some time with me in Roskilde. Allow me to show you what I do. Let's get to know one another better." His eyes twinkle as he draws her close.

Emma curls her arms around him, savouring the warmth of his body, and lifts her face expectantly to his. "You must promise not to sail off in your longboat."

He grins, and then kisses her lips tenderly. "Yes. I promise."

Author's Note

The inspiration for this story is a beautifully embroidered tapestry made by the women of Maldon and housed in the Maldon Heritage Centre. It depicts a history of the town beginning with the battle in AD 991 when a Viking horde sailed up the Blackwater Estuary intent on invasion.

The novel is a work of fiction although there is some contemporary evidence for Eirik Hakonarson, who is known to have become the Earl of Northumbria. He was the son of Hakon Sigurdarson of Norway and took part in the Battle of Hjorungavagr, and in the conquest of England by King Cnut. The early part of his life is less certain as is his death sometime in the 1020s.

The Jomsvikings are legendary, but like most legends there is often an element of truth. Esme is a completely fictional character, as is Saxstow, her home; Edmund, her husband; Father Aidan and others.

Historical characters for which there is evidence are Thorkel the Tall, Olaf Tryggvason and Sweyn Forkbeard, whose sister Gunhilde apparently lived in Britain and was married to an adviser of King Aethelred. To this day members of the Danish royal family are said to be descended from Forkbeard's daughter, Estrid Svendsdatter.

To find out more about the author visit the website:

https://godsendbooks.wordpress.com

or email

gaynor.lynn.taylor@gmail.com

or

godsendbooks@gmail.com